I0548929

Down to Earth

(A Book of Improvisations)

Gladys Swan

Down to Earth

(A Book of Improvisations)

Gladys Swan

Serving House Books

Down to Earth

Copyright © 2018 Gladys Swan

All rights reserved.

No part of this book may be used or reproduced in any manner whatsoever without the prior written permission of the copyright holder except for brief quotations in critical articles or reviews.

ISBN: 978-1-947175-04-4-

Cover art: Painting by Gladys Swan

Serving House Books logo by Barry Lereng Wilmont

Published by Serving House Books
Copenhagen, Denmark, Florham Park, NJ

www.servinghousebooks.com

Member of The Independent Book Publishers Association

First Serving House Books Edition 2018

For those who will cultivate the garden.

"Energy is eternal delight"
—William Blake.

I.

A Visitor

The Kid wanted to do something for me—and the question was, would I let him? He's on his way up in the world these days, and there's no telling how high he'll soar. I figure he's got the goods, but when I put my mind around what he's aiming to do, my breath catches. Really what Dusty struggled to do on the grand scale—take the world by the tail and change things at the core. It takes a kind of high-feathered ambition all right—to think you're the one who's going to make a difference. On the outside it looks like arrogance. And it takes a powerful imagination. Sometimes I can't help thinking it's an affliction, when the idea gets to buzzing your brain worse than any horsefly and keeps biting at your rear when you're not looking. I watched Dusty take his knocks, let me tell you, thinking he could create some kind of grand celebration at the heart of the city—carnival and circus all rolled into one. And all it finally added up to was one little ragtag outfit and one big question. Would it make it from one day to the next?

What the Kid has done is put together a circus that sends your heart soaring and keeps your blood tingling. I've seen it. You just never want the show to quit—one great act after another, full of zip and daring, and comic routines to double you over.

Something to celebrate all right. And I keep thinking there must be something to it after all, the way it lightens your foot, puts a glow around the edges of the day. It would be enough to gladden Dusty's heart to have an heir to carry on his dream. That way—if only he could know about it—he could maybe think the struggle wasn't all for nothing. But then the Kid knows magic, what it's supposed to do— it can change you, even if the world gets caught in the same old snags.

I'd sat with the Kid's letter a month or two—time is pretty sluggish down here in the Retirement Belt, one flawless day floating up on top of the other. The light comes up gradually, bleaching away the dark, as though to save you from the shock of a new day, time passing—time running out. Then when you're free of all surprises, the sun tilts up on the horizon, a red ball into a net of cloud, setting its glow on the day. Breeze warm and wet, salty as a lover's smooch, while the folks up north are shivering in their long johns and digging out their cars. Oh, we have our moments, enough to scare the socks off the citrus growers. But mostly you sit with a glass of something inspiring, waiting for a pelican to sail on over and fling itself down tail feathers over wing tip into the waves for his fish, or else for the resident egret who makes the rounds to mooch a few shrimp from anybody who'll give it a handout. Knows a good thing when he sees it. Expensive tastes. But then I've never known a creature that didn't want to improve its standard of living, up its bracket, so to speak.

Hadn't been able to lift a pen to reply. Had hardly done a thing the past year or so. Hard to think of a new life when the old one is shot to hell. Even when you spend a good many hours wishing it all had been different. Dusty gone—a hard going. Everyone I'd known scattered to the four winds. And what was I any more? An old piece of goods marked down below cost, lying on the shelf with the other unsalable merchandise. I'd thumbed through my fifties still flinging the old body into a few good times, but my sixties had hit like one of those late summer hurricanes, knocking out the power lines and tree branches. Nothing you can get insurance for.

Then here comes somebody knocking at the door and what-do-you-know, it's the Kid himself, standing there big as life and twice as handsome, in jeans and pale blue shirt, denim jacket and sandals—looking pretty spiffy. All of it just right, like it suited him. Like he knew where he was going, maybe even how to get there. He gave me a grin and a big squeeze before I could get a greeting halfway off my tongue. I had to keep from crying—last time I saw him was at Dusty's funeral—in the big tent with various friends and connections on hand. The Kid had taken care of it all. Lots of people came, even those Dusty still owed money to. And they gave him a tribute that kept me dabbing my eyes. Spoke of all he'd aimed for, what his example meant for the circus in America, and how he'd left his imprint on the coming generation. As though you could let go of all the failures, the misbegotten ventures, just forget them, and leave something shining—better than a slug's trail in the grass.

"Kid—My God—what are you doing in these parts?"

"Coming to see you—what else would I be doing?"

"I keep reading about you in the *Circus Record* and the *Spectacle*," I said. "I've followed you all over the place."

"We had a great year," he said.

"And the one coming up?"

"Wonderful acts," he said. "Yeah, we're in our own place now—it'll be a challenge." I saw a little catch of hesitation in the midst of his enthusiasm. "We've got a reputation to live up to. And we've got to build on it—sky's the limit."

News to cheer me, that's for sure. "Come on inside," I said, "and have something to drink. I've got some scotch and some fixings for a piña colada." Actually I'd been itching for a little pick-me-up, though I admit it was ahead of time.

"A little early for me," he said.

"Here, there's no early or late," I assured him. "Time is whatever you slice it up to be. You can cut it in little squares or turn it around in circles and add a few curlicues—"

I got him settled in the visitor's chair with a glass of iced tea, slouched down with an ankle over one knee, and as I sipped my whiskey, I took a long look at him. He'd changed—as if a certain set of qualities that at one point had been contradictory and out of balance had moved together into something you'd call maturity. Yet he hadn't gone hard or cynical. Manly—with his wavy brown hair and blue eyes and healthy skin. Good teeth to put a dazzle in his smile.

"You're opening in three or four weeks, aren't you? You got the jitters?"

"I have no doubts about the acts. And you know there'll be those few days on the edge of chaos to make things come together. If Morgan delivers with the money like he's promised and keeps out of my hair, we'll go great guns."

I was sure of it. I liked seeing him there. At ease, but you could still feel the energy pouring out of him. Open. None of the old suspiciousness and the big *Keep Out* sign. Maybe an old suffering had turned up a gleam of reconciliation, for there was a kind of humor playing around the edges. A light in the eye. If life was a joke, he was no joker. Well, it had been a long time coming. He could have gone down the tubes just as well as up the ladder, so to speak—either way, considering what happened after Billy passed on. Left a hole in his life bigger than the state of Texas. Just when the Kid had finally got the father he needed. After Billy left us, he went to pieces. And I won't say what I was like. Billy and I were soul mates in some fashion—it felt like half of me had been ripped out. The Kid had lost the hand that steadied him and taught him magic. And I'd lost the magic. Couldn't do a thing with him. Like trying to tame a tornado or pet a wounded tiger.

I was actually glad when the Kid cut out for God-knows-where. Pointless to try to stop him. We lost track of him—thought we'd never see hide nor hair of him. I know Dusty was relieved. Then all of a sudden, he turns up, comes to see us. Had found a lost city, he told us, somewhere in the hinterlands where we'd traveled before, in the Seven Cities Territory but even more remote, or so it seemed, but now "discovered," with everybody beating a path to this final, most "authentic" city. And then when you got there, a bunch of crooks and bullies. Totally corrupt. For all the phoniness, he'd had some kind of experience there that opened his eyes. He babbled on about a great love, his inspiration—Aurelia. Only she'd disappeared and he'd been trying to find her ever since. But she'd been the one to send him back to the land of the living. I had no idea what he was talking about. But she'd done him a turn—whoever she was—turned him inside out and ripped out the old lining. He was off drugs, off the booze, ready to find his work in the world.

Reality, he said—the old bitch. Now he was ready to face up to it, come down to earth. He got on in Las Vegas with his magic act, but he didn't like the nightclub scene. For a while he teamed up with a fire-eater and a sword-swallower. Did some gigs on the road with them.

Then he got into a hot little one-ring circus out of Phoenix. Became a founding partner with some fellow—I forget his name—who was producer now, an old hand in the business. Had brought circus acts into his nightclub. Plenty of contacts, people who owed him favors. Someone to woo backers and brainstorm with the Kid about the acts they'd scouted. And the Kid was left to come up with the conception, work his ideas out with the performers, put the whole show together.

He told me about their new location—in a depressed area of the city, where they'd been given a contract to settle on. The city had given them that space, along with some support, hoping the circus might bring new life into the area, for kids and grownups alike. He hoped it would go, as well as draw people in from outside. They had to have those, too. It had taken a lot of work to convince his partner. He talked about all the top-notch talent they'd gotten together—a great Cossack riding act, some hot stuff on the high wire and trapeze. I had the feeling he was trying to draw me in, though he wasn't looking at me directly. Every once in a while, he'd frown as though something prickly was lying behind his eyebrows.

I was pouring myself another little booster, when he said, "I meant what I said in that letter, Alta—I want you to come along with us this season."

I suppose I should have been flattered he'd taken the trouble. "Oh. C'mon. To do what?"

"Something you'd like. Maybe wardrobe—take care of the costumes."

"Hell, I can't stand anything to do with a hot iron or a needle and thread. I did it when I had to—did a little bit of everything. But I don't come with domestic talents. Anyway, what do you want with an old bag like me?"

He frowned again. "What do you mean? Because that's your life, it's always been your life. You know it inside out, start to finish . . ."

"Just look at me, will you. You know what people come to a circus for. What would I be doing? Don't condescend."

"You think I'd do that?" the Kid said.

Well, no, I didn't.

"Besides you're getting too comfortable," he said, looking around.

I had my habits, I'll warrant. I had my platform rocker, and I spent a lot of time in it. When I wasn't out in the garden or having a drink with one of the neighbors or by myself, there was a big stack of magazines I could leaf through, courtesy of Clytie, former queen of the liberty act, really a wonder with horses. She lived across the way. I didn't give a damn about them, the articles about fifty-seven ways to keep your man (I'd had my innings) or forty dozen possibilities of goosing up your sex life—how to do it from a chandelier or in a diving bell—or how to fix up the tastiest dish with rutabaga or carrot tops or horses' ovaries or shrimp toes. I'd read enough about the latest cure-all, a small exotic fruit the size of a raspberry from the tropical islands off Tasmania, and the seven infallible steps towards becoming a millionaire in real estate or graft. I liked the pictures. Mostly I'd drift off to some little spotlit moment of the past. The same when I watched the game shows or the sitcoms. I'd put on my own show; the others were too dumb to watch. Time killers—and I mean, killers. Like the slow poison spiders use to kill their mates. Paralyze them first, then eat their hearts and brains.

"You want me to take on life's challenges?" I said. "Screw that, Kid—I've had my fill."

"Damn it, Alta," he said, "I want you to be part of this. Think of what you did for me."

So there was gratitude in him—I hadn't banked on it, but there it was. Mostly it should have gone to Billy, who'd taken him under his wing when he was only half a step up from being a savage. Taught him magic and transformed him. All I did was cook his meals and keep an eye on him and act like he was halfway human. Thank goodness he made the grade—didn't end up in jail or dead of an overdose. I don't know what you're supposed to do when somebody's got all that loose feeling playing around—he had his life now, and I had the leavings of mine.

"I want you to be part of what I've got, while I've got it." From one moment to the next, I couldn't tell whether he figured it was a sure thing, or whether he was in the midst of some real uncertainty. "You need to give me a chance." He said it lightly, with a little smile. Then he added, "You could be part of the chivaree."

"What—come in with the goat?"

"You could wear any costume you like."

He knew me all right. I didn't tell him I still had two or three hanging in the closet, maybe looking for an occasion, though I hadn't found one recently. I've always liked decking myself out. Color alone can make me drunk, set me on fire.

"Who knows what you'll come up with," he said, giving me all of earth and outer space to forage in. "I want people to invent, improvise. I've got ideas in my head all right, but it takes the rest of you to make things come alive, to give them that special zing."

Oh, he'd found room for his imagination all right. I was looking at him through a haze. Hadn't given my mind to invention for quite a spell—it takes all your moxy. Then once you start, you're caught up in what lives in your head—just ripe for a pounding from outside. How could I stand it anymore? He didn't know what he was asking of me. To open up again all the old worries, setting up your heart for a target. And all to help him out of his gratitude. What I had now was easy enough, even if you could call it a hollow blessing: not having to get up every morning wondering if we had enough to eat and to get everybody through the day or whether some sheriff was going to close us down for not having the right friends or connections or for not slipping him enough moola to make it worth his while. None of the old burdens. Feeding hungry egos, straining to see that the show held together when the old no-fail glue of ready money was not forthcoming. All that sweat and labor to keep the wheel on the track. All the dreams—gone now, like smoke. But that's what it is with dreams—when they vanish, they don't leave a trace.

I was used up. All that effort . . . I'm not what I was, I was trying to tell him. Even if I shed thirty pounds I still wouldn't be, though I don't feel any age in particular. Just now there's nothing pressing. The money I've got gets me by. Courtesy of a cousin who cashed it in without any other kin—.

One day this lawyer turns up and says, "I've got some great news. What's the best news you could get?"

"You really want to know?" I said.

I admit I went through the family phase. *Thought: here I am all alone—I'll look up a few of those kinfolks I haven't seen in years.* They were nice enough—they even invited me to dinner. There was a little jittery bobbin of surprise running under the surface when I appeared—I could sense it. As though some strange creature had dropped from the sky, one they had to acknowledge but couldn't make any decision about, but nevertheless had to take me on because I was kin.

Their furniture was worn but comfortable, having given hospitality to various kids, dogs, and cats. The house was full of kids' voices and screen doors banging—the grandkids were visiting. I liked the autumn scenes on the walls and the family photographs with all the faces I didn't recognize. Family, but sure different from mine.

The chicken-fried steak and carrots and peas, the au gratin potatoes and strawberry-rhubarb pie were the best I'd tasted in years. Even grew their own rhubarb. They told me about the church bazaar and what their grandkids were doing in high school and college and beyond.

And then after we'd packed away her splendid meal, my cousin Ellen said, "Tell us about the circus." They were all eager.

"Well," I said, "it's taken me wandering with all kinds of folks." I don't know how that grabbed them. They'd spent their lives in Jefferson City, where Mitchell had good work as a contractor, the family looked forward each to their vacations in the Ozarks. Wandering around, spending a few nights here and there sounded pretty strenuous to them.

"You don't know the half of it," I said, "but the show must go on." That's all I could get out. How could I tell them what it felt like up on the trapeze, faces of the crowd just a blur below, and you're flying across the tent under the hot spots. Or the way it was, all of us together for the sake of what we could do out there, as though that made us what we were. Loyalties and jealousies and sickness and dark days, just for the sake of those few moments. The craziness of it all.

All my experience just shrank up into a little knot the size of a walnut. All I could say was, "Well, there was some excitement in it. And lots of grownups and kids to entertain."

They were very gracious to me, I will say, but that didn't keep me from a great sense of relief to get back to Sarasota—my trailer, my cat, and my platform rocker.

Here, I don't have to talk to anybody I don't want to. Just take care of my assorted plants and Calypso, who is going to have kittens any day now. Have my early morning walk along the beach to pick up a few shells or shark's teeth, whatever the tide's tossed up. Stand there half an hour looking out over the ocean and maybe watching a shrimp boat on the horizon, knowing it's not going to move. A stationary point, for that moment anyway. Then after a few chores, shopping for groceries, taking my time for decisions in front of the fish counter—a little pick-me-up. And another after lunch. Then maybe a nap. I can fill out the rest of the afternoon sipping wine and playing a little circus music, save the whiskey for later in the day after the piña coladas. These days I appreciate a little nightcap too.

"Come on, Dream Girl," he said.

He could play dirty, that one. A pang went through me. The name I went by during my glory days on the trapeze—what Billy always called me. *Dream Girl*. Oh, Billy—oh, Dusty. I suppose the Kid knew what he was doing to me, tearing a huge hole in my resignation. A shark, that one. A tempter.

He wasn't a magician for nothing. He'd come down to rouse me out of my funk, beckoning with his wand: *Come, come, come, come.* The Pied Piper. And already a voice struck up in the head: *Go for it, Dream Girl*—despite that ancient sluggish side, going down to the deeps, that just wanted to drift there in the haze and vegetate. A sort of blankness. Not that I was unhappy—I was too numb for that. Or else too pickled. Nor was I at peace. Something still ached below the surface, as though all the sap hadn't hardened yet, but still waited to be used. Despite all I could do to stifle it, something throbbed. *More, more, more.*

"I'll think it over," I told him. I could see disappointment congealing in his looks.

"Alta," he said, "please come. I don't even know myself why I'm asking. It's just . . . I've got some kind of feeling—"

A raw note. I looked at him, trying to figure out what he was really trying to tell me. I was so caught up in my own confusions, it hadn't occurred to me he might be asking, reluctantly, for some kind of help. Still I couldn't make it out.

"You in some kind of trouble?"

"No, not yet. I don't know—Morgan bothers me—I don't know quite where he's coming from. The way he talks. Now that we've had some success, I think he's got caught up by the glitz. He sees millions pouring in. Like he's some new incarnation of P.T. Barnum himself. All the big outfits—he's impressed by them. That's not where we are. We can create something, work our way into it . . . make it real. But it'll take time."

"Who is this fellow?" I said, with a sudden sinking feeling. No, it couldn't be—it was a common enough name.

"Juan Pablo's his name. Descendent of the pirate—you know, Henry Morgan—that's what he claims."

"Juan Pablo!" I said. "I can't believe it."

"You know him?" the Kid said, clearly astonished. "But I guess you know everybody."

"Yeah, yeah—way back when." I didn't want to say anything about it—it had all been so long ago. We had a history, you could say. "Used to juggle swords and daggers. He loved his costumes—all that pirate stuff. Does he still wear a mustache?" I lost track of him years ago. "Where'd you link up with him?"

"Las Vegas. He had a club there—did some circus acts along the way. Then after the season ended last year, he turned up. He was looking for a new challenge. Liked my style."

"Well," I said, not knowing what to make of it. "Imagine him still being on the scene."

"Only—" the Kid looked troubled. "I'm beginning to think we don't see eye to eye."

"That can be a tough in this business." And the money arrangements?—I didn't dare ask.

"Yeah. That's what I'm afraid of, in my worst moments. Everything sounded terrific when we first started out. Maybe I'm just jittery. It's just that everything hangs on this. I don't want to fall on my face."

"You won't," I said. "I'm sure of it. Not just from what I saw in that one wonderful show."

"The show's fine—I have confidence in it. But there's all the other stuff that can get in the way—you know about that. People you were counting on . . ."

I knew all about that all right.

But he wasn't going to dwell on obstacles—he was all caught up. We were in a new era. The circus—the one-ring circus—is being reborn from a place where it mattered, where it reached the public in a different way from other entertainments, really drew them in, made them more than spectators. That's what they were mostly reduced to—just sitting there in front of the TV or a movie. Even sports events—there to look. And what could be better than real skill, real daring, real danger? Being invited not just to watch, but to risk something, see things pushed to the edge. Showing people how far the magic can go. Helping them bring a little glow back into their lives. A change of perspective. The Kid reminded me of Dusty all right. And the animals—he liked that connection. They make you acknowledge your kinship. The comedy, too, of course. Clowns at the heart of it. The circus is going to be more important than ever—a place to explore and experiment. And dream. Oh, he had a bad case all right.

He was coming to a crossroads, I could see that. He had to make it work, he said, almost with anguish. He had to do it for *her* sake as much as for his own. She may have disappeared, but she was never out of his thoughts. *Aurelia.* He spoke her name as though it was almost too precious to say aloud. It was all for her now—for what she stood for. And what could I say for myself that would have any parallel? That it was all for Dusty? or Billy? or whoever—whatever they'd been striving for? I'd just leaked out into my surroundings, hadn't really kept much of anything to hold onto. As I looked at the Kid, I thought, *There's still a touch of craziness in him. And it's probably catching. So what are you going to do—sit here and wait for the final curtain? Without even putting on a show? Damn!* I thought, trying to ignore whatever was playing with my head. I couldn't stand to refuse him, couldn't stand to do it to myself. "You're on," I said.

"I knew you had it in you."

I wasn't sure I could bear his triumph.

II.

Talking Heads

So now I had to tear myself out of this place, what I'd gotten used to, succumbed to. I might as well say it—I was moping—that was the long and short of it. Trying to let go, but that doesn't happen all at once. Even when I put the blame on Dusty for the rotten times he took me through, somehow it didn't stick. What would I have been without him? without that life? Nothing I could feature. It was the lick of anticipation that kept us going, the high of those moments under the lights, the smile running through the audience. Laughter erupting out of pure delight. You just wanted to tickle it into existence. Looking at the world out there, all the misery, you think it's something you can do, remind people that poppies can grow on top of the graves. It was the bright thing that kept us together traveling down the years. And when cancer hit Dusty's lungs, I wouldn't believe it. Not even when I had to call the ambulance to take him to the hospital.

"Come on, Dream Girl," he said to me. "Let's go to bed and cuddle one last time."

He knew he wasn't coming back, but I wasn't buying it. And I knew what I'd always known. I loved him even when I wanted to kill him, maybe for what lived in him—the striving for something beyond what put bread on the table. Billy was a part of that too. Maybe that's why he stuck with us. He did his magic tricks with a little sideways smile, like maybe it wasn't anything of consequence. But he was the magic, and it made all the difference. Now here was the Kid taking on the next round, walking past all the failures, looking neither left nor right, but ready to take off right beyond them.

After the Kid left, I sat there with Calypso on my lap, all bulging with her kittens, looking out over the birds of paradise, elephant ears, and flowering kale and the other stuff I'd gotten to grow. Picture me out there digging in the dirt. I'd come to like it, actually, watching all the ideas nature and nurseries put together sprouting into leaves and flowers. Like I say, it was color that got to me. Any little scrap of gorgeousness—pink red yellow purple—it just conquers my heart. Like the notes of a scale—music for the eyeball. I was a sucker for it. That's how I spent my time, hovering over my flowers and jawing with the neighbors. That way I kept reasonably sane.

Plus all kinds of circus folks lived in the environs—trapeze, high-wire acts, animal trainers, specialty acts, and enough jugglers to populate the Pentagon—which might be an improvement. If I wanted to talk trapeze, I'd take myself around to Iliana Markova. We'd relive our aerial flights, our somersaults and backward flips. The close calls. Twenty years of it and she'd had enough. Figured she'd take up a life more in tune with gravity, so she took to training dogs and chimps. Now she was sewing costumes for a ballet company. I had to hand it to her—show biz all the way.

When Dusty went, any ambition in that direction left me as well. We'd all been special in our way—the circus is where everybody's special. Now we had our yellowed newspaper clippings and programs and photographs and memories. But the Kid wasn't going to let me settle for that. Well, I figured, I could humor him for a season—probably do me good to get my backside up from the cushions.

I felt both excited and irritable—there was the future again, coming at me with all the question marks dangling from it in little hooks. I fidgeted around for a while, then put on a pair of sandals and trotted down the lane. I had to find Dollie and tell her what was going on. Dollie and me, we went back a long way.

I figured I'd find her sitting by her fishpond. She'd sunk her money into a little grotto with moss-covered rocks and water trickling down into the pond where gold and black and white speckled carp lazed through the water. Maybe she'd learned how to read the future from them. Fortune teller supreme. I'd watched her in action twenty-odd years ago: the Celebrated Madame Selena and the Talking Heads. That was how we presented her.

A lot of people came and went over the years, as Dusty gambled for the winning combination. A little more circus here, a little more sideshow there, as he tried to weld it all together, that giant celebration at the heart of things. Too great an ambition or maybe too wide a focus. Carnival for the Gods. *You were in it to the hilt, Dusty.* Tears welled up. And here was the Kid working me up again. What should you aim for anyway? And was the game worth the candle? Artistry pushed to the limit—that was one side of it. Then there were the bills to pay, though God knows Dusty left enough of them owing, even when he tried pulling people in to look at the freaks. Freaks of nature and freaks of circumstance. And folks with their tongues hanging out to get a look-see. But it sure enough went over—for a while.

"Give people what they want," Dusty would say in one of his cynical moments. "Barnum had the idea. People will look at anything—till they get bored, then start itching for the next spectacle." Dollie and the Talking Heads were a huge fascination.

Sometimes I'd find Dollie in the trailer shuffling through all her stuff—you could hardly find a place to sit down. She collected curiosities from all over the globe—she had a whole box of splinters from what various folks claimed were pieces of the true cross, bits of gold dust from various strikes, bottles and dried flowers and petrified wood. On her wall she had some little doodad, a flower arrangement made out of human hair, popular for young girls to make way back when. She showed me a pelican all made out of shark's teeth, big ones and little ones fitted together. I'd never seen the like. Junk everywhere. Plus piles of clippings from newspapers and magazines. Faces. She studies them. She's got a knack—let her look at a face and a whole life history pops into her mind and rolls off her tongue. The way she can look into character, tell you things you don't know about yourself . . . it's a marvel.

She even has a pile labeled *Folks I'd Like to Know*—as if she might meet up with them in some other dimension. I leafed through some of them. One was a "mad" doctor, a German Jew who tried to rule a tribe in the Congo while collecting specimens of birds and insects. Another was a fellow who sliced lox at a local delicatessen, loved by everybody, always trying to make matches between his customers. And a woman who went around collecting stray dogs in the city and giving them a home. She had a houseful.

Dollie would pore over the society page, looking at engagement and wedding photos.

"Well, that one's headed for the rocks in about five years," she said, or "She's going to strike out with her best friend's husband in just nine months."

She'd shake her head bemoaning the fate of kids as yet unborn. I think she wanted to be a specialist on love, though that might take more brains than any of us have got. She'd been married herself once—a disaster. But then how can you see yourself with your own eye?

"What do you want with all that stuff?" I asked her the other day. "You can hardly work your way to the toilet."

"Opens up a doorway," she said. "Lets me keep a finger on the pulse. Besides, it's the stuff of history, pushing up between the so-called facts. All the stuff that nobody knows for sure but thinks they do. Ari knows about it—it keeps pouring through his brain, though he can't do anything with it, poor guy. Some souls can get to deeper levels, deeper than I can. Nobody gets to the bottom."

That was the other part of what made them unique—and amazing. The Talking Heads were her brothers, who'd started out in the womb as twins but ended up melded into one another—two heads and necks, one chest, one heart, and the right number of arms and legs for one person—some vestigial limbs removed in infancy. They were two separate personalities for all they shared the same body and went by one name, Armand. Privately, they were Ari and Mando, total opposites. Ari was the dreamer, a poet and musician, who composed songs and even a ballet.

Mando was like a sponge, reading everything he could lay his hands on—science, philosophy, the latest researches in psychology—you name it. He loved being the center of attention at cocktail parties. People liked to show him off at their gatherings, though Ari hated being dragged along. Couldn't stand crowds and chitchat. Mando, on the other hand, was playful, full of outrageous puns and limericks. He had a quick thrust that sent you spinning and a wicked tongue. Nobody could beat him in an argument. I loved all his hijinx. Women swarmed around him, but he was too rational for the battle of the sexes, really wedded to the workings of his own brain. As long as the groupies admired his mental powers, he was amused. But he bored easily, especially when he wasn't at the center of things and would simply nod off in the middle of a conversation. I've seen him do it sometimes in the middle of a sentence.

Then Ari would blossom, shyly. During one of Mando's longer periods of boredom, Ari actually proposed to a young acrobat from Bulgaria named Katerina. Mando was incensed—utterly betrayed, as he put it. He almost created a crisis by refusing to come to the wedding. But finally he acquiesced, being forced, as he put it, to play the donkey. Ari and his bride were married in the circus tent with all of us there—a big feast afterwards.

It was, as you can imagine, a pretty rocky marriage. Not just problems of the connubial bed, though that was the bedrock of the problem, if you'll forgive the pun. Ari claimed he was being spied on, but Mando insisted he was too bored to care what gyrations their shared body went through. He insisted he got his best sleep then. All the same, Ari was fearfully jealous, and finally their quarrels became so fierce the poor girl ran off to another circus. As I recall, she hitched up with a lion tamer. Mando was delighted to get his concentration back. "A woman just screws things up," was what he said. He and Ari weren't on speaking terms for quite a while.

Together with Dollie they had an extraordinary mental life. They all played a part. Let a person step in front of Ari, and a flood of images went through his mind, as though the person's life was unrolling before him like a film. Some of the images were fanciful, things that could never happen, so it was hard to know if he was seeing actual occurrences or images that pointed in some other direction, like you'd find in a dream. Mando was a kind of reader of the script and could translate some of the bizarre elements that crept in.

But Dollie was the one who could really take it all and put it all together. She'd listen to them, then go into her trance, I guess you'd call it, and come up with a picture where most of the pieces fit. She could separate the wheat from the chaff, what really lay at the center. Really amazing. Sometimes when she gave out with what came into her head, you swore it could never be true. Wait a little while and then suddenly there it was. What's more, she could read fortunes with cards and coffee grounds and tea leaves and would have done it with entrails and bird flight if you'd put in a special request. Nobody did.

So here she was in the same trailer park after all these years. I'd never expected to meet up with her again. But—as she'd said to me when we'd parted the last season I saw her, "We'll pick up where we left off one of these years."

Not that her abilities are exactly a blessing.

"Come on in," she says whenever I go over. "I'll give you a read-ing—compliments of the house." Then I start to worry.

"I smell something in the air," she told me the last time I was over. "I think you're going to travel a little, turn a corner." She gave me a slant look—her left eye is a little off center.

"That's right," I said. "On my way to grocery, I'm turning down the street for that big four-family yard sale. Maybe I can find me a Venus stomach-clock. Always wanted one."

I was putting her off, you see, and I could tell she was offended. But she'd sent a tremor through me. You can be looking at the horizon one minute, and suddenly a crack streaks across it, and half the sky shatters like glass, with something new bleeding into the atmosphere. She took my breath away—because on just such a day a few months before, I'd found her rocking back and forth in her chair, her eyes closed. Rocking and moaning.

"There's going to be a wreck and a drowning," she groaned. "Only there's one alive—a little boy. He'll be in the eye of a hurricane." After they found the little Cuban boy, I had to believe that's what she'd seen.

It was her gift. Claims to be Romany. Says her grandmother was known throughout the gypsy world for her powers. So her ability had come down the matrilineal side. Though it skipped right over her mother, who couldn't catch a pan burning on the fire, let alone see into the future. And maybe there's a virtue in that, instead of fetching up with all kinds of things you can't do anything about.

I had a brief spell of clairvoyance right after Billy died. Figured it was the shock that brought it on. If Dusty was the love of my youth,

Billy was the love of my middle age. And when the magic drained out of the world, a terrible longing seized me. For a spell it was like I'd drawn back a curtain and could see beyond my grief, look past a threshold into the fiery seeds waiting to put on flesh. One day during that period, when I was out walking in the fields, I saw a black Percheron grazing with a bunch of regular horses. I thought, that's a circus horse. What's it doing there? I stood and watched it for maybe a quarter of an hour, then walked on, but when I came back, it was gone. I looked for him and waited for him, but he didn't appear. For some reason, I was all upset and I went to find the owner. He told me they'd had such a horse years ago, but that it had died quite a while back. A ghost horse? I said a little prayer to whoever takes care of horses.

I'm wondering if there aren't different sets of eyes handed around, some for the surface, some for the shifting ground underneath. Call it other dimensions. But for the time being I'll stick to surfaces. I wouldn't let Dollie tell me what she saw in my future—sometimes you learn more than you can use.

When I walked over to her place, I found her in a lounge chair in front of her trailer and Timon, her tiger cat, sitting next to the fishpond in deep concentration, tail twitching. Those fish were a challenge.

"Don't get up," I told her. It would take an effort—she's a bulky woman—and she looked comfortable, leaning back all relaxed. She didn't have a turban on, and her hair, still black with only a little gray, was falling loose down her back. But as usual she was dressed as Madam Selena in her Florida mode. This time it was a mou-mou decorated with sun, moon, and stars, plus the figures of the zodiac. Other days you get to look at chalices and pentangles or various flying creatures, animals with human faces and lion bodies, or bolts of lightning ripping through dark places with yawning chasms. You could watch a whole drama unfolding in her dress from day to day.

"I've got a surprise for you—I was just about to ring you up," she said, before I could give her my news. "Armand's here. He's inside mixing up a pitcher of piña coladas and putting together a few things to snack on. You came at the right moment—I always knew you were psychic. Mando!" she called, "Bring an extra plate and glass. Guess who's come over."

When he came out, he just stopped in his tracks like he couldn't believe his eyes—almost dropped the tray. "It isn't—" he said. "It can't be." He put the tray down and just stood there. "Alta," he said. "My God!"

"I thought you wouldn't recognize me," I said. "A few things have changed."

Mando waved them away. "Not the essentials."

Before he offered me a drink and we could sit down—even though Dollie kept nudging his arm—we went through a half decade of reminiscences and exclamations. I was about to die of thirst.

Being with him took me back. Mando wasn't paying the least attention to Ari, whose eyes were closed, his head leaning against their mutual shoulder. Unsettling. For Mando, it was like Ari wasn't even there. And Ari—how could he sleep through all the excitement, as though we weren't present or the world had disappeared? What was I to say after all these years? Dollie had more or less kept me up on things since I'd moved into the retirement belt, though I sensed a certain holding back whenever I started asking questions.

Mando was balding a little but, if anything, looked younger than I imagined.

"I hear you're a new kind of celebrity," I said. I'd even watched him on television a time or two.

"Yeah, basking in the limelight," Dollie said, a certain irony in her tone. Was she jealous?

"What d'you think of that?" Mando said.

Seems his and Ari's brains had become of vast interest to neurologists, psychologists, and assorted experts. Now Armand lived at a special facility devoted to the study of the brain, where there were continual experiments and interviews concerning their combined mental life. Mando had written a book describing it all from the inside, from his earliest memory on up, and it had been on the best-seller list for months. Had sold three or four hundred thousand copies so far. He'd been hosted on talk shows and asked his opinion on everything from education to women's rights and was continually sought after by advocates and groups trying to free the country from poverty, crime, racism, pollution, sexism, and even boredom.

"Over a thousand letters a month, not counting e-mails. I don't even have time to read them all. Not to mention interviews and articles. A good thing I have a little protection at the Center," he said, "plus the use of a secretary. Otherwise I'd never get anything done That's the trouble," he went on, "with having one of the most advanced brains . . ."

I will say that for Mando—he'd never been afflicted with any kind of false modesty. But what about Ari? I wondered. Was he totally out of the picture? Or had he permanently withdrawn beyond the interests of the researchers and whoever?

"Dollie gave me a copy of your book," I told him. "Maybe I'll run back later for it and get you to sign it." I confess I hadn't had the ambition to read it.

"With pleasure," he said, finally serving me up a piña colada.

"Yes," he said, "now that I've been on TV, the books are selling like hot cakes. I won't even tell you how many copies have been scarfed up by my devoted public. Curiosity," he said. "The insatiable maw. How eager they are to visit the inside of my brain, when most of them have scant acquaintance with their own."

"But you're—"

"A freak—of course I am."

"That wasn't what I was going to say. You're beyond us all."

"That's the trouble. Only I'm not beyond the beyond—that's what they're asking me about—where we are going, how to stop the AIDS epidemic in the world, what to do in the Middle East. Hell, I don't even know why I'm like I am or what I'm supposed to do with myself."

"You've got a public," Dollie said. "You can tell them anything."

"You're rich then?" I offered.

"Rich? It's like I've been given the golden touch. More green stuff than I'll ever spend," he said. "Flowing in from an inexhaustible sugar tit. And my accountant insists on putting it where it'll make more. I can't even think of things to spend it on."

"And what does it come down to?" Dollie said. "It's all paper, honey. Strike a match to it and it burns right up."

"Cheers," I said, holding up the glass. "Here's to—" Only I couldn't think what to drink to. Fame and fortune didn't seem to be on target. Old times? The future?

"Well, here's to—the next round." I guessed that would do it.

"May it be rounder than the last round," Dollie said, sitting down finally. "Here's to more nonsense after that."

I glanced towards Ari, eyes closed, leaning heavily. Must have had an awful crick in the neck, not to mention the strain it put on Mando.

"Asleep for the duration," Mando said, irritably. "Snuck out on me. You can't wake him, they tell me, not unless he chooses. Otherwise, the shock would be too great; his very skull would shatter." He looked at me.

"No," he said, reacting to my expression. "I kid you not. He's entered the world beyond— much good may it do him. Everything down below. All things half-forgotten or half-imagined. Time past and time future all rolled into heaven knows what—that's his—he's only missing the *now*— closed off the little doorway—"

"What d'you expect," Dollie muttered. "When you've sold out on him."

I wasn't sure he'd heard her or just ignored her. Maybe it wasn't a new piece of friction between them, but I was beginning to wonder what I'd walked in on.

"Must be damned drafty down there," I said. "Sounds like eternity."

Mando was giving me the willies. I tried to read him, but as I remembered, his was a polished surface. Gave you back your own reflection. Plus a bunch of scattered glints and glances. A bundle of conjectures and speculations, odd moods, fits and starts, though he always claimed he was a perfect rationalist. He was sporting a mustache, which was lighter than his hair, a square of reddish-brown fur. A little piece of vanity, I suspected—for the TV audience. Something of the dandy about him in spite of all the disclaimers—And he dressed meticulously—linen jacket, dark pants. He liked the attention. I wondered if the women still trailed after him.

"They can read his dreams," Mando said, as if speaking of someone in another town. "They fussed around with some new contraption they've been working on day and night. Then they planted a chip somewhere that would throw up all his mental activity on a screen."

"Used to be Ari'd tell us what he was seeing," Dollie said. "Now they can project it—Imagine! That's science for you. Looking at your mental guts, prodding and poking."

"I have to watch the stuff and give my commentary," Mando said, as though it was a great imposition. "Be the superior translator. Mostly it's boring as all get-out, like a continual television without the sound—the good, the bad, the banal thrown together without rhyme or reason. Just try to sort it out. All the interior dust and feathers we carry around. In the midst of it, now and then, a zing, a little leap—and you get a gleam or two. A notion nobody's thought of. Wait a while, and some canny soul will fish it up and presto! a new discovery. Or else up comes something bizarre enough to blast you out of your wits. A bit of the future that nobody can recognize till it's on them like a hairy monster. Believe me, I've seen it all and then some."

"It was different in the old days," Dollie said.

And I could remember how sometimes when the crowd was flocking around them, Ari would sit bolt upright, his eyes fixed, and the words that came from him sounded strange to the ear. It was like he was seeing new things in the world the way Leonardo saw flying machines, images of things people had never seen. A hush would come over the crowd. Then Mando and Dollie would offer some kind of explanation. Not that anybody believed them, but I'm sure Ari saw the first trip to outer space. He was just a boy then. He kept talking about overcoming gravity.

Mando gave a shrug. "I'll let the boys and girls play with the stuff on their own. I like being a kept man."

"A great waste," Dollie said. "You used to have something together, you and Ari."

But Mando waved it all away.

"I'll just stick with my piña colada," I said, and took a drink.

Mando paused to do the same. "Actually, I hate pineapple," he said, looking at the glass as if it were medicine "Give me a good martini any day."

"Nobody's forcing you."

"I'm just minding my *p*'s," he said.

"He's in his Peter Pan phase," Dollie explained.

Which didn't make any more sense than the rest of what he'd been telling me. "Oh? Well, you certainly have the bloom of youth," I told him. He was a study all right for a whole pack of psychologists.

"It's the world according to the letter *p*," he explained. "I do it to amuse myself and the science boys. I eat only pork, peas, popcorn, polenta, pasta, pizza. I've taken up philately and the piano, sometimes painting. I enjoy pinochle, poker, and pornography. My favorite tree is the ponderosa pine. My favorite body part—the prick, naturally."

"It's better than his Samson phase," Dollie said.

"All nonsense," Mando said. "Mental tricks to use up the time."

For years he'd been an avid reader, Dollie told me—a book a day. But that just added too many ingredients to the stew. Past and future no longer interested him; even the *now* had gone pretty dull and empty. He went over to sit by the pond and stared down at the carp.

"It's good to get away from the place," he said, as much to himself as to us. He pulled up a lawn chair, sat down, and leaned back "I'm weary of being a mental prodigy." He looked hot in his jacket.

"You see," Dollie said. "Bored to death."

I exchanged a bit of gossip with Dollie, who told me they'd made contact with Ari's ex-wife. She wasn't performing any more. She'd dislocated a shoulder years ago, and it kept giving her trouble. She'd been eking out a living coaching acrobats. Now Mando was supporting her. Didn't want to see her—it might be too much of a shock to the system.

Then I remembered the reason I'd come in the first place. I'd gotten so caught up in seeing Armand again, I'd let go of my own news. I told them about the Kid's visit and how I'd finally agreed to join him.

"So I thought," Dollie said, nodding as she took it in. "Come over here," she ordered Mando. "If you want something to liven you up. I've been telling Alta she's on the way to something new," she announced. "She wouldn't believe . . ." Dollie gave me a triumphant look. "What do you say we activate the sensor and see what's in Ari's head. Maybe we can offer a little advance news."

"I'd have to get up," Mando said.

"Don't go to the bother," I said. "You're on a Sunday visit. Like meeting your doctor on a social occasion and asking him to look at your elbow."

"We're family," Dollie said. "It's a different thing entirely."

Mando didn't argue that. He finally got up and followed Dollie and me inside. Dollie bustled around. She cleared one of the walls of snapshots of herself and the brothers and pictures of circus friends and their acts—a lot of them people I knew. She was piling things here and there, stacking piles on piles. I couldn't help wondering how she'd manage to find anything again.

Mando sat down so that he was facing the wall Dollie had cleared, and she drew the shades. Then they switched on the gadget that projected Ari's mental functioning. We were treated to what looked like a home movie, only it wasn't. More like the sweepings from a film editor's floor, the outtakes from every silent movie you've ever watched, only lacking any kind of order. Crowds of people moving you couldn't tell where, horses running through a town, elephants hosing each other down, a flock of crows, a gaggle of kids throwing snowballs, men looking ready to fight, women peeling potatoes. Mando was right—it all got pretty boring. And I couldn't figure out what any of it had to do with me. "We're getting static," Mando said.

"Which it mostly is," Dollie added. "Sometimes I think it's because of what's going on up here. It's affecting what's going on below. Corruption everywhere."

I'd never seen her in such a mood.

Mando glared at her. "Always happens at first."

I figured he ought to know. Hard to say how long it went on. Mando was sure some of it had to do with the future of Madagascar, but Dollie pooh-poohed the idea. I thought they might have a squabble.

Then here comes a parade, a circus parade like they used to have in the old days. A big crowd on the sidewalks. Elephants all decked out with spangles. Only they were huge elephants, like mastodons. And horses, even bulls, with fancy harness and bells, their riders in gold tunics—but they too looked different, like creatures drawn on the walls of ancient caves, before they knew the bridle. And there was a kind of wildness in them that kept them tossing their manes and lowering their horns. So the riders were on their backs for only a moment, then leaping down into the street. Then here comes puppets with masks, larger than life, dancing their way through the animals before all of it was gone.

It didn't have anything to do with the Kid's outfit, as far as I could tell, but it needed only the touch of music and the reaction of a crowd to bring on the old thrill. Pretty lively action. I was really getting into it when something went wrong. I was watching a clown tumbling in with a violin case. Then came a commotion somewhere in the audience. A running figure. I couldn't tell what was happening but I felt a surge of panic.

But that was all fanned away by a curtain of smoke, and from it acrobats emerged, tumbling through. A young woman came twirling in. I couldn't really see her face, just caught a glimpse of her large eyes, her lithe body as she spun. Her skin was golden. An elephant lifted her up and she danced along its back, then took a leap as if into the air as a crowd of bird wings surrounded her, blue, green, yellow in a kind of crescendo. She could have been a bird herself.

"How's that for spectacle?" Dollie said.

"Well, if I get to see anything like that . . ." I could see why Ari might not want to wake up. All he had to do was let everything pass through—he didn't have to feel any of it, or wonder how it was going to turn out. But this meant he was missing everything else, too, never have any experience. But then why did you want it?

"Think Ari'll ever wake up?" I asked them.

Mando shrugged. "Who knows? Maybe this dimension is too much for him."

"And what am I supposed to make of all this?"

Mando shrugged. "Possibilities. Who can tell?" It was a disappointing response, considering all his brains.

"You're not much help," Dollie said, "after all your writing and speculating."

"You're the clairvoyant," Mando reminded her. "I just write about what I see."

"Which doesn't go beyond the end of your nose."

Then I saw the black Percheron. It stopped my breath.

Before I could even say anything, and before some kind of squabble could break out, we were in a new moment none of us had predicted. A hideous noise from outside. We got there in time for a great splashing and howling. Timon had fallen—or leapt—into the fishpond. Water was not his natural element. Between the three of us, we rescued him, furious and dripping, clawing like the tiger he was. Scratched up Dollie's arm something fierce.

"Ungrateful beast," she said, wiping away the blood. "Ought to let him drown down there with the fish." He was a rag, every hair clinging to him—tail like a rat's.

"Well, Cat!" Mando said, as Dollie bundled Timon up in a towel and tried to mollify him, "The best fish, spelled with a *ph* are to be found inside a can." Dollie dumped the cat in his arms and went inside to get some sardines. A tidbit for the whole experience. Maybe they'd lure him to jump in again.

I was glad for the interruption. Like I say, I'm leery about knowing things ahead of time. Oracles are never clear or simple, even when what they're telling you is straight from the horse's mouth, or so you think. They're winding up for a curve ball when you think you're seeing the straight shot. And you get left, holding the riddle and the consequences. As far as I'm concerned, the only thing coming out of the horse's mouth is a horse laugh. Just at that moment, I was peering down into those horse teeth. I didn't know what I knew—I was just hot and bothered over nothing you could pin down.

Anyway I took the moment as a signal to leave, but not before Mando put his palms on my shoulders and looked at me with an expression I hadn't seen before, like something was melting at the core.

"I envy you, Alta," he said. "I really do." I could tell he meant it.

"There's an energy in the circus right now, and you'll be part of it. Something new coming into the atmosphere. A place of discoveries. A place where you can make a difference—I'm sure of it. With everybody, not just the kids. I'd give my eye teeth to be there—to be part of it."

He took me by surprise. "With all the things you've yet to discover? The inside scoop. Books to write. You've got an audience in the palm of your hand."

He waved it all away. "I just sit back and laugh. The public hanging on my every word like I've got the inside track. Yeah, I'm great on talk shows. They're translating my book into twenty-three languages. They're talking film rights."

"Some folks would sell their soul for all that."

"Yeah. Oh, they love me all right—clever fellow that I am. They want me to write a sequel. But I'm nothing but a damned guinea pig, come right down to it. Getting poked at. Interviews from all over. So they can rush off and publish their articles. *New Knowledge.* And what do they *know*? The more bizarre, the more they love it. Move towards the extremes and what do you get? Beauty? Maybe just a new kind of ugliness."

Suddenly I caught his drift. To his mind, he was still a freak, putting on an exhibition. Though there was something more to it once—I was sure.

"Maybe you come up with a few ideas," he went on, as Dollie, who'd been off changing her outfit, came up, "—but where do you go with them? What is the brain anyway—this much patched affair that's come up over the millennia? First the reptile. All that aggression and cold cunning and cruelty, still living with us. And stuck on to that the mammalian part—so you might get a little love and caring out of the creature. But not enough. Never enough. And on top of that, Mind. Consciousness. Trying to figure out what to do with the whole enchilada. Maybe just write a few dirty limericks."

"Sounds pretty impressive, if you ask me."

"Yeah, I know. Only I'm stuck with it. You get to find things out by pushing your limits."

"Don't you?" I challenged him.

"It's not the same."

"How's that for jaded?" Dollie said.

She turned to me. "Why are you dragging your feet? Who knows what's waiting for you?" she said. "Maybe you'll come up with something absolutely stunning."

"A little late in the game, isn't it? I'm past my glory days."

"Think of the challenge—the experience."

"That's what I'm thinking of all right—having to let things matter again."

"Beats the hell out of where I am," Mando said. "Trying to make experience out of the whole mess—this body, these minds. One mind divided between two heads—and one of them out of it. I envy Ari here," he said. "Gone through the escape hatch. Continually entertained— He doesn't have to do a thing."

"You know," I said, "I'm beginning to think you're the dreamer."

"Don't pay any attention," Dollie said. "He's just in one of his moods. Wait till Oprah or somebody like that calls him up. Then watch him preen his feathers. He'd be bored stiff without his mind."

"Yeah," he said savagely. "I'm a spectator sport all by myself. The greatest show on Earth, an infinity of circuses. If I could only see something beyond—" He didn't finish.

"Anyway," Mando said, "think of me." He leaned over and gave me a kiss. Ari swayed slightly. It must be, I thought, a great burden to carry not only someone else's dreaming that was partly yours, but the dreamer as well.

"I'll take care of your place while you're gone," Dollie offered. "You leaving Calypso?—I'll feed her and make a box for her. Let me know when you're taking off. I'll have sandwiches for you." She was always good to me.

I was tired, done in. All the excitement had taken a lot out of me. I pointed myself in the direction of my trailer and hoped for the best. My brain was surging on wings of color. Buzz of words, glut of images—all mixed up with the piña coladas. A surreal state. Maybe I could have inspired a new generation of painters. All the colors and costumes I'd put on over the years—sequins and satins and velvets, the scarves and tiaras! I soared as Dream Girl and was grounded as wife to an enterprise. I was a lover of sorts, a mother of sorts. Except for my time in the air and a few hot moments in bed, nothing was ever enough. Maybe that's why I needed to pour myself into another drink. I knew as soon as the Kid got me back into things, the old longings would take hold of me—to get beyond gravity before it pulled me under. The matter with matter. At the same time, something's pushing you from the opposite direction—take it easy, just let it all go. Push and pull. A certain excitement rising—you can't help it. Go pack your bags.

III.
Back to the Big Top

A flare of brilliance! Red and white stripes running up to the top of the tent into a red peak. A glory! How it gladdened my heart to let my eye ride up to the top, with its flags fluttering in the breeze. I always loved watching the tent rising up. Canvas just lying there on a flat piece of ground one moment—nothing special there, then the poles going in and the canvas billowing up all fresh with promise. The hammering and the pounding, the stakes and ropes pulling it all in place. I remember once Dusty had the help of three elephants to put all the poles in. They seemed to like the work. Then chunks of bleachers being carried in and set up in rows. The archway and curtains, the platform for the band. The lights and rigging for trapeze and high wire. Nothing like seeing it all come together. For two weeks—or if you're lucky, two months—it's where you'll live and breathe and work like hell to make the show come together. You hold your breath as the first performance begins, and you listen and try to get a take on whether the crowd is with you, or not. All in that canvas castle where afternoons and nights of spectacle unfold.

Then it's all over, the last show, and it gives you a pang to watch it all come down. Get the crowd out from the final performance, and you've got a little time for food and celebration. Then there's the crew right on your heels taking things apart, everybody happy if it has been a good run, yet kind of at loose ends, too, now it's all over. You wanted to believe it could go on forever. Back in their caravans and trailers, the show folks are packing up, ready to move on, some that very night, taking their acts to a show they've got lined up somewhere. Or maybe going back to New York or Florida to teach in a circus school or try a little theater or nightclub work, waiting for the next year's prospects. Maybe you'll see them the next round, maybe not—who knows where you'll be? What had been family is all splitting up, heading into the four winds. And the next morning there's that flat piece of ground again, a few scraps of paper snookering around in the breeze, not a sign of last night's dazzle.

"What do you think?" the Kid said. "Terrific, huh? We got one of the best tents on the market."

"Sure looks good." I was thinking of Dusty. Towards the end—the much-patched canvas. A much-patched life.

I'd landed and gotten my stuff into the rented caravan and had a decent night's sleep. Now the Kid was showing me around. His voice kept its enthusiasm, but I could tell he was kind of jittery. Kept jingling the change in his pocket. When I made some comment, it would jerk him out of some train of thought he'd been following, and I had to repeat what I said. The usual chaos before a show, I figured. People coming in, or sending messages about being delayed. Things wrong with the sound equipment or replacements needed for the wiring or the spots. Right now he and the manager Kitty Bailey, an energetic young woman who'd been with him for a while, were doing all the shuffling. Morgan was off beating the bushes somewhere for money.

But the tent was all you could ask for—the only bright spot in the cityscape. For the rest, the town was beaten up old warehouses, some boarded up, and vacant lots where buildings were torn down, and fenced off so kids wouldn't get hurt in the debris. Down the street a-ways were what had been some fine old houses, on the downside now, badly needing paint, divided up into apartments for those who couldn't come up with the ante to make it to the suburbs. Blacks and Latinos mostly—a few Orientals—some who had businesses there but who lived elsewhere. We'd be getting our food from a Chinese takeout around the corner, the Mexican place down the street, or else from the pizza palace farther on. We'd done Chinese my first night.

The section had an abandoned look, like it would turn back into something scarred and pitted like the surface of the moon, unless things turned around. The sort of place where you didn't want to walk alone even in the daytime, let alone at night. Not because you weren't safe—though maybe you weren't—but because the life of the place had sunk so low—down to the dregs. The streets had no kids' voices in them, and there were more than cats and dogs worrying around the dumpsters.

"Well," I said, "it's not exactly a glamour spot. I thought they'd give you a place in one of the parks."

"The city fathers didn't want us trampling up all their grass. Thought they'd have to spend a lot of money on cleanup." The Kid looked a bit ruffled, I thought. "The park would have been good—lots of room and something to gladden the eye. But the way I see it, here's where we can make a difference. What's important is right here, under our eyes. Think of what has happened to make it like this. We got to do something to lift it up again."

He got it right, that one. But it would be a hard go, and I knew it would be a struggle. I felt proud of him for taking it on.

"At least we've got room for the horses on those vacant lots across the street, and the elephant. Babe—she's quite something."

"Hey. Have we got time to go get acquainted?" Now that I was there and reasonably settled, I wanted to meet everybody, find out everything that was going on. The old curiosity leaping up. I was a sucker for all that.

The Kid consulted his watch. "Sure, there's time. We've got half an hour." The Cossacks had arrived the night before and the riding act was scheduled for a rehearsal. The Kid had seen their tapes, but it was his first chance to look at them for real. I wanted to be on hand. But for now, the Kid and I wandered over to where Babe's trainer, Tony Sanchez, was filing down her toenails. It took a little doing. She was standing, not altogether patiently, with her foot resting on one of those round stools she climbed on in the ring. Every once in a while, she'd get a notion to pick up her foot, and Tony had to convince her to leave it where it was. We watched the operation, then waited while he invited her out into the yard, and hosed her down.

"Be right with you," he said. He stood stripped to the waist, a solid-looking man, in his early fifties I'd guess. "Soon as I get her done, she'll pick up a trunk-load of sawdust and throw it all over her back—you can count on it." He laughed.

When he got her wetted down, he turned off the hose and came

41

over. The Kid introduced us, and Tony introduced me to the elephant. "She'll put on the show for you,"

"I had to meet, Babe," I told him. "She's quite a gal."

"That's for sure," he said, "You can't believe how smart they are. More civilized than us humans, I keep thinking."

I could feel her taking me in, figuring the percentages. Her trunk moved in our direction, the end of it working. "No, no, Babe," Tony said. "Don't beg. She's always hoping for a little treat." Babe slipped her trunk under his arm, around his middle—a little caress.

She was new to the outfit. The Kid had bought her from a circus that was disbanding after they'd lost their sponsor. Love at first sight. Tony had come with her, had been with her since she'd first crossed the ocean, an orphan from Africa, where her mother had been shot by poachers. She's wasn't full grown yet. She was a beauty all right—wonderful ear fans and an eye that seemed to go as deep as a hidden spring.

"She's a real quick learner," Tony said. "You can teach her a trick in an hour. A big ham too. You should see the way she soaks up the applause." He was proud of her, you could tell.

"He spends a lot of time with her," the Kid told me when we were walking towards the back of the lot. "You ask him to go out for a drink, and he says he's got to take care of Babe. There's really nothing he has to do—and there are others around who could check on her. He's like a doting father."

The horses were stabled further on. "These are horses for the Cossack riding act," the Kid said. "Wait'll you see it. They've been in the Moscow circus, and they can ride like demons. It'll be the last act in the show." We looked over some prize Arabians, piebald, black, and chestnut, with long sleek legs and finely shaped heads. The Kid reached in his pocket, pulled out a bag of carrots, and offered them to the horses one by one. "I like to be on good terms," he said.

As we started back towards the tent, I caught a movement from across the lot and stopped in my tracks. There he was—a black Percheron.

"What's the matter?" the Kid said.

"Nothing." It wasn't anything I couldn't expect. Coincidence. Maybe I even saw him in the last show—I don't remember. Déjà vu. Call it what you like. Only for me, it wasn't just any circus horse. He'd been in Ari's head, and on the screen. It scared me. I'm superstitious like a lot of circus people. Never wore yellow, for instance, or whistled. Supposed to be bad luck. I'd never heard anything against black horses though. And this one was a handsome beast. Only I was too startled for a moment to appreciate him for just being horse. He came up to the fence to greet us when we walked over—solid enough. His coat was satiny and fine to the touch, and I admired his fine heavy legs and great hooves.

"Viola's our bareback rider—terrific somersaults." The Kid checked his watch again. "Fifteen minutes."

We'd just opened the gate and entered the big lot when a fellow, full of nervous waiting, jerked up to the Kid. Tall fellow, smooth moon-shaped face. Looked like he'd been young only a little while ago, but already his hair was receding, and he was shoveling on to middle age, a bit down at the mouth. "Can I talk to you?" he said anxiously. "I'm looking for work. Lots of stuff I can do. Anything that's stuck, broke, bent out of shape—I can fix it." It came in a rush, as though he'd be cut off before he could get it all out. "Lost a key, I can pick the lock. Doesn't run, I can get in the motor." He was trying to stand close enough for conversation, but not too close to be in your face. Looking pretty unkempt, like he'd slept in his clothes. Hadn't bathed for a while—you could tell.

The Kid considered. "Well, we've got a full crew already."

"I'll be up front," the fellow said. "I've been in some trouble and I'm on probation. It was a setup— I got suckered in. Thought it was a joyride, only they were out for a break-in. I wouldn't hurt a fly— honest. I need something bad." This, too, in a rush of breath that could have kept on coming till he'd spilled out his guts.

The Kid gave him a long look. "Well, I've been in some tight spots myself," he said.

An upbeat look, the one a cat gets in its eyes when you've got the can opener and the can in your hand.

"Are you above carting off the trash?" the Kid said. "All the cans and bottles? They're going to mount up. Lots of stuff from each performance. You can get the deposit money. I'll give you a few bucks in addition."

"Sure thing. I've got a good arm. You need hauling, I can haul it. You need breaking it up, I can do that. Anything anybody wants—or doesn't want. I'm damned if I can't do it."

It looked like he was ready to demonstrate the whole range of his talents on the spot. I expected him to drop to the ground or run up the side of the tent for good measure.

The Kid pulled out his wallet and gave him a ten. "See that caravan over there. Ask for Kitty and tell her what you're going to do. She had someone lined up, but he hasn't showed."

"Name's Dooley," the new crew member said, reaching out a hand for the Kid to shake. "I thank you. I never hurt nobody," he reassured us.

I could see how the Kid was thinking. All for the fresh start himself—anybody was entitled to one. Myself, I was of two minds. Whatever this one could fix, it looked to me, it couldn't keep him from wading beyond his depth. Maybe just blunder in and find he'd pulled the wrong wires and set off a rocket, when he was only trying to splice a cable. But then maybe he had to have his chance. Throw him off the lot if he made any trouble. I guess the Kid figures sometimes you have to gamble.

Maybe I heard his name wrong, or maybe it was something perverse in me, but Doodles was what I came up with. The name stuck, seemed to fit, and I think he rather liked it. After that, when I saw him around sacking up the cans he'd collected, he'd bend my ear, or anybody's ear, just rattling on. Seemed like he couldn't forget anything he'd ever seen or heard, all there just ticking inside of his brain, and he had to get it out.

After the Kid sent him off, we went for a soda from the cooler in front of the Kid's caravan and stood outside the tent waiting for the groom and the riders to bring up the horses. The Kid seemed to be waiting for someone else, too, the way he kept looking over his shoulder.

44

Then I knew who he was waiting for. I suppose I'd have recognized him anywhere, even though it had been what?—twenty years, maybe more. Something about his shape and the way he walked, like he had the goods, and it was all so valuable you'd better give him all the space he needed. Tall, well-built, with the sort of good looks to make you turn your head when he passed you on the street. The wave in the hair, the eyes blue as fire. And still quite a figure in his blue linen jacket and white slacks. He'd kept himself trim. Only the thick gold hair had thinned—he was combing it over a bald spot. The reddish-blond mustache had gone pale. And the lean face was heavy now, the skin coarsened, deep lines driving down under the cheekbones and a large, fleshy nose—had he been hitting the bottle? But the smile was gorgeous.

"Dream Girl!" he said, coming up with open arms.

"I can't believe this," I said, suddenly folded up in them. "Morgan, what are you doing here?"

He gave a hearty laugh—I'd forgotten how deep his voice was. "Putting on a show," he said, "What else? Do you realize this is the girl I almost married," he said, turning to the Kid, who looked from one to the other, kind of dazed, like somebody had socked him the Adam's apple.

"That's right—you knew each other. You were telling me down there in Florida."

"You don't know how I've been waiting for this moment," Morgan said. "Could hardly sit still." He moved back, gave me the once over. "You're still terrific, you know that, don't you?"

"C'mon," I said. "Don't give me that old line."

"I loved her the first time I laid eyes on her," he said to the Kid. "She's been my Dream Girl ever since. I've followed your career for years."

"Now look—" I said, "There's a lot of water under the bridge."

"Some things never change," he insisted.

"Well, I hate to break up the reunion," the Kid said, "but there are a few things we need to go over."

Morgan still hadn't let go of my hand—kept smoothing with his fingers. He was like that, always coveting a little flesh to smooth under his palm. Start with a hand and work up—hadn't let go of the habit. Lets you know the old switches are still, haven't quit operating. Keeps up the old interest, keeps the juices flowing. I don't deny it. And when I was letting my eye rove, he was a prize, I'll have to admit—if I'd just been settling for looks. And why hadn't I? It was a question, just why I'd sent my frisbee sailing in other directions. He'd outlasted Dusty, and the girls would hang onto him till he was ninety. At the moment I didn't know what to think. The past was just that—done with. Not worth digging up any dead cats. If his talents were set to working up a few sponsors, loosening the wallets of a few widows with money to burn, he was likely to be top-notch.

"You checked the advanced sales?" the Kid said.

"You know, Kid," Morgan said casually, and I thought a big patronizingly, "I've been thinking. Now that I've been talking with the backers, we maybe have to shift things around some, I have a few thoughts about the narrative."

"We open in less than a week," the Kid said impatiently.

"Well, you know. Something that'll grab people up right away—really take them in. There's still time to make a few changes." He gave me a wink.

"I thought we'd been over that. We agreed, remember. I've got a free hand—that was the agreement—right?"

I started to move away—at least I got my hand back, but the Kid reached for it, signaling I should stay—maybe he wanted me there for moral support.

"Wait a minute," Morgan said, holding up the hand that had let go of mine. Nicely manicured, I'd noticed before. Good moons, no ragged edges. "Let's just go over things once more—that's all I'm asking. The acts are strong, but it's the timing I'm worried about. Particularly down here. Considering what they're used to. I've been checking around." Then he added, "The ticket sales are down, way down—really disappointing. We've got to get some publicity that'll turn things around."

"Okay, but give us a chance, will you?" the Kid said. "Let's at least see what we've got, when everyone's here, when it's all together and the enthusiasm is high. I don't mind making changes, we made changes along the way. But it's the conception that's important—"

"Listen, just one suggestion and then I'll shut up. Just this one thing. How about bringing Bruno in on the elephant—right away. Then the chimps. Work up the comedy angle."

The Kid threw up his hands. "Look—it's a matter of tone. That's not how it works. You're putting the cart before the horse. Without the narrative there's nothing to hold the show together. I've been through it with the whole gang—they know what's expected. You're going to jinx the show—throw everyone for a loop. When I was on my own, we did fine—That's what got us together, remember?"

"Look around you," Morgan said. "This ain't Vegas."

"Okay, it's different," the Kid said. "But we're trying for something different. The posters, remember? 'The Dream of Circus.' That's the theme—that's what we stand for, that's what we're taking them into. We're trying to work them into it—into a different feeling from what's down here. You don't have to jump in all at once."

Morgan, too, was heating up, accentuating his words, clearly, carefully, appealing to logic or even good sense. "It's just a catchy phrase," he said. "You don't have to get bent out of shape about it." He glanced at me like he wanted to make some sort of pact—two adults trying to make the wayward kid get back in line. I wasn't buying.

"Look, Kid, I know you're an artist, a true artist, and I admire you for it. You might think I can't appreciate, but I do." He appealed to me to see his heart was in the right place. "But it's a business too. Entertainment is business. And I mean *BIG* business. You know how it is with entertainment—competition left and right. Barnum knew about that, knew about showmanship—that's why he was a great man. He knew the entertainment values."

"You think I don't," the Kid said. "Damn it, they're waiting for us. I'm late."

"Just look what we've got around us. Christ, the neighborhood. Not even a decent park. If I'd known they were going to give us this piece of shit—" Morgan said—voice stripped down to the raw. "We're

47

starting off down in a hole as it is, with two cement blocks on our feet."

The Kid was already off, halfway across the lot.

"Always on the run. Hard to catch and make him sit still for the news," Morgan said, trying for a more amiable tone. "Believe me, Alta, I'm just trying for his own good. You and me," he said to me. "We're veterans—we know the ropes."

"Well," I said. "I've seen what he can do."

"Right," he acknowledged. "Something to appreciate. I just don't want things to come crashing down. He's got a will of his own, that one." Shook his head. Maybe admiring him for it, maybe counting it a double-edged sword. But with a shrug, he let it all go. "But what am I thinking of—forgive me, forgive me." He reached for my hand again. "Really, Alta, you can't imagine how I thought of you over the years. And when you were down in Ventura City . . ."

I was curious to see where he was heading, but I wanted to be at that rehearsal. "I've got to go," I said. "Don't you want to see the rehearsal?"

He looked at his watch, "Hate to miss it, but I've got an appointment. Listen, I count this a great day—to be followed by others," As I turned to go, he gave my arm a final squeeze. "We'll see more of each other," he promised.

Lots of folks get caught in the nostalgia trap, especially when the glory days are over. I figured that was his problem. What did bother me was the way things were shaping up between him and Kid. The Kid had hinted at something of the sort when he came down to work his magic on me. And though maybe neither of us knew what it was, maybe he was asking something of me. Anyway, I went on into the tent to watch the horses.

The next days were so busy for the Kid I hardly saw him. He wasn't getting a whole lot of sleep, I could tell. I spent some time visiting Babe and talking to Tony about his days with the big cats at Ringling Brothers, then wandered over to the horses, admired them, got acquainted with the troupe. I'd met the acrobats and the aerialists. I felt a bit out of sync, though, still not knowing what I was doing there. The new crop comes along and people forget you were ever on the roster. Maybe you knew their folks from way back when, but that was about it.

People were busy all around me, practicing their acts, working on the equipment, feeding their animals, paying attention to their families. I'd got caught up on some recent gossip, if that's worth anything. It wasn't the time for me to sit and spin a few anecdotes about all that had been in days gone by.

I did stick my head into the wardrobe trailer and looked over costumes, trying to figure out what I could fit into for the chivaree. The Kid and I had come up with the idea I could carry the trained rooster in on my arm. I was deliberating between a pink gown with full net skirts and a purple velvet, rather elegant. It would be hotter, than blue blazes, but then I didn't have to live in it for long. I opted for the velvet and a wide-brimmed hat with plumes.

Only Morgan made a little phizz in the blood. I didn't see much of him, but every time I did, I'd get hit by a burst of enthusiasm. "Hey, let's find some time to get together—we've got lots to talk about." Yet somehow he made me want to avoid him—it bothered me. I'd see him and the Kid in a huddle now and then, talking and gesturing, but so far, the Kid was doing things the way he wanted, though it looked like he'd never be done arguing for it.

Finally, though, it was going to happen. Things were ready—everybody was there for the cue rehearsal. When I walked into the tent, the acrobats were still doing handstands and flips, and others were juggling rings and pins. The band members were climbing up to their platform with their instruments. The leader, Ginger, started calling their attention to passages of the music and reminding them which pieces went where. A slender energetic redhead, who'd taken her place on the drums, launched into the roll that would start the show. A keyboard struck up a tune, a fiddle came in, then a bass and a sax.

We were a few minutes late. The Kid was talking confidentially to Bruno, the clown, who I'd heard about but hadn't really talked to. Then he turned to Kitty, the house manager, who was standing there with her clipboard, looking at some notes. I started talking to Whitney Bowser, who was handling the front as well as joining in the juggling act at the end. I'd heard about him for years—one of the country's top jugglers, who'd taught a whole generation of jugglers. Started learning the art when he was a kid, picked it up from old vaudeville performers. You could tell he lived and breathed circus. I wanted to hear his stories when we had a free moment.

We took a seat on the bleachers as the Kid glanced through the cue sheets.

"Everybody here?" he wanted to know.

"The Barclays aren't in yet," someone told him.

"Yeah, Kitty told me. Delayed in New York. Stand in for them, will you, Bruno? We'll have to get them in here tomorrow. I've set up the rehearsal schedule for the week on the bulletin board. We need the acrobats here tomorrow morning eight o'clock sharp. Dress rehearsal tomorrow afternoon."

"Okay, everybody here and ready?" He looked around. "Where's Scott?" he asked.

"He's already left," Kitty said. "Family crisis."

"Oh, I . . . That's right. You'll all have to take turns on the back curtain," the Kid said. One of those last minute improvisations we all know about. "Don't know if he'll make it back or not."

"I can do that much," I volunteered. Didn't even stop to think— It just came out like somebody else said it. Seemed the thing to do. I could still do the chivaree if I wanted. Walk in with that rooster and be part of what was going on. Walk around the ring and look at all those faces turned up in expectation. A thrill in that.

There sure wasn't any glamour in the back curtain—I might just be stuck with it. But it would be something useful. At least I could be part of the aesthetics, so to speak. When the front curtain's open, you just want the audience to see whoever's ready to come on, not what's going on in back: folks talking, kidding around, practicing juggling, the crew standing around waiting to bring out the next prop. You don't want the folks out front to be staring into the harsh light bouncing off the white wall behind the tent. Spoils the illusion. Just like you don't want to see the actors and stagehands and all the ropes and pulleys back stage. So you keep the back curtain closed while the front curtain's open. The performer gives you a little nod and you open up. Then you wait, make a little peephole so you can check when the front curtain man, or whoever, is opening up for the act that's going out.

"You sure you want to do that?" the Kid said.

"Why not? I got nothing better to do."

"Okay then, let's get going."

The hours that followed were exacting work, getting all the performers cued into their entrances and exits, and the crew ready to run out and prepare the ring before and after the acts, bringing the necessary props and removing them quickly. Then, getting the music in sync with each stroke of the performance. Sentiment when it was called for; drama and excitement when needed. The right horse music. The right music for flying through the air; the right beat for walking across the high wire; music for juggling and tumbling. Music for the dog act and elephant entrance. The clown needed some emphasis here and there, a little satire from the fiddle, or a crash and clatter from drums and cymbals.

Whitney and I had to know everything that went on and off, so we'd be ready with the curtains. I got hold of the little notebook where I jot down things I need from the store. I tried to keep track of the cues. Exacting work indeed, but we got through the first round anyway, with a few hitches here and there. Always were. It would take a few performances to smooth out the rough edges. I was glad when we got it all worked out and were free to grab a bite to eat. I'd been working up an appetite. We opted for pizza. Something had been niggling at me all the time I was trying to concentrate on the rehearsal. Morgan. I'd been thinking back to the old days, when he'd made a big deal of being related to Morgan the Buccaneer. He dressed the part—came out in his high boots and braided jacket and plumed hat and sword. Then with a flourish, he swallowed that sword down to his navel. He juggled daggers and swords like you wouldn't believe and could balance a sword on his chin. The audience ate it up. We were together a couple of seasons with Ringling, before Dusty and I got married. The rivalry between them was intense for awhile. But there was something about Morgan that couldn't quite convince me. Maybe he looked too good to be true.

We went our separate ways—that was after Dusty and I got married, and we didn't run into him for a while. Then suddenly he turned up when Dusty and I were trying to put our show together. He was there with all kinds of friendly interest, was hot to be in it, and for a while Dusty was willing enough—Morgan was a crowd pleaser, and he was even going to put up some money to give things a boost. But then he and Dusty had some kind of go-around. I never knew what it was. Was Dusty afraid he'd try to get around me? Or was it something else? All I knew was, one day he was gone. I heard about him from time to time. He'd worked up a nightclub act and was pretty successful with that. Then I heard he was in the nightclub business. Now I kept wondering what had gone on between him and Dusty.

After the rehearsal, the Kid wanted to get a moment of quiet before the momentum caught him up, so he drove us to a tavern a couple of miles away.

"Give me a beer quick as you can," he told the waitress, "I'm dry as a bone." A beer was a little mild for me just at that moment, so I put in for a scotch on the rocks. When the beer came, he took a long swig, and leaned back with a sigh. "That's better," he said. "God, I'm tired—I am so tired." Then he smiled. "You still in one piece?"

"Still hanging in."

"Well, we're moving to the takeoff," he said. "If only that goddamn worrywart would get off my back. I'll wait for dress rehearsal to see what you think." He shook his head. "Now if the Barclays get here tomorrow when they're supposed to . . . Can't wait for you to see them." Enthusiasm began to work back through the fatigue. "Great act. Foot juggling and acrobatics. Their timing is a wonder. And if nobody gets sick or screws up . . . And if the folks from uptown will come down . . . Oh, God I hope it all works the way I can see it."

He went on like that, excited and nervous, full of the show in his head, seeing how it could be, hope trying for glory. He drank his beer, called for another, talking all the time, foot swinging back and forth, fingers drumming the table. He was Dusty all over. I remember those nights, him all revved up, couldn't hardly sleep, rising up with a new shot of energy to take over the day. It was catching, too. If you didn't have any of his enthusiasm, you couldn't have stood to be around him. A dynamo. A bundle of jitters, too. I just let the Kid go on talking till our food came. If he'd had to keep it all bottled up, he'd probably have exploded.

"Damn that Morgan," he said, "He cramps my style. Always on my neck. Wants to throw a monkey wrench into things before we're even underway." He took his napkin and played with a wet spot around the beer bottle.

"He's worried about the ticket sales, I take it."

"Yeah," the Kid said. "He's the bottom-line man. Okay, it's a risk—nothing guaranteed. I figure we are not going to get the big crowds right at first. We got to convince them to come, and I'm hoping for better as we go on . . . They're worried about this part of town. Getting mugged, having stuff ripped off from their cars. We'll have guards on the lot keeping an eye out. Okay for the matinees. But the evening show—that may be what's worrying them. I'm not going to think about it anymore. The show's the main thing right now. And to scuttle what you know is good—that's the old fear business."

He waved it all away, looked eagerly at the pile of fried sole and potatoes that had just arrived and dug in. Amazing what a little food will do for the cast of things. No use fretting ahead of time.

"The thing is," he went on, between mouthfuls. "I don't know how much I can trust the old pirate. He's always thinking the money side of it—okay, so that's what it takes to get a show off the ground. But if that's all you're thinking about, before you even get a glimpse . . ."

Morgan the Pirate. Now he'd turned into a businessman. But once it was his signature. Claimed his great-great—I don't know how many greats—but way back when—grandfather was the natural son of Henry Morgan. From a Costa Rican girl he met up with in Barbados. Might be true for all I know. His father tried to get the court to declare he had the sole right to any treasure found in Morgan's territory down around those Caribbean Islands, but the courts threw him out. After that, he tried to float a stock company to finance treasure hunts.

Colorful character. For a while, I remember, Morgan was trying to sell his father's story to some feature magazine. I don't think anything came of that either.

"He sure is taken with you," the Kid said. "He really wanted to marry you?"

"You know, I wonder about that," I said, thinking back. "He'd say to me, 'Alta, you're the one for me—marry me and I'll be the happiest man on the continent.' But you know, I always had the feeling that if I said, 'Okay, let's do it,' he'd have turned and run like a fox with a hunt behind it. Maybe that's why I left things up in the air."

"He's never married," he told me.

"He didn't have to—all the gals flocking to him. Why spoil a good thing?"

The Kid laughed. "I'm sure he's had his innings. Maybe still does."

"Didn't you say he had a nightclub out in Las Vegas."

"That's where he got into the entertainment business. Only he had some bad luck, he told me. The place burned down—there was some question about the insurance. I don't think he was able to collect . . ."

A little odd, it struck me. "But he got back in the business?"

"He'd started doing circus acts in the club, the only one in Vegas. Only he said he missed the real thing. That's when I came along."

I had trouble sleeping that night. Next day was dress rehearsal.

And then it was for real. It's a wonder we made it through. The Kid was supposed to be in charge, but you wouldn't have known it. Morgan sat there on the edge of the circle, jumping out like a jack-in-the box, throwing out suggestions, running up to the performers to tell them what he wanted done. The Kid was ready to tear his hair. I could see him getting red in the face. Finally he went up to Morgan and told him to get the hell out, he was getting everybody riled. It was unprofessional. If he wanted to watch, he'd better sit there without saying one more goddamn word. Morgan tried to hold himself in, but you could tell it was a hard go. He started once to say something during Bruno's act, but the Kid glared at him so savagely, the words just dropped to the sawdust. The rehearsal went on fairly smoothly after that.

54

I figured I'd try to get out of there before they beat each other up, but the two left the tent without exchanging a word, and I paused on the way out to tell Bruno how much I enjoyed watching him. With a flourish, he pulled out a bouquet of artificial flowers. "They don't make them like this anymore," he said, as he started to hand them to me. Then he pulled them away. "These are such lovely flowers," he said, "I believe I'll give them to myself."

Morgan came up to where we were standing, beside Babe's pen just behind the back opening. A funny thing happened. As he approached, she put a foot on her trunk and blew through it. Sounded just like a raspberry. We all laughed, even Morgan. "That's a greeting for you."

When I got back to the caravan, I found a letter from Dollie in the door, telling me the news from down south. Calypso the cat and her tiger cat had made friends after a rocky beginning. There were now six kittens, all doing well. "Make friends with the elephant," she wrote me, "so she won't take you for a rival. Remember, where there are elephants, there is victory." Another of her peculiar pronouncements, but then she'd always been a little strange. I'd say we were all a little strange. Came with the territory.

IV.
The Comedy of Bruno

What would the circus be without a clown? All the razzle-dazzle, lights and action. Aerialists and acrobats. Dogs and elephants doing tricks. Illusion that dances past the eye. Real skill and daring. Beautiful—all of it. But still you'd look around and think, *Something's missing*. The figure with the sad face and floppy shoes trying to sweep up the spotlight into a dustpan or falling over his feet while he stands there singing to his lady love, or climbing to the moon on a ladder that breaks into pieces under his feet and lands him on his ass. Folly's red heart, redder than roses, red as blood. More real than real. Always dancing along the edge of things and taking a pratfall. And what do you find when you've taken hold of folly and gone to the roots? Enter BRUNO, with his potato nose, and downturned mouth painted on his white face, creases in the forehead, the shaggy brows—a hulking dark figure in a tattered black coat, patched at the elbows. A black beret to top it off.

Let him walk in with his mandolin or sweet potato pipe or trumpet or watch him juggle or borrow a baseball cap or two from the audience to see if he can make a trade. I'd stood at the back of the bleachers watching him shake hands with the kids, borrow their popcorn to juggle, letting a piece or two land in his mouth. After that, I stayed behind the curtain, trying to figure out from the laughter I was hearing just what hijinks were going on.

A minute or two later, the Kid is yelling out, "Places everyone."

I take my cue from Bruno to open the back curtain and wait for him to enter the chute, as he stands up in a little red car, steering with one hand, while a great yellow balloon floats above, *Bruno's Dream* skipping across in shining blue letters. This performance is Bruno's Dream of Circus, with him leading off the chivaree. I have to work quickly in time with the music, so everybody can parade in an unbroken circle before the audience. Babe is next in the chute, with an acrobat ready to do a handstand on her back. It's not a great crowd, but they're with us, and the cheering continues as the horses enter and the aerialists and acrobats make their appearance in their brilliant costumes. The old thrill is still there.

One by one, I was getting acquainted with the folks in and around the show. I didn't have all their names straight yet, but I was getting there. Wally, the other clown, and his wife, Minna, an acrobat. The trapeze artists, Wanda and Ivan. Columbo, who did the dogs—they all slept with him, a very crowded bed scene. I'd been wandering into the tent during rehearsals, sitting on the bleachers, with or without the Kid, and watching. Acrobats. Equestriennes. The high-wire folks. The balancing chair act. The Cossack riders—as they did their workouts.

I'd gotten to know Katya and loved watching her lead her dancing horse. She put him through his paces, a beautiful high-stepping piebald gelding. Then her three brothers, and I never got tired of watching them, riding a dark bay horse, a black beauty, and a white—leaping to the ground and back into the saddle, working under the horse's belly to the other side, while the horses went at their breakneck best. Training and practice—coming together with confidence and skill. Down to the action itself. Even without costumes, music, or lights, it sent your blood racing. I was able to catch their act every rehearsal, for it was the climax of the show. The curtains had to be tied back out of the way as they moved in and out. Afterwards, they wiped down the horses, who'd worked up a lather, and led them back to their stalls.

Some of the performers I had only a little time with. If they weren't rehearsing, they were busy with their families or trying to get some rest. But Bruno was around a lot, seemed to be at the heart of the show. Generous with himself. There when the Kid needed him, looking in on people, speaking a friendly word in an accent I couldn't figure out. But practically his first words to me were in praise of the Kid: "The Kid, I love him. He's not afraid to dream. Trying to make something grow in the midst of stickers and thorns. Always a big risk."

When he was in costume, everything he did made you break out laughing, as though he was made only to be funny, but get rid of the shoes, and nose, the mop of hair, the mask of white paint, and he stood there, a tall man, with brown eyes ready to take you in, whatever you were, and welcome you, at least for a while, into his life.

He liked to talk circus. He wanted to know about my career, where I'd played, whether I knew so-and-so. He described spectacles he'd seen, performers he admired.

"Trapeze, eh?" he said to me, the first time I had a real chance to talk to him. It was after the cue rehearsal, and we were breathing a little fresh air outside the tent. Though why we were standing there was a wonder. We'd gone without lunch and were hungry as cannibals.

"Were you ever in the European circus?"

No, I had to tell him—we'd had a couple of offers, but things never panned out. One of things I wish we could've done, among others. "I've never even been to Paris."

He kissed his fingers and let the kiss fly into the air. "Ah, Par—ee. My beautiful Par—ee." He looked as though he was studying my expression, trying to come to some feeling about me. "Yes, you *must* go there—I think you would love it. The City of Light . . . That is the truth. Maybe you can go one day."

Really? Was it possible? I'd never thought of it.

For many years he lived in Paris, he told me, and he loved being part of the circus there. His first job was working the spots.

"Such wonderful circuses there. The Bouglione, the Cirque Plume, Zingaro, the Cirque Baroque and, of course Le Cirque Romanes. Very small but with gypsies singing. Nothing like it." He had put an idea in my head.

"I'd love to see them."

"And the city itself—such a great place to walk around so much to see and taste. Even though I missed my beautiful Prague—who can forget her? I have had my two mistresses. Now my home is here." He gestured towards the tent.

"Mine too—" being as it was the only one I'd ever really known. The trailer was a place to park—convenient. I wanted to ask him which circuses he did his clowning in and where else he'd traveled, but a shrill voice summoned him like a whistle. "Bruno, dinner is waiting. Everything is almost spoiled."

"Olga," he said. "Come, please, and meet her."

I started in her direction, but quick as lightning she turned and disappeared inside the trailer, maybe to rescue something on the stove.

"She manages me and the chimps," Bruno said. "Keeps us all in line."

I didn't know how to take that. I hadn't had much chance to see her, she made herself scarce. I'd caught a glimpse of a small woman in jeans and T-shirt with dove-colored hair piled up on her head. Faded and a bit pinched, I thought. Pretty once. Slender.

"I hope you can join us sometime," he said. "Olga can cook, I tell you. But then, I taught her everything she knows. *Duck* à *l'orange*—her specialty. Ooh-la-la. You'll have to try it."

Somehow I had the feeling Olga wouldn't favor it. The whole time I'd been there, I'd hardly seen her emerge from the trailer, except with her chimps, who shared a large cage at the side of the trailer. They swung from their bars and ate their bananas and picked each others' fleas, eyed the passersby until it was time for their act—a barrel of monkeys. Then they were into it, yammering for attention, trying to outdo each other, clasping their hands above their heads in triumph if one got more applause than the others. Riding their unicycles, turning cartwheels, balancing on each other's shoulders. All over the place. Pure show biz—the kids loved it.

Maybe the chimps took all Olga's energy for being social, or maybe living with Bruno used her up. It would have been a challenge.

He was like a bandleader inventing the entire world as he went along. Taking up anything at hand. Always getting the worst end of things— Getting pushed around. Everything he touched led to chaos: tables and chairs fell apart; doors stuck or flew in his face when he tried to pull them open; strings popped on his fiddle or guitar; his horn refused to make a sound. His feet and arms betrayed him. His little dog, Hercules, would send him running around the ring, tearing his hair off in clumps, yelling for his life as the creature tore into his pant leg and wouldn't be shaken off. All this he looked upon with wide-eyed wonder, a crooked smile in his creased, genial face, as if

59

he would never come to the end of the ways things could blow up in his face, turn inside out and upside down, or plain self-destruct just when they seemed under control.

He was an endless store of jokes and anecdotes. He had me splitting my sides all the time he was waiting to go on. He would come in paddling an imaginary canoe or doing a little dance while he juggled pins or teased the young contortionist or tried to talk to Columbo's dogs.

"He's had quite a life," the Kid told me. He filled me in on some of it, and I got the rest in bits and pieces from Bruno himself—though it took me quite a while to get the whole story. He was from an old circus family, went back several generations. His parents had survived Treblinka because they were performers and could entertain the Nazis. There was a troupe of dwarfs who'd survived as well, and the youngest was still alive. Bruno was very fond to her—she had known his parents. So had the other members of her family. Bruno was born after the war, but although his parents survived the camp they didn't last through his childhood. Nine years old and he was an orphan.

He went on both in the theater and in the circus, doing any kind of work he could find. He learned juggling, was a magician for a while, and then began working with animals. His real love was the animal acts, he told me a lot about the animal acts. He had a whole string of them at various times—foxes and kangaroos, chimpanzees, a bear, an elephant, a gray African parrot of high intelligence.

"I never had a hippopotamus like the great Durov," he complained. I tried to imagine him in the midst of this menagerie. It was his great regret. "That man taught her to do somersaults—a marvel." He loved the animals—they spoke to him. Each one a syllable of existence, he called them. "Each with a voice. One day they will speak."

I noticed that he spent a lot of time around our animals, feeding carrots to the horses. Taking treats to Babe. Petting the Shetland. Talking to the goat.

Later I learned that he'd performed in Prague all during the Communist era. "You should have seen the way I used those animals to make my comment on the state of things," he told me. "I had a wonderful set of monkeys, and I pretended to be a bureaucrat making them jump through the hoops. The audience knew what I was doing all right. That's when I started figuring out I was really a clown."

"He's the funniest man I've ever known," the Kid said. "You go through all he's been through, and maybe all that's left is laughter."

Bruno was a real contrast to Wally, the other clown, who was a shy young man, who spoke with a slight stammer and had trouble talking to people. Once he got into his whiteface though, he was a different person—his arms going in all directions, twisting himself like a pretzel into impossible shapes. I liked him, too, and his wife, Minna, an acrobat. He and Bruno were good friends.

"What about Olga?" I asked the Kid.

"Hard to figure," he told me. "Always hanging onto Bruno like he might get out of her sight. I don't know—doesn't take to people much. Doesn't trust them. I never stay around her long—she's generally in one of her moods. She does her job . . . does it well, in fact. She's got those chimps eating out of her hand."

And the Kid's job was trying to get all the different egos and moods and temperaments to work together to put on a show. I remembered all that from years back when. Even now, with my little part, I still had to work to do—getting the cues right for the curtain. The show still had some rough spots during the dress rehearsal, people slow on their cues, the crew confused about taking off the props for the dog act, one of the jugglers whose timing was off—things like that.

"Think it'll come together?" the Kid asked me when the last rehearsal was over.

"Sure it will," I told him, though it would take a few performances to get things really smooth. You had to expect that.

Morgan had kept pretty much in the background since he'd made a nuisance of himself the two had had it out. There wasn't room for two people to direct things, especially if they didn't see eye to eye. Morgan was supposed to handle the money and publicity side and let the Kid do the show. I kept wondering what sort of arrangement, or contract they had worked up— I worried about it.

The Kid wasn't conceding a thing. He'd done the thinking and the planning, had worked up the show with the performers. He wasn't about to throw it away and make a mess at the last minute because the old fear had crept in. The performers were behind him. Circus for them was daring, not being afraid. But Morgan was an unknown quantity. And I had the feeling he was just waiting, biding his time to see which way the wind blew.

But whenever the two of us came together, his tone was like a lover's.

"Alta," he'd greet me. "I've just got to spend time with you. We have a lot of catching up to do. When things calm down a little . . ." And he was off in a rush. I was just as glad. I wasn't eager to summon up the past, especially any part of the past that included him.

Saturday, the day of the first show, a matinee, you could feel the tension in the air. Jake, the head of the work crew, was up at dawn, finishing work on one of the props that had broken. Kitty, the wardrobe mistress, had been busy ironing costumes and had them hanging up where a set of curtains had been strung up for those who needed to change quickly. The donnikers had been cleaned out, and Doodles was on hand to collect the bottles, cans, and garbage. Slow work. He hauled the bags of stuff out on a kid's wagon he'd found or pinched from somewhere. He still looked like he'd slept in his clothes in an alley somewhere with a piece of cardboard for his bed. The Kid told him to come around between the afternoon and evening shows as well.

The concessionaires began setting up their tables and booths with piles of T-shirts and caps with the circus logo, posters and stuffed elephants and chimps and key chains and pennants. A big popcorn machine was working away, and the cotton candy vendor was pouring in the syrup; the candied apples were on display, and the stomach-twisting smell of hot dogs and sausages being grilled was in the air.

I couldn't resist the aroma and treated myself to a hot sausage with lots of mustard. It tasted wonderful going down. Took me back to youth and longing. A smell like that hits one of those sensitive spots that must have evolved like the eye, a longing that goes deeper than food. The smell comes at you, suggesting that something might exist to satisfy the heart, and that the stomach might be the path.

It was the circus after all, and I was feeling frisky, young in my bones with things bright in the air. That was the trouble. I could feel a spot of weakness in that direction. If you ever figure things out and can ever move on past time and regret, I want to know about it.

I walked around the lot, crossed the lot to see how it was with the elephant and the horses, shot the breeze for a while with Tony Sanchez, who told me about his boyhood days with a little mud show in Torreon. He'd worked with the animals there, though all they had were a few birds, a couple of ancient horses, fit for glue, and a toothless lion. Didn't matter—he'd loved them all, especially the horses. The Russians were grooming theirs, and I paused to admire the sleek beauties.

Cars were beginning to pull into the neighborhood and park in the lot as I walked back to the tent. The cans and trash were all gone, but Doodles was still hanging around. When I asked if he needed anything, he looked sheepish and hangdog and said he hadn't eaten that day. I gave him a fiver for a hot dog and whatever else would fill the space and told him to come back after the performance.

"You think I could watch?" he said, with a kid's eagerness.

"Sure you can—I'll put you in a spot on the side the bleachers near the back. If there's an empty seat, you can sit down. If not, you'll have to stand." He was ecstatic.

I took him in and stood there with him for a few minutes. I was nervous as a cat, watching as folks started to come in. It would be mostly kids in the afternoon, an older audience at night. The Kid was hoping that the matinees Saturday and Sunday would draw a bigger crowd to make up for the evening performances if they were thin.

I went out the back opening to wait, sat down in one of the folding chairs with several of the acrobats and Sara, the equestrienne, who'd walk in with her little daughter, Yvette, and their pet rooster on the back of a goat. The Kid appeared in top hat and tails, ruffled shirt, and vest of gold and silver thread, looking every inch the ringmaster. "Eight minutes," he announced. Bruno came over, raised an imaginary glass and tossed down the imaginary contents. Then he went out to do a little business with the kids, work up the crowd till showtime. I walked to the side of the bleachers to watch him as he carried in his tiny dog to do a few tricks, catching the pieces of popcorn he had the kids throw.

The center sections were full from the ring seats almost to the top of the bleachers. But the other sections were thin or almost empty.

No time to think about it. They were all there in the chute, and Whitney opened the front curtain for the Kid, who stepped out to a great fanfare to announce the beginning of the show. And here's the music, making a lively time of it, with Bruno and the company behind him, brilliant in their costumes under the colored spots. How many times I'd seen some variation of this, only now I could only hear the music and wait for some break to catch whatever act was going on. They all filed out and the show was going up.

And so the performance begins with a solitary man in the spotlight, Bruno, a traveler with a battered suitcase, searching through the world for the home of magic. He has no car now, and the balloon is floating high over his head. He goes through various gyrations trying to catch it. Much laughter from the audience.

A great crow hovers in front of him, raucous with warnings, and every obstacle awaits him. A monkey runs away with his suitcase, opens it, and doves rise into the air. When Bruno collects them into his hat, they turn into scarves that he pulls out one by one. Worn and weary, he takes refuge in a park bench, but Hercules, hardly bigger than your hand, chases Bruno around the ring, leaping at his back, tearing at his pant legs, hanging on as he runs. More frantic movements as Bruno shows his terror, while the crowd explodes with laughter. He finally captures Hercules and lets him balance in the palm of his hand, but then he loses him in his many pockets. A mad search as the dog pokes its head up, now here, now there, as Bruno races around the ring, jumps, and finally dives into a summersault. The kids love it, of course. And so do the grownups.

When Bruno comes back to the bench, Wally, skinny as a stick, dressed as a cowboy, is sitting in the middle of it—arms stretched out along the back. You think he is no match for Bruno, but every time Bruno tries to sit down, some part of Wally is in the way. Won't let Bruno have an inch. Bruno grabs up a huge papier-mâché club, threatens to beat him, chases him around the bench. Then Wally gets hold of the club and chases Bruno. How they fight over the bench, chasing one another, climbing on it, pushing each other off, it all keeps the audience right with them. Then, just as you think it's over, with Bruno and Wally both finally sitting on the bench, the dogs run in, climb all over them, then race over to a slide, run up and down, leap through hoops. Bruno, in pursuit of his dream, watches in dumb wonder while the acrobats form their pyramids. Maybe things would be better from up above? Enter Babe to lift him up on her back, but he gets stuck halfway up—and gently she sets him down. No, he can't get off the ground. Claudio enters with the balancing chair act. Bruno tries to climb to the back of one of them, but takes a pratfall instead.

Between the acts, there is always one of the troupe to remind Bruno of his dream. The balloon appears in various colors, carried by a boy on roller skates, by one of the horsemen, and even by Wanda on the high wire. So we watch the various acts unfold—Claudio, splendid in a red satin suit with gold braid and sequins, set up four bottles on which he balances his chair, climbs on the top of them, piles up chair after chair, till six of them balance one on top of the other, and he does a handstand on the back of the last one. It's all too much for Bruno, though he does manage to make it across a tight rope a foot off the ground, balancing an umbrella. He invites the audience to applaud his triumph. He looks up as though to see if he can, after all, leave the ground.

Here are Wanda and Ivan to show him how, and I'm reminded of when Dusty and I were Gold Dust and Dream Girl, sailing over the heads of the crowd. Wanda, all in her youthful loveliness sails though the air like milkweed and Pearson is there to meet her. I watch her climb up to the top rung of the trapeze, pump back and forth several times, Ivan below her. Youth and strength and beauty—oh, it's a glory. Then Wanda goes into a backward flip, diving down, and Ivan reaches out, catching her by the wrists. The crowd gasps. Every time—you can bet on it. No nets under them. Then it's the last act of the first half.

The Flying Marvels on the high wire with their bicycles, going back and forth, Leo's daughter standing on his shoulders, various pyramids and their extraordinary feats of balance.

The rest of the circus unfolds, continues the story—Bruno's dream. And it was like a dream, the way it takes you out of your seat into another space.

From where I was sitting on the stool near the ropes, I had a little spot where I could see some of the action; the rest I knew from the rehearsals, I could tell that the audience was with us all the way Through all the moods and rhythms. The laughter, the thrill with the edge of fear when they were watching the trapeze act and the Flying Marvels on the high wire, the astonishment that rose from the experience. The excitement of the Cossack riding act, and the final glimpse of Bruno, now back with his suitcase, the balloon in front of him as he races out of the ring.

A great show—if only there had been more people to see it.

The evening crowd was about the same as in the afternoon, and on Sunday, though we'd hoped for better, they weren't exactly pushing to get in. The first week, in fact, was pretty dismal as to numbers, though not with the enthusiasm. No complaint there. The show went over big, you could tell. And the cheers and clapping made it seem like the crowd was double the size. That gave a lot of energy to the performers. And one by the one they were working the kinks out. At first the sound system rumbled, let out an occasional shriek. Now it worked like a charm. The show was coming together. The music sounded terrific.

There was to be a party that night after the performance, a chance to see everybody together, get their feedback and try for a sense of combined effort. The Kid sent out for a dozen big pizzas and salad and beer. The musicians were on hand, and the crew. Pretty soon others came around to the back, after they'd stood at the exits, giving their farewells to the crowd, cleaned off their makeup, and changed out of their costumes.

"Went well, don't you think?" the Kid said, undaunted by the turnout.

"Yeah, they loved it," Morgan said, "but I'll bet we didn't have four hundred in the seats."

"We're new here," the Kid argued. "People aren't used to us yet. It takes time for the word to get around. Anyway, I look to the future—it'll all work out."

The pizzas arrived, we were more than ready for them. I went off with Minna and several of the others to help set up the tables, while some of the men brought in the ice chests with beer and soft drinks. Morgan was standing next to me. I was trying to forget I was tired and wasn't much in the mood for talk—just wanted to feel my way into what was around me. One of the musicians was having a go at juggling and making a mess of it. The others were laughing at him. Despite the thin crowds, people were in a good mood, you could tell—things were falling into place, and the audiences couldn't have been better.

I liked that enthusiasm. Made me feel buoyant, as though I were up there again myself, ready to take a flying leap. Only that was just one way of looking at it—things were up in the air, and that felt a little scary.

There was a certain impatience in Morgan's bearing—he had something on his chest and was bound to get it out.

"All the energy," he said, following the juggling efforts. "Even after a performance."

"Think of what we used to do," I reminded him.

"Yeah, I know."

"Often just trying to get from one day to the next."

Odd to be standing there with somebody from the old days. We were young hopefuls then, with the world just opening up. Scrambling for gigs, going for a reputation. Then trying for our own show.

"And fixing things when they broke, sewing things when they ripped, standing in to assist with the dog act, or helping the snake charmer. I wonder now how we managed."

"Maybe we had more stamina," he said. "It's a great outfit, this one. I just hope . . . The Kid's still young—he doesn't know how tough it can be," he said, giving the conversation is downward thrust. Seems like you could always count on him for that. "I've seen outfits like this start up, all energetic and hopeful . . ."

I didn't want for him to finish his sentence.

"You don't know the Kid," I said. I wasn't going let him be like the great crow hovering over Bruno. And where was Bruno? People were already at the tables filling their plates. Actually, he was sitting with Olga off to one side, as though they didn't want to talk to anyone. He seemed to be two different people—Bruno by himself was something like the clown in the ring, full of jokes and little inventions, as if his only mission in life was to make people laugh. Bruno with Olga stood apart, as if he could only be a spectator, and what he saw had no connection with what he was. Her expression was neutral.

"Come over to the trailer afterwards," Morgan said. "I owe you a glass of wine for old times sake. You can meet Jamaica."

"You better let me get some sleep this round," I told him.

I saw the Kid wander over to them, and Olga seemed to brighten up. He stood talking with them, and she seemed more animated than I'd ever seen her before. The Kid gestured up towards the top of the tent, and then turned and pointed up again, but I couldn't guess what they were talking about—the lights maybe. He'd said something about taking one of the spots off Bruno when he needed a softer light.

"Well, you know, Alta, I still have some fond thoughts about you. Seeing you hasn't changed any of that. Just brought it back to life."

"I think we better get something to eat," I reminded him.

"But you will come over," he insisted. "Before dinner even—or maybe I could grill a couple of steaks for us."

"You're on," I said. We walked down to the tables, where we heaped up our plates. I sat down with Minna and Wally, and we got into a lively conversation about a wonderful acrobatic act that Minna had seen in Orlando. I don't know what the Kid had said to her about me, but Minna had taken it upon herself to look out for me. She was always bringing me a glass of iced tea or a soda to drink during the show, and I'd had lunch with them in their trailer. After a few days, you begin to see friendships forming here and there; sometimes people had to learn to stay clear of someone as well, because their chemistry just didn't mix. Mostly people are careful of each other, seeing as how they have to work together for their own good. Under the spotlight you're a big deal, but you're not the whole show. Every once in a while, you

68

get some whizz who's got to be the star, shoves everybody else aside, and tries to grab all the luster. Then it takes a few words.

The pizza sat rather heavily on my stomach during the wee hours, but I managed to get enough sleep. The next morning the Kid came around with the local paper. Not just a glowing review, but an editorial as well. We took turns reading it:

For those of us who love the circus, the piece began, *the city has taken a unique step—giving a home to the New Downtown Circus. From among the warehouses and decaying buildings you see its jaunty red and white-striped tent rising up, promising riches for those there for the show. Once inside with your bag of peanuts or popcorn, you see that promise fulfilled. Enter clowns and laughter . . .*

Next thing the article praises the various acts and all those who've made it possible, with special praise for the Kid. It goes on:

Let us say more of what the presence of the circus makes possible: The Dream of Circus, so the poster tells us. A dream we can enter and let our imagination soar as we enter once again the realm of childhood. How necessary in this era of the computer and the cell phone to leave a space beyond technology, beyond the pressures of day-to-day life—here in the city. And for those who are struggling down in the inner-city, here is there chance to dream of possibility—a way to a better life.

Then it winds things up:

If you haven't been to see the show, let me urge you to do so. Ticket prices won't eat up your wallet. Believe me, it's worth the price.

"We're a success," the Kid said.

"I hope it'll goose up the sales," Morgan said.

"What do you say we get some skywriting?" the Kid said. "Or we could have a banner: 'Follow your dreams to the ringside.'"

"Right now," Morgan said, "We'd better keep down expenses and get something more solid in those seats." But even he was lightening up. A corporation was possibly interested in becoming a sponsor. If we got their backing, we could breathe a little more easily. But the Kid was not to be done out of his skywriting. The sky, after all, was the limit.

V.

The Mystery Prankster

It was a mixed bag throughout the week. The tent was never filled to capacity, but we hit a Wednesday matinee with a crowd nearly double what it was the night before. That got everybody excited, and it was a whacking good performance. I could tell from behind the curtain that everything was a notch or two above what it had been. And every moment I could, I stepped through the side curtain and went to stand at the side of the bleachers with the crew to catch a glimpse of what was going on.

Friday night attendance was down, but the Saturday performances and the Sunday matinee were booked pretty solid. We figured the news was getting around. The editorial and the review were bound to catch some attention. Plus the newspaper sent a reporter down to take pictures, to work up some feature stuff about Bruno, the Flying Marvels, Babe, and some of the others. The Kid was riding high.

"See—look," he said, pointing out phrases from the review. "They're calling it 'innovative' and 'appealing,' 'full of beauty and surprise—an astonishment to watch. Pure magic.'"

"That's something to go to the corporation with," he told Morgan. "That's something tangible. Even if this first season doesn't put us in the black, it's something to build on." He thought, though, that in the next couple of weeks we'd make up for lost time.

Morgan was typically cautious. "I'd sure like to see us out of the hole. Corporations like to put their money where it doesn't evaporate like water."

"You can't guarantee anything the first year," the Kid argued. "The city people know that, too. It's what fund-raisers are for."

Sunday night, the crowd dwindled to what it had been during the first week, but the Kid refused to be rattled.

"The word'll get around," he insisted. "It's a great show."

But Morgan didn't have the Kid's buoyancy. We were off Monday and Tuesday, and I'd planned to go down to the laundromat with a bundle of clothes to wash and then shop for groceries and catch a nap later in the afternoon. I'd just come out of the caravan for a breath of air after breakfast, before I got things together, and there was Morgan striding over from his place, with a newspaper under his arm.

"Look at this," he said, coming up, and turned to an ad for the show that would be moving into the city the next week: *Bigger, better—three rings packed with excitement.*

"They have a long history," he said. "We're competing with that. They'll be stealing sales right from under us. They can afford to give out baskets full of complementary tickets."

"It's true," I said. But then, as the Kid had said, we were different. We were trying to build a reputation for the future—trying to be part of the city. It might take a while. I was concerned for the Kid, though. He had a long view of things. He had a vision—wanted to take other folks along and open up some promise for them. But there are always those looking at the immediate picture. And they can get desperate. When things get too far down you're tempted to do desperate things. I saw it happen to Dusty.

For the money part, the Kid had left everything to Morgan to handle. The Kid wasn't a business type. But Morgan had run a club, had dealt with circus people, knew management. He'd arranged with the city for the space, though he wasn't happy with how things had turned out. And he was the one looking for contacts and connections. Sometimes he watched the show in company with potential donors. And occasionally, I'd see him glad-handing some suits around the lot, with or without their wives, secretaries, significant others—who knows. He handed around tickets, hoping somebody would pull out a checkbook.

After I got back with the laundry, I sat down to read a second letter from Dollie. The kittens had their eyes open now and had started to get their legs—three calicoes, one black, and one white.

"Calypso wants you to come back and see them," she wrote. "She meowed it to me last time I went over. I go over to the trailer every day. Cute as a bug's ear all of them. Bad news on the home front. Mando collapsed from fatigue the other evening, he's had a nervous breakdown, and is now at a spa in Hawaii for healing. I saw the Eiffel Tower in a dream I had a couple of days ago. You thinking of traveling?"

I was trying to take all that in when I looked up and saw a couple of men get out of a sporty-looking car and head up through the gate. The first was young—a big man, athletic, with upper arms the size of some men's thighs. Thick blond curly hair and pink cherub cheeks that must have got him a lot of kidding, but I wouldn't have wanted to tangle with him. I caught his look when he came up, and his eyes nailed me on the spot. The sort of eyes that could undress a woman and strip a man to bone in a look. The other was an older fellow with a gimp leg, but quick-moving in spite of it. Face so weathered and exposed to the sun, it was like a piece of old leather, hook nose in a sharp face. As he went past, he gave me a smile, ingratiating, that wasn't any favor, teeth all crooked in front. Like he wants your favor but doesn't intend for any good to come out of it for you. He was the brains of the outfit, I figured—the other one, the muscle. They weren't here to see the circus, you could bet on it.

I asked them if they were looking for somebody in particular.

"A fellow named Morgan," Pink Cheeks told me. "He's here— right?" Then he muttered, "Better be here—we been looking all over for him. He was supposed to be in Las Vegas."

I pointed out Morgan's trailer but told them he was probably off in town. He gave a look to his sidekick, if that's what you could call him, who went over and banged on the door.

"Any message?" I said, curious now about who they were and what they wanted.

Pink Cheeks considered. "We'll be back." And they went off together.

I put the clothes away, tidied up a bit, and went over to see what Minna was doing. She'd told me to come by for a cup of coffee when I had time. I'd been doing so pretty frequently, or else she was over at my place. I liked her company, and for whatever reasons, she liked my stories. Curious and eager to find about where I'd been, what I'd done. Full of admiration, too, as though it had some significance. I will say it's flattering to know your life matters to somebody, especially when nearly all the people you lived it with are underground or scattered to the four winds.

"Wonderful the way you survived," she said. "You never gave up."

"Just because the bottom of the hole looks scarier than any place at the top," I told her. Doesn't take any courage—just running scared. Her youth was refreshing to me, the promise of it. The smooth skin of it, the bright look in the eye, not dulled by disappointment. She was a fine little trouper, limber as a spaghetti noodle, and I was continually amazed at the shapes she could twist her body into. I knew something of the feeling when I was flying through the air. Somehow this piece of life you've been endowed with in the shape of bones and muscle and tissue and cells seems more like a bit of lightness that you can take towards a place outside of gravity, outside of boundaries, and shape to the point of astonishment. And all the hours of stretching and exercising it took to get there.

It was strange sitting there watching the Kid's show. Suddenly I'd be thinking to myself—*Am I really what I am? Is this the final gesture of it? Maybe there's something else.* When you're in that mood, anything seems possible. Even going to Paris. I think I'm a natural sucker for keeping my sights on the horizon. Whenever Dusty got going on some new scheme, there I was, too. Except towards the last, I got a bit weary of having to keep things going, food on the table. Gravity finally got him—me, too.

Only I must be a hard case. Now that the Kid had sent me off in the old direction once more, I couldn't resist. And though my heart took a nose-dive when I kept looking at those empty seats, I was with him up to the hilt. Maybe my thought was to inspire Minna as well, her and Wally. I gave her a history of the Kid and what happened when Billy died. I talked a lot about what Dusty had set out to do and how the Kid had put on his mantle and was aiming high, and how far I thought he'd go. It was a good little pep talk.

"You're a wonder," she said. "Really." She poured me another cup of coffee and put out some chocolate-covered cookies I had no business eating. But my hand always reaches in spite of me. Sweet tooth like you wouldn't believe.

"You're getting the reputation around here—," she said, all of a sudden, "of a real *femme fatale*."

I looked at her—her smile had a little curve at the corner—she was enjoying herself. We live in a fishbowl—everybody knows what's going on. But even if I'd had the inclination, I was a little short of material, unless I wanted to rob the cradle.

"Now, who's been telling you that?" I'd had my moments in the past, same as most of us, but I figure that didn't make me any sort of Calypso.

"Olga," she said. She didn't tell me then what Olga had really called me: *a dirty old woman.*

"Olga! How would she know?" I'd hardly exchanged a dozen words with her. Mostly when she passed me, she had her eyes on the ground, and if I said hello, they darted up and away like she was a startled cat. But then she was almost always in her own space, and if she sat outside her caravan under the awning, I never went over to join her. Didn't feel welcome. The only person I'd seen her really talking to was Tony Sanchez, maybe because Bruno spent time working with him and Babe. Lately, she'd glared at me a time or two when she passed me or turned to look at some object of absorbing interest on the lot, but I didn't know as I'd done anything special to earn a cold shoulder.

"She thinks you're after her Bruno, trying to lure him away from her."

"What?" That really shook me up. I had to blow it off. "I exercise my feminine wiles whenever I get the opportunity—I need a lot of practice." She laughed. "Listen, when you get to my age, you're lucky if a man even glances in your direction, much less makes a pass." Morgan didn't count. With him, I figured it was all folderol and fiddle dee dee. "Besides, Bruno's a good deal younger than me."

I tried to think what it was could have put Olga's nose out of joint. I'd have to say I liked Bruno as much as any man I'd come across in a good while, and we'd get to kidding and joking there back of the curtain. Sometimes he'd put an arm around me and look at me with

74

crossed eyes or some other expression to make me laugh. But then, he did that to any woman within reach, or else with the kids. He was a clown in the ring and outside it, no boundary to mark a difference. At least when anybody could see him. I did come across him once after an evening performance—I'd forgot a bag with a few things in it just by the steps leading up to the band platform. I found him sitting on my chair, leaning his head on his hand, jacket falling open, feet splayed out. He looked not just tired but down at the mouth. He perked up when he saw me and launched into some joke about a dog in a bar. He'd grabbed it out of the air, just to be talking. Though I didn't think about it at the time, I'd caught him in one of those rare moments when he wasn't putting on an act, and when I thought about it now, I had to wonder who he really was.

Well, I figured, if he'd had a rough life, maybe she'd had a rougher one, a woman alone, separated from her man, dodging around to escape from wolves and tigers who wanted to slam the iron gates on her. By that time, I'd listened to a further chapter in the "comedy" of Bruno. For a while, during the Prague Spring, they had it pretty good, since they were entertainers; they traveled with the show all over the country, and even to Paris. Their mistake was coming back. He signed a petition for free expression that Vazclav Havel had started, and after that a number of people were arrested for signing it. A number of times he was called in for questioning.

"They didn't have anything on me, but they wanted to scare us. They threatened to throw us in prison and let our children starve. That put terror in my bones." They fled when friends warned them they were going to be arrested for real. He sent Olga off first, since he was the main one they were looking for. Only he got out, and she never made it past the border. He waited for her in Paris, trying through friends to get her out. Finally, after fifteen years, they were reunited.

The experience had put lines in her forehead all right. Wouldn't make her exactly trusting or friendly, and even Bruno no doubt had a dark side to his moods. But it seemed a little off the wall for her to suspect an old horse like me.

But then I thought of something else. Back a week or so before,

Bruno had come out of the show wincing with pain. He'd pulled a muscle in his shoulder alongside his neck.

"Sit down on this chair," I told him, "and I'll give you a massage." I'd gotten pretty good at that sort of thing over the years. Happens all the time, somebody straining or pulling a muscle so it tightens up something fierce. If you can't go running for a chiropractor, it's good to have somebody who can fill in for the time being.

Anyway, I worked the muscles around his neck and shoulder, and that helped some. I did it the next day too, rubbed in some Tiger Balm, and then I went to work on one of the acrobats. I could have started a business. Maybe that was what got Olga bent out of shape. Strange, though, that she'd have a fit of jealousy about it. Minna said she was hard to get along with, and once Bruno had made a joke about it. "You know what Socrates and I have in common?" he'd said to her. "Our wives."

I worried over it a little that evening when I was visiting the incidents of the day, but I wasn't going to let it bother me—her problem, I figured.

But when Bruno asked me if I'd give him a neck massage after the Wednesday matinee, I wasn't sure what to do. Why make trouble when you can avoid it, but on the other hand, it seemed pretty mean to refuse.

"Sure," I told him, and sat him down in one of the chairs outside the back entrance. Some of the performers were still on hand. Wally asked me if he could be next in line. "You've saved my life," Bruno said after I was done with him. And he gave me a big smack on the cheek—a clown's kiss.

"It's a good thing it's only your neck I'm massaging," I said. Just being wicked. Bruno made his eyebrows dance, then went off to his trailer to rest up for the next performance. I turned my attention to Wally.

After that, I went down for some Chinese takeout and was sitting in front of my little caravan to eat it when Olga herself came up. Forewarned is forearmed, so I figured it wasn't a friendly visit—though I acted like she'd come to pass the time of day.

"Why, hello," I said, "Glad you came by. Haven't seen much of you. Sit down and have a few of these noodles." So much chaff in the wind.

She stood over me, her face working as though I'd stolen her thunder and she'd have to come up with a new strike. Rage has its own language.

"You touch Bruno again, I spit in your face."

I stood up then. "Wel-l-l." I wanted to laugh. That's the difference about where I am now. I'd had my moments, too. I remember when Dusty took up with a rising young protégée—he was always finding ripe little peaches to promote to stardom, impressed by what the Big Man could do for them. I'd caught them in flagrante (only Latin word I ever learned) in one of those typical balancing acts with you-know-who on top. I'd thrown the little twit out half-dressed, clothes and purse sailing after her, all her little items dumping out in a heap on the ground. Legitimate rage, I figured. I think I pulled her hair while I was at it—should have been his. Felt kind of bad about it afterwards. I laid a few claws on Dusty, too, extracted a little blood and some promises. Not that he kept them. And then it got to be too much trouble. I hate spying on people. I just went my way—I got in my innings, believe me. What's good for the gander can also soften the life of the goose. I'd laid too many eggs.

Maybe I should have been flattered that Olga could be jealous of me, had it not been so ludicrous. I had maybe a dozen years on her—she was younger than Bruno and not bad-looking. Probably had been a beauty in her time, before her blonde hair had dulled and her complexion gone mottled and coarse. She'd gone through the wash a few times too often herself.

"Look," I told her, "you're barking up the wrong tree. I've had my men, and I'm not hungry. Plus a circus isn't any place for making trouble."

But she'd worked up her rage and needed an outlet for it. She looked like she was itching to slap the plate of food out of my hands.

"Whore!" she yelled and turned and ran back to her trailer.

It would have been funny, if it hadn't been so outrageous and even sad. Ordinarily, I'm not taken by surprise, but I admit to being perfectly astonished.

Didn't know what to do, except let it pass and keep my distance from Bruno. No fun in that, and hard to manage unless I gave him the cold shoulder. But why should I? He'd come up and sit down next to me, and we'd banter about one thing and another till showtime, or else he'd stand around after the show was over, sometimes with the Kid, and talk about the performance. Nearly everybody did that. You'd hear the three men and two women of the Flying Marvels making little adjustments to their high wire act. Seemed like they analyzed every movement, went through every moment. But then their lives depended on getting it right.

Dusty and I did the same when we were on the trapeze. Imagine—the kind of trust you have to have, not just in your own body and every move you make but in your partner's timing, nerves, and muscle. No room for a false step—no nets below to catch your mistakes. Funny thing—I could trust Dusty's every move when we were up on the trapeze. But I couldn't turn my eyes away once he was on the ground. Now that he's under it, at least I know where he is.

Bruno and I hit it off, that was clear—I liked matching wits with him. Maybe even the notion of that aroused her fears. We laughed a lot, reveled in each other's company. And now what? It was going to be hard to continue as usual. I was conscious of myself—and I didn't like that. Didn't want to keep looking over my shoulder as though I might be caught in something underhanded. Like I really did have some hidden motive. Start thinking about yourself like that and it sours everything, takes all the energy from what matters. Bad vibes, as they say.

And maybe the Olga business was a symptom. Something creeping in below the surface that wasn't supposed to be there. Then something you're not prepared for happens.

It had been a slow week, and Friday night was no exception. We were into the second half of the show. Everything going smoothly, and then the new element is there somehow, like a wheel that has jumped from a cable or somebody falling. It is like part of a dream gone awry. But it starts like every dream. I left my chair to go stand near the bleachers. And what am I seeing? Bruno in the center under the spot, takes up his harmonica and shapes a tune, a little tune you'll probably hear over and over in your head afterwards. The harmonica goes into his pocket, and he pulls out a piccolo and toots out the tune again. But that's not enough. There's a trumpet in his coat, and he belts the tune out of that. But finally, he turns to a row of bells, and Wally runs with them to various folks in the audience to give them each a bell so they can play along with Bruno. He brings a large man into the ring to be Bruno's assistant. Then all of a sudden, like the sudden appearance in a dream, here comes another clown in white-face and clown costume running up into the stands. For a moment Bruno stops, makes a few antic gestures. But it's clear he has no idea what's going on. There's laughter in the audience as the clown runs up to a young woman, long blonde hair, shapely, and starts to kiss her, but it's edgy laughter as he holds her struggling in his arms and keeps kissing her. They take it for part of the act, but now the young woman is yelling and trying to push the clown away. Finally, she gives him a sound slap—the audience roars with laughter—and he draws back, surprised.

It's clear Bruno's surprised, too, but he's running towards them, waving his arms, yelling, "It's not part of the music," which brings another wave of laughter from the crowd. The clown throws up the woman's skirt, turns, and runs out along the top of the bleachers, down one side. And is gone.

Afterwards, I had to marvel at the way Bruno brought things off. The young woman was standing there in complete confusion, almost in shock, but Bruno—the show has to go on—goes over and kneels in front of her, raises his hands as though to beg her pardon. Then gently he takes her hand, limp at her side, still with the bell in it and raises it up. First a little tinkle. Then he shakes it harder, until finally the bell is going wildly. She's being a good sport about the whole thing. The audience yells and claps. Thunderous applause. Wally leads her back up to her seat, as Bruno runs back to the center to make one more clamorous round with the bells.

So the audience is left with the impression it was all part of the act, while the rest of us are wracking our brains about who could have pulled such a stunt. The Kid is furious. Some of us were standing around in back trying to take the whole thing in.

"Sabotage," he said. "How did that creep get in here?" he kept asking. "Who'd do a thing like that?" He'd looked for the young woman in the crowd when the show was over, taken her aside, and apologized. Morgan took it as a joke.

"Some guy figured on a little fun. It can't hurt us," he said. "Once the news gets around, folks'll start coming for a little excitement."

"What do you mean? That's exactly the sort of thing to keep people from coming down here. My God—there's enough fear already without women thinking they might be harassed or even raped. You call that excitement? She was all shook up—she was scared out of her wits. A miracle the asshole didn't hurt her. I had a helluva time getting her calmed down, even though I told her it didn't come from us." You could see the Kid was overwrought himself. "She could make a lot of trouble for us, and who would blame her? We've got a reputation to keep up. We don't want people feeling threatened when they come."

Morgan shrugged. "Did you see those empty rows? What's going to get them in here, I'm asking you? Okay, even a little notoriety doesn't hurt. I tell you I've seen the show that's here in town now. They are putting up a couple of acts really have the audiences going—erotic as all hell."

"We know about them," the Kid. "Some hunk stripped to the waist in red tights, struggling in a cargo net up in the air till he's exhausted, then dumped on the ground like so much garbage. Or a guy in long hair and black leather twisting around among the straps, like he's gyrating in bed."

"You've got it, and he's doing it in a leather jock strap . . ."

"And what kind of image is that? What would we be giving them?"

"A little excitement," Morgan insisted, "Sex is what it's all about, isn't it—the juice that runs things? Probably give them a little some-thing to fantasize about when they get home."

"Damn it," the Kid said. "They get it all over the place—that's the trouble. Thinking that's all there is."

"May as well face it," Morgan said. "A little dash of spice . . . a little ad lib."

"What d'you mean?" the Kid said, ready to shake him till his teeth rattled. "Even if the crowd took it as part of the show, what does that do for us?"

No better than what happened. The next day a headline sat over the entertainment page, *Circus the scene of Mystery Prankster. Insinuating himself into the clowning, a stranger entered the performance last night of the Downtown Circus.* The article went on to describe the whole incident, ending with the question of who the mystery clown might be, and whether he'd appear again.

Just the thing to give the show a bad name. And how did the guy get in, past the notice of everyone else? No one could remember seeing him. He hadn't taken anything out of the wardrobe trailer. We were going to have to be more careful about people getting in on the lot. As far as Morgan was concerned, a little notoriety never hurt anything. And he brought it to the Kid's attention that the numbers were back up to where they were during the top nights.

"You see what brings people in," he said. "We ought to be thinking of a few erotic touches, if nothing else."

He'd put the Kid where he wanted him. The crowd would likely be expecting something, and the Kid was on the spot. "I hate this kind of monkey business," he said. "Worse than the old Barnum mentality. What's wrong with what we've got, I ask you? Why do you have to appeal to the worst—the cheapest?"

"Only it delivers the goods," Morgan argued. "Old P.T. was dead right about the public. Like he said, Nobody ever got poor underestimating . . ."

"Yeah, only maybe you never get to know what the public might learn to like, if they had the chance. Maybe something besides sensationalism."

"Show me," Morgan said. "Prove it."

"I was right, wasn't I?" he said, after the next night's performance. "It brought in the numbers, didn't it? I wish he could see . . . trying to do poetry when you needed brass tacks."

All the Kid wanted to do was get rid of the bad taste in his mouth, change the image, improvise something, and make it part of the show. The next morning he got together to brainstorm with Bruno and Wally. And before noon, they had a sudden burst of inspiration.

Morgan's prank, as he called it, was transformed into part of the theme—Bruno's Quest. That night Bruno, sporting a cardboard heart on his chest, went up to various women in the audience, professing his love in pantomime, looking for a kiss. If he couldn't find a woman willing to give him a kiss, there was Olga planted there in the audience to offer one. She was painted up as the most sour-looking creature imaginable. Bruno got the laughs— And then a kiss from a large grandmotherly type around my age. He began to add a bunch of business to his forays into the audience. They loved him. The routine worked beautifully into Bruno's act. Now he was a man in search of his love.

Was Olga jealous of those kisses bestowed on him by the women in the audience? He never had to go to his own wife—there were always women there ready to give him a kiss.

"Hey, you know, I'm beginning to like this," he told me. "And how about you?" he said to me, after the evening performance. "Why aren't you up there in the crowd? Aren't you always looking for a part to play?"

"Sure," I said, with a laugh. "The curtain would have to stay closed, and Olga already has the part." Though I didn't say so, I thought it would be fun to actually have a place in the show. For the sake of domestic tranquility, I'd have to be one of those refusing to give Bruno a kiss.

VI.
Tête-à-tête

When Morgan asked me if I'd come over for a glass of wine after the Wednesday evening show, I was game. He'd been after me, but one way or another we'd both been occupied.

"Hey—more out of curiosity than eagerness, you know, I've got so tangled in the day-to-day stuff, I've been neglecting you. I owe you an apology. We've hardly gotten re-acquainted." He gave me a look suggesting that the omission was the biggest mistake of his life.

C'mon, I thought, *give me a break.* He was a puzzle to me—was he clinging to that emptiest of fantasies, what might have been? I suppose we all have a touch of that. Trying to make up for lost time? Somehow I wasn't buying it. I was trying to look down into the closet where he kept his motives and see if there was a tip of one sticking out, and what might be the size and shape. I wasn't easy in my mind about a number of things—what had happened the other night and his reaction to it. The Kid was pulling one way and he another. But what was his game, and what did he expect to get out of it? Like I say, there'd been some business in the past, and Dusty had gotten stung—I know that much—maybe it was Morgan's revenge on him for marrying me. Who knows?

The question still remained about who had broken into the show and sparked the business in the bleachers. Eddie, the retired cop they'd hired to keep an eye on the entrance and check on things around the lot hadn't seen anyone suspicious enter or leave. But then he spent a lot of time gassing with whoever'd talk to him. And how could he know somebody in costume on the lot was an intruder. Whoever it was had managed to put on his costume and makeup unobserved. Not in the wardrobe trailer. And then after his little trick he'd managed to disappear. The incident cast a shadow, especially for the Kid. We all wondered if it was an isolated prank, or whether there was something afoot to sabotage the New Downtown Circus. Somebody in the city opposed to our being there, wanted the land for his own purposes. Maybe that was just the beginning. And what else did he have up his sleeve? Enough to get your paranoia grinding away.

"You know," the Kid said to me the morning after it happened, "I have this sneaking suspicion Morgan's behind it somehow. The way he reacted—big joke. Only I can't think he'd be that stupid—with everything that's been going on about harassment, I can't figure it out."

Morgan's gimmick? If it was, what did he think he was doing? He was still talking about getting the corporation interested. He'd managed to convince some of the higher-ups to come to a performance. And I will say, the show was better than ever—even he had to admit it. For one thing, Bruno took over his new part like he was made for it. But then he was the sort of clown who could pick up any object, enter any situation, turn it upside down, deliver it over to laughter—like Buster Keaton, his idol. In spite of himself, the intruder had done the show a favor, made Bruno rise to the occasion. But the Kid still chafed—the incident violated the sort of pact he'd made with himself and with the audience.

Maybe some folks had gone to the carnival only for the freaks, to the circus to see a trainer mauled by a cat, an aerialist fall to her death—the worst you can imagine. That's some people's idea of excitement—back to the days of blood and gore. But the Kid wanted to encourage the others with the skill, the beauty, the daring that's already there. Maybe hoist it up a notch. Why cheapen it with tricks? Besides, the threat of danger is always in the background anyway—that's what makes you hold your breath and sometimes gasp. No wonder the Flying Marvels pray before every performance. Sensationalism—the Kid hated any smell of it.

Something else struck me. A day or so after the incident, Doodles hadn't come to haul off the trash. We were worried about him. He'd been so anxious to please he'd fallen all over himself, so taken with the circus he was practically part of the scenario. He hung around even after he'd done his job, though he was scrupulous not to be in the way. Every once in a while, we put him to work doing something extra, taking a food order for us or going for a length of rope or some wire. He was always waiting to be useful. Everybody knew him by now, he was such a talker. He came up to you like a dog looking for a home, looking at Wally and Minna, the Flying Marvels or Bruno or the Kid, even me, like we were celebrities. He was all agog.

He was a farm boy, he told me—could hardly believe he was there in the city. He seemed innocent of everything—the way the world ran. Constantly open to surprise. Doodles. Mother died when he was a baby—his aunt taught him how to read and write. Father stayed drunk, beat on him—till one day he was bigger and taller than his old man. Then once when his father came at him, without thinking, he put a fist into his face. It was still a source of surprise—he didn't know how he did it. His father had him locked up.

Doodles shook his head. "Lots of things go on in that jail," he said. "You wouldn't believe the things that happened to me." He said it with a certain amazement, like he'd wandered up the wrong street, and what-d'you-know, a house had fallen on him. But his experience, whatever he'd suffered, just washed over him, leaving him without bitterness or blame. Though maybe no wiser. Or maybe he knew more than any of us.

Till now he'd never seen a real live circus performance. The Kid told him he could watch anytime there was an open seat at the back, and he was there most days. You'd see him come out with the shine of wonder on his face. The trapeze: "Why it looks like they're flying." The high wire: "How do they stay on like that?" The Cossack riding act: "I was so excited I nearly forgot to breathe." But the clowns won his greatest enthusiasm: "All that fun! And they just make it up. I never laughed so hard."

No sign of him, and the trash was beginning to pile up. I kept thinking about him—wasn't like him not to show up. I was afraid he might have blundered into some new kind of trouble—he was too simple-hearted to be loose on the streets on his own. I don't mean dumb—he was bright enough. But wide-eyed and trusting, without any thought for the evil in the world. Dangerous to himself. He might as well have walked with a sign on him, saying, *Take me for everything I've got.*

85

A couple of days later, a rather tall narrow-chested black man with a bad cough came around early in the morning to see if he could haul off the bottles and trash. Apparently, he knew we needed somebody. Kitty consulted with the Kid.

"I can't figure it out," the Kid said. "We had a fellow, only he's disappeared." The black man nodded. "You know him?" the Kid said. "You know where he is?"

"I saw him yesterday—he got one of them big bottles of wine. Looked like he wasn't going to be in circulation for awhile."

"You know where he is now?"

"No, 'fraid I don't. I could use the work, though," he said simply. "I been out of work for the past three months, looking every day—I got a family—two kids. I see he was doing all right, getting some cash off them cans. He told me all about it. Said the circus was the greatest thing ever happened to him. If only he could be in it."

"Why isn't he here?" the Kid said. "I think he's still got some money owing. But we need somebody . . . You don't know where he is?" he said, forgetting he'd already asked.

"He did say something about going back home—some place down the river. Can't recall the name."

The Kid took him on, Jason Foote. We were still puzzling over what could have happened to Doodles—why he'd blown his chances. But then we remembered he was on probation. Maybe things had gotten too much for him. We had to let it go. But my mind kept getting snagged. I put things together in a way that made a certain kind of sense—all conjecture. I managed to put the whole damned thing aside during showtime, right until I watched Bruno do the new version of the orchestra act, searching for a woman in the audience to give him a big smack of a kiss. Then I thought of Doodles, and I thought of Morgan too . . .

So I accepted his glass of wine. I was a little beyond playing anything like Judith to Holofernes, but I could at least see what a little booze and sympathy might do to limber up the tongue and see if anything slid out. Besides, I was eager to thumb through the past. The For-Old-Times-Sake routine—for whatever he still meant to me or I to him. And what he was up to now. I wanted to look into the man and see what was ticking there inside him. I wished Mando or Dollie was around to give me a few tips. Right now, I wanted to see the future, what makings of it Morgan had in his head. What it augured for the Kid and for everybody else. After all, the Kid was on probation, too.

I didn't say anything of this to him. After the crowd had scattered, he was too occupied to give me any notice, trying to pin down a problem with the spotlights Carl was operating. We still weren't up to capacity that night, though the performances had met with high enthusiasm. Once again, the crowd was really with us, and of course, that brought out the best in everybody. The hitches were all smoothed out now—a strong showing.

I went into the caravan to change out of my circus garb, white blouse and red skirt, into something more comfortable, as they say. Except for a couple of costumes that might come in handy, I hadn't brought anything all that special. But I did have a pair of blue trousers with narrow legs, and a silk blouse, satin blouse, soft as a dove's breast. Around my waist I tied a woven sash, yellow, green, blue, from Mexico. I figured a little lipstick wouldn't hurt; I'd given up on the eyeliner.

Then I started out across the lot for Morgan's RV. It was a warm evening, rather humid, and the stars were difficult to see over the city lights. Sometimes down on the Gulf, it seems like you could pluck them right out of the sky.

A striped cat turned and ran under the caravan of the Flying Marvels, and I thought of Calypso—whether I'd be tempted to keep one of her kittens. And then I found myself thinking of my little spot down there and when I'd be going back to it. And what I'd want to do then. I lingered over that a little. I had a letter from Dollie that afternoon telling me that Calypso and the babies were thriving. The kits' eyes were open, and they'd be ready to take on the world pretty quick. The rest of her letter was pretty dismal. Mando was back with her, more depressed than ever, giving everybody fits because he was refusing any longer to let any of the various scientists poke into his mental life.

"It's dead," he keeps telling me. "My brain is completely dead." I didn't know what he was talking about, so I kept after him. Finally I got him pinned down.

"Ari's gone," he said.

"Gone, what you mean, gone?"

"Even when he was sleeping, I knew his thoughts. Now he's not there—he's left."

"He's not—"

"Can't you see he's breathing?" Mando got all worked up. "Only he's gone—right out of our body. Can't you understand? There's no dreaming without him. I could read his dreams—some beautiful, some terrible, some full of color and lights and gleams of ideas presaging the future. But now there's nothing. Can't you understand—I'm unable to dream?"

Strangest thing I've ever come across . . . And right there in my own family. I'm worried as hell. I've never seen him in such a state. Wants to get out of the country and go where nobody'll find him. There's a kind of shame hanging over him. I think he feels he's had something to do with Ari's leaving.

Talk about having problems. It's hard enough for one person inhabiting a body all on his own, let alone dragging around a whole separate set of feelings and opinions. I don't know—sometimes I've felt like two different people myself. "He's had too many letters," Dollie went on:

Too many people thinking he's got some kind of answer. They heard him say it wasn't any good paying off the farmers in Bolivia when the problem with cocaine and heroin was right here.

"And why do people want it?" he said. "That's the trouble, isn't it? Because they've reached into the sack and found it empty. And they want something else—something for their lives. Isn't that it? Something more thrilling than junk and an eight-to-five in a boring job."

Now he gets all kinds of letters from parents about their kids, their in-laws, and their mates. People pouring out their hearts. It's got him down, driving him nuts—the way things are going in the world.

Poor Mando . . .

Morgan was sitting in his living room, the air conditioner pumping away. I could see him as I went by the window. He was at the door the moment he saw me. "Come on in out of the heat. I've been waiting for you, Dream Girl," he said, as though he meant *all down the years*.

For my own good, I couldn't believe him—yet if I wasn't careful, he was going to get to me. Maybe being alone makes you susceptible. All the same, it was a liberty, the *Dream Girl* business. If you weren't Dusty or Billy, you were stepping on my toes.

I stepped inside his RV, into the cool living room.

"What have we got here?" In the corner sat a bird I'd never seen before, glorious in all his plumage. He had a blue head—a soft yet shining blue—with orange skin around his eyes. The blue became a greenish sheen on his wings melting into yellow, and his breast was yellow, and the long tail feathers were yellow, with a band of red. His beak and claws were black. He gave me the eye, side-stepped along his perch, a bit jittery maybe for my coming in.

"Is that some kind of parrot?"

"Macaw."

"He won't take a chunk out of me, will he?"

"He's pretty civilized," Morgan said.

I admired his colors. "You do brighten up a place," I told him.

"Brighten, brighten—" the parrot gave me back.

"What's his name?"

"Dah. Sometimes Doddie. I've tried calling him Jamaica, but he won't respond. Got him off a Jamaican sailor. Says he's an old tar."

"Alter, alter," said the macaw.

"Oh, shut up, Doddie. Sometimes I wish he'd say something original."

"Original, original."

"He's been on treasure-hunting expeditions. Thought he might be holding a few secrets. Maybe he knew one of my ancestors."

"The macaw?"

"That's what the old man told me when I bought him. Says he could recognize the spots treasure was buried, if you hit one of them."

"Well," I said. "Have you got a ship fitted out?"

He gave me a wry smile. "My ships haven't exactly come in. I think I was better off when I was swallowing swords." He was looking a bit worse for the wear, I thought. Skin spotty, blue veins in the nose—the heavy jowls. "But who knows—?" he said, working up the old devil-may-care, "Anything can happen, can't it? We're looking to the future, aren't we?"

"I've been sticking pretty close to the here-and-now," I said. "It's kept me pretty occupied."

"I figured we could do with a little celebration. I have a bottle of champagne on ice," Morgan said. "And a few things to go with it."

"Oh, really? A special occasion? What are we celebrating?" I hadn't expected anything so elegant. But here he was taking a plate of shrimp from the refrigerator, a weakness of mine, and a wedge of brie and other cheeses with little crackers to send them off.

He had a nice little shelf of bottles. Jack Daniels, some good scotch, gin. I'd been behaving myself pretty well since I'd come up—an occasional glass of wine when we had dinner out. Hadn't even kept anything on hand. I figured I owed it to the Kid.

"Why we're celebrating being here, you and me. A reunion of two people who should never have grown apart. That's enough, isn't it?" He motioned for me to sit down on the couch and handed me a glass of champagne. Then he sat beside me.

"I've never lost sight of you," he said, huskily. "Believe me. Dusty was a lucky dog—he didn't deserve you."

"Well, there were times I'd have agreed with you, but then—"

We clinked glasses. "To us," he said, "to our new—friendship."

It was so new it hadn't yet been born, but I let it go at that.

"How long has it been?" he said, "—that first time? Over twenty-five years ago, I'll bet. You and Dusty with that great act. For me the circus has always been the trapeze—nothing more thrilling. Just watching you gave me the goose bumps. Me down there below, no wings to fly—stuck with my swords and daggers and whatever else I could toss in the air. I was sure full of myself."

"Oh we all were. I thought sure we'd land in Paris the next season."

"I realize now I never had a chance, but at the time— You can't imagine how jealous I was."

"He used to send me roses."

"I should have thought of that."

"Only what was the deal with you and Dusty—" I was changing the subject.

"Don't even speak of it! He claimed I gave him a bad check, but the money hadn't been transferred—that's all. Then he picked a quarrel, blamed me for welshing on the contract. What I really think is, he wanted me out of the way—didn't want me around you. He wouldn't have anything to do with me after that."

So here was another way of looking at things, if I was to believe him. I knew how territorial Dusty could get those early years; only that didn't prevent him from doing his share of roaming himself. Didn't seem to notice when he busted in on somebody else's territory.

"And then when I found out you were in Ventura City . . ."

"What?" I was really surprised.

"Sure. I had the Go-Go Inn—that was mine. Dusty, some of the others came in one night. I came over and we all reminisced for a while. And when I told Dusty I wanted to see you, he said, 'Sure, sure, come on around.' Only when I got there, you weren't on hand. I think he'd seen to that."

"Well I'm damned." I was trying to remember his club, and wondering why I wasn't there with Dusty and the rest. We cruised a bunch of those clubs. It might have been one of those nights I was feeling fed up with it all. But any memory of it was lost in the blur of lights of all those joints that lined the gulch and the mobs of people at the gaming tables, watching the shows. I suppose Dusty had been to every likely place in the city, Dusty thinking he could make his way with some of the owners. He'd hobnobbed with them all—

"I left you a note," Morgan continued, bitterness in his voice. "I just wanted to see you just once—that's all. Just to remember what I'd been so drawn to. A little piece of folly. Dusty must have laughed."

Peculiar. I was more mystified than ever. You go along trying to live your life, doing what you do and wrestling with the results. And all the while, someone else is playing out the drama with a whole different set of characters and cues. Only he's got the main role, and it's a different play. I suppose it was in Dusty to sandbag a rival, and maybe it was in Morgan to keep a flame burning. The whole thing sent a chill down my spine that had nothing to do with the champagne. It was nothing I'd asked for—and where was I in all this?

When I looked at him, I had a few questions. What was he seeing when he looked at me? Not what I was now—a woman who'd had some life behind her—experience, and then some. He was seeing a young thing with a mane of chestnut hair and green eyes, who could fly through the air and who flew above the cheering crowd. But the soaring bird had come down to earth. And he was still up there with his fantasy.

Then he had to tell me all that had happened to him since. A fire did in the Go-Go Inn, some kind of mystery fire. (*I thought that was in Las Vegas.*) He lost everything—he'd been late paying the insurance premium. From there, he went up to Reno, where he took over a small club and made some money. Then moved on to Vegas. Had a big house somewhere outside the city. Designed by a protégé of Frank Lloyd Wright. Nearly all glass—even a glass roof with trees growing up through it. Trees from five continents—a whole tropical garden, a pond in the center with rare pink water lilies. And birds, the rarest of the rare. Including one called Montezuma's gold, all black with yellow wings and yellow collar. Not to mention cockatoos and *chachalacas.* He'd brought Doddie with him for company.

He described his closet with his thirty-three suits and fifty pairs of shoes—must have taken some trouble to keep them all counted. He had handkerchiefs from all over the world, including one embroidered by a nun who'd lived with Mother Theresa. He'd commissioned it the last time he was in India buying an elephant for one of his shows. He owned a Rolls Royce with seats covered in leopard skins and had a Filipino housekeeper who doted on him and cooked the best food in the world. Didn't know a word of English, just went about her work and kept the place so clean you could eat off the floors. Had a raft of visitors—he was always throwing parties. Sometimes that pond of his was floating with orchids he had flown in from Florida, even Hawaii, just for the occasion. His friends kept sending him urgent messages to come back, their lives had grown so dull without him. All this was what I'd missed, he was telling me in so many words, my old admirer. I'd gone off with the loser.

"Only, what does it all add up to?" he said, waving it away with his hand, like a genii who'd conjured up a castle and didn't know where to put it. "There's something so tired about it all." Indeed he looked tired, and it seemed like the skin of his face was drawing up, becoming so dry it might peel off and reveal another layer. "I've known many women over the years—I don't deny that—but your image has lived in my head—unspoiled." His face was flushed, and I had to wonder if it was from all he was feeling or whether he'd gotten started on the Jack before I got there.

"Then when I first met the Kid and I learned you were backing him, I felt, I don't know—it was like there'd been a bolt of lightning, and suddenly the world presented a new opening—"

The note in his voice seemed true enough—the other stuff he had piled up in front of my imagination was like a set of prizes on a quiz show I'd missed the answer to. Now, though, I was listening hard, thinking he was trying to tell me something.

"Believe that my whole aim is for your good, for the Kid, the circus, all of us." An arc, a sweeping circle, took all of us in. "The Kid is like a son to me—the son I never had . . . The two of you in my life now . . ."

Unexpectedly, there was a knocking at the door, loud and insistent.

"Damn," he said. "What fool at this time of night?"

When he opened the door, I could see a couple of shapes standing there below, and they brought to mind the two men I'd seen some while back looking for him.

"Mack, Lonnie—what are you doing here?" he said with clear surprise.

"Why do you mean what—what are we d-doing? What d'you mean c-clearing out? We didn't know where you were," the one called Lonnie said. "Are you in this oper-operation or not?"

"Of course I'm in it," Morgan said, getting hot. "Who the hell told you I wasn't?"

"Look," he said, suddenly remembering me, "I've got a guest—it's not the time . . ." He didn't ask them to come in.

"We're in a pinch," Mack, the wiry one, insisted. "Damn it, why didn't you let us know where you were? We've wasted a lot of goddamn time, trying to get hold of you in Las Vegas."

"I left word with Connors," Morgan said.

"Connors is out."

"How come?"

"Said he wasn't going to throw any more bucks down a rat hole."

"No f-faith," Lonnie said. "We're onto it this time, I s-swear to you."

"You'd better be," Morgan said. "You know what this whole thing set me back?"

"This time we're on—I swear. And we can't let it go—we're too close," Mack said. "We gotta do something before the news gets out. There's lots of competition."

"Okay, okay," Morgan said. "Where are you going to be tonight?"

Lonnie rummaged around for a piece of paper as Morgan went to his desk for a pen. "What's the name of the place anyway?"

"You're a big help," Mack said to his partner. "There's a motel down the street—maybe four blocks on the left. Look, I'll draw you a map."

"I'll be there later," Morgan said.

They left then, and I was ready to leave, too.

"No, stay," Morgan said. But if I had come with any sort of expectations—which I hadn't—I was too much waylaid by curiosity to indulge them.

"Who are those guys?" I said.

He shrugged them off. "I've been in on a sort of treasure-hunting operation," he said. "I should've quit years ago for all the results we've had. A handful of coins is about it. Now they think they're onto something. They always think that."

"Treasure—pirate treasure?"

"Any kind we can find," he said. "My old man got me interested. He spent every cent he had. Died broke. I guess it runs in the blood.

94

I keep dreaming I'll hit it big. And then," he said with a laugh, "there's always another circus."

Good grief, I thought. *He's as bad, if not worse than the rest.* Then he started in the old groove about how great the show was and how much all of it meant to him.

"Then relax a little," I put in. "Give the Kid a chance. You never know how things'll shape up for the future."

"What do you make the future out of?" he said, looking at me seriously. "When I think what's happened . . . trying to untangle . . ." The champagne was giving him a head, I could tell.

"Help me, Alta," he said, reaching over, taking my hand.

"Tell me what you have in mind."

But he just looked at me, looked at me as though something inside had started to melt and dissolve. His eyes were bleary.

"Just help me," he said thickly. Then his hand slipped away from mine, his head flopped to one side, and he was gone for the evening. I hadn't found out what I wanted to know. But I had the feeling that when I did, I wouldn't be any better or happier for it. I had to wonder if he'd make it to his crucial meeting.

VII.
Fighting the Shadow

I didn't really have much hope of finding Doodles again, especially since Jason had said something about his going back home. But there was still a good deal unsettled in my mind, and I wouldn't be satisfied if I hadn't made the effort. Not that things would necessarily be any clearer if I found him. Whenever I went out to one of the cafés, I kept an eye out for him, asked the waitresses, even people on the street, if they'd seen him. Then one morning, here he came, looking for all like he'd not only slept in the gutter but had set up housekeeping there. His clothes were a wreck, shirt all torn, pants caked with dirt. He hadn't washed, or combed his hair, and he looked both dismal and ashamed. He sneaked in, trying to avoid anybody seeing him and went round to the Kid's trailer. But I caught him—I was right next door—and quick left my coffee and went out to him.

"Doodles!" I said, forgetting that I'd never called him that to his face. He looked at me strangely. "That's our nickname—I didn't mean to offend you. Where've you been? We've been worried about you."

He stood silently for a moment, as though he were trying to take it in, then his face lit up.

"You call me that?" he said. "I've never had a nickname before." He gave himself a smile. "Doodles," he said, trying it on, like it was the main thing he had to think about at the moment. "Doodles—think of that." He put aside the pleasure and came back to where he stood. "Mighty sorry about the trash. Just sorry about everything," he said, ducking his head. "You find somebody else?"

"A fellow named Jason."

He stood awkwardly for a moment. "I feel like I can't even show my face. It's only because I don't have a cent that I've come . . ."

"Come on inside," I said. "The Kid'll be back directly. Come in here and have some breakfast." What I really wanted to do was send him off for the benefits of soap and water and find him some clean clothes and get his hair combed . . . But first things first. And food in the stomach was it. How long had it been since his last meal?

"After what I've done?" he said.

"You can tell me all about it when you're done eating."

I got him inside, poured him a cup of coffee, and then worked up a pile of scrambled eggs and toast. He ate like he was trying to fill a pit. "Oh, that was good, real good," he said when he'd cleaned his plate, swallowed the last crumb, drained the cup, wiped his mouth, settled back in the chair.

"Now then," I said. "You were getting along fine here. We missed you. What happened?"

"I'm not supposed to let on," he said. "Only you and the Kid and Bruno and Wally—why you all have been my family. And I thought the clown bit was gonna do something for the show . . ."

"You mean what Morgan put you up to?" I was being bald about it, jumping in with a set of assumptions with no proof behind them, just a nagging suspicion.

"You know about it?" he said, amazed. "You knew it was me? I didn't intend any harm. I didn't know it was a piece of meanness," he said in a rush. "Not till I heard the Kid all bothered about it. I hid under a pile of canvas and stuff, waiting till everybody was gone. 'Molesting'—that's what he said. I'd never thought of that. I thought it was just playing a trick—being a clown," he said. "And Morgan kind of teased at me—said it was just the gimmick the show needed."

Morgan could really believe it, I could understand that now. We just hadn't realized how blind he could be. And Doodles didn't need much persuading.

Doodles's mind was working in a different direction. "There's nothing better than being a clown," he said, his voice husky. "When I think of Bruno . . ."

No wonder he'd been so willing—he'd found himself an idol. All Bruno had been through—had he sensed that? Seen his own path through his miseries? I wondered if all clowns were the same.

". . . he's just the greatest."

So Morgan could twist him around his little finger, till the poor fool didn't know up from down. I could have punched him one. The fellow was not just ready, he was primed, waiting only to imitate his idol, fulfill his dream.

"Morgan gave me some money when I sneaked out and told me to get lost and not come back. I wasn't expecting that. I cried—I really did. Then I got drunk and somebody stole my wallet— I didn't know what to do. I thought maybe if I saw the Kid— I had a little money coming to me," he said. "I'd get it and clear out."

Though he didn't have the Kid's rage, I was reminded of the Kid, when I first knew him. All savage innocence, ready to tear the world and himself all to pieces. Just a boy then. It had taken Billy to pull him out of that chaos, channel all that violence. And turn him into a magician. Not that it happened all at once. I remembered how the Kid used to follow Billy everywhere, as though he had to see everything through Billy's eyes, imitate every gesture, pick up every word that fell from his lips. And here was another. Already grown, but still hanging around at the doorway, like a hunk of putty, without any notion of what to do with himself. Only the violence had been beaten out of him.

"You'll have to wait for the Kid," I said. "Only right now you've got to clean up and get yourself into some decent clothes. There might still be a chance for you. I'll have talk to the Kid first—okay?"

He sat wonder struck—couldn't believe his ears. He kept his eyes fixed on me like I might suddenly disappear and leave him doubting his senses.

"Here," I said, handing him a twenty. "Take yourself down to the Goodwill Store and get something to wear, and some shoes. You know the neighborhood—there ought to be some place where you can get yourself cleaned up. Come back after the matinee. I'm counting on you—there won't be a second chance." I meant it. It would give me a little time to prepare the ground beforehand. If I knew the Kid, he'd find something.

The Kid finally came along just before lunch. He looked distracted, preoccupied, like he had forty things going and they weren't settling into the right slots. I told him Doodles had come back and what shape he was in and what I'd done and asked him if he could help out with the concessions. "Do you know what happened to him?" he said.

"Yeah, unfortunately."

He had to know—I couldn't keep anything back. When he heard how Morgan had put Doodles up to the little show in the bleachers, the Kid turned red and bit his lip. "Damn that bastard," he said. "Somebody should stick his head down the toilet—and call it a joke. Though he'd probably start bragging about how he'd sparked Bruno into a great bit of routine. Damn him anyway."

I knew it would set him off—I just thought it was better coming from me.

"Can't keep his hands off. Telling you one moment the sky's going to fall— Scheming out some angle, what'll go over, what'll draw the crowd, what kind of publicity stunt. The next moment he's off in the stars—sure we've got the sponsor who'll see us through all our troubles." He put his hands up to his head. "I've got one colossal headache. And he is it."

"He's running scared—I'm sure of it. Keeps telling me how much the circus means to him. A whole new world. The dawn of a new day ..."

"Well, I hope he brings it off, that sponsor—" the Kid said. "Everything I own is riding on it."

My heart sank. "You put up money?"

"Just about everything I have—to get us started."

"I thought he was raising the capital."

"He put up the rest—equal partners—he showed me his check. Then he started beating the bushes for donors."

"The check," I said. I tried to sound casual, though my lips were dry. "And the balance in the bank?"

"I left it all to him—we had a contract. I take it you don't trust him." He looked at me. "Right now he's riding high. Five years and we'll have troupes all over the country. LA, Las Vegas, Dallas, Chicago, New York."

Dusty had those fantasies, too. True—some folks make things happen. Dusty had bad luck, I'll grant you—though some of it was plain bad judgment. Like I say, he was so caught up in his dream, he made his mistakes on the practical side. Trusted the wrong people and got snookered a time or two. Looked like that for the Kid, too. Morgan was a different kettle of fish; only every time I looked there was a different fish.

I didn't have the heart to tell the Kid about the two guys who'd turned up the night before. Would it make any difference? Would you know any more about what was going on?

"Well, at least some of the businesses are kicking in," the Kid said. "I looked over the list of contributors—it was pretty impressive. Morgan must have rubbed a few of the right elbows. He can be convincing—I've watched him. Puts on a suit, combs his hair over his bald spot, and talks a good game."

"If he's got some money out of the corporation and a pledge for more . . ." He gave a sigh of impatience. "But it sure gripes the hell out of me when he meddles."

We left it at that. He had things to do before showtime. I went back to my trailer, opened up a can of tuna, made myself a sandwich, and poured out some lemonade. Morgan was still going round in my head—you know those things keep grinding away at you; the more you think about them, the more they get under your skin.

Oh, we went back a long way. I could see him then. Talking about costumes, he had a whole rack full—different one for every show. All the colors. Sequins and gold braid and what-not. Wild stuff. Speak of vanity. And he knew he was good—it showed in his eyes, the set of his jaw. You can tell when somebody's conscious of himself: *I am one helluva dude.* And he liked to work the buccaneer stuff with his fancy boots—red ones, black ones, silver ones. He was a celebrity, no two ways about it, and went to hang out with other celebrity types, always trying to cotton up to the beautiful people. He was handsome enough to do it.

But though he never let on, he'd grown up in the sticks, some little town in Indiana or Oklahoma you could never remember the name of and were hard put to find on the map. He name-dropped all over the scene—this bigwig was going to bankroll him to the top—that one had connections with the biggest show in Paris. But I don't know if any of it ever happened.

As I thought about it then, I wondered if any of the stuff he told me was true. Owning a club. Maybe somebody did bankroll him for that. But the rest of it—the house he lived in, the tropical paradise. Did it exist? Or the stuff going on in his head? What he thought I meant to him in the past. What he thought was happening in the future. It might have sounded real enough to him, even if he was making it up as he went along? If he was, he was certainly a convincing liar. What struck me was the look on his face when he said, "Help me, Alta." I think he meant it. He was in some kind of trouble. I just hoped the Kid wouldn't get sucked into it.

I put my stuff away and went to sit in one of the chairs at the back entrance. Soon the others started to gather. Bruno came up to banter a few minutes before the matinee. I told him Doodles had come around. "Did it occur to you he was the one who grabbed the woman in the bleachers?"

Bruno cocked his head. "Of course," he said. "Of course, it was him. I can see it now. My head was all—" he made his hands go in circles. "I just acted on reflex when things started getting out of hand. Clown stuff—I'm full of it." He considered. "Yes, but I didn't pay attention to him. I'd see him around—he'd always greet me like a long lost relative. Once I stopped and juggled a few of the cans he was collecting and let them fall on the top of the heap. You have to impress yourself sometimes." He gave a little twitch of the shoulder. "But Doodles—that's what you call him, huh?—It fits—he looked like some savage who's just discovered fire."

"He's easily impressed. And he thinks you're the top of the line. The greatest. Been watching your every movement."

Bruno mugged and swaggered "Ah, worship—the thing we crave. But I owe him something myself. Because of him, I get to look for a beautiful woman to give me a kiss. Not that the beauties want to kiss me—mostly the grandmothers and the little kids. But I'm not complaining. You take what you can get. So long as it's somebody besides Olga," he said, beaming happily on her as she passed by the tent opening. But she was outside the joke and just went on.

"The one thing he wants is to be you."

He laughed. "He doesn't know what he's asking for. I can show him a few tricks, teach him the techniques. Maybe it is good for him, yes. Very good for him, to clown away the shadows. Let him fight his shadow—that would be the trick for him. Just suppose. And everybody doubling up with laughter. It is a trick it has taken me years to perfect, though I have never performed it—fighting with the shadow. And always the shadow wins—you can't take it by surprise. See. Look. I have tried. I whirl around—like this, and this." He whirled and twirled, took a pratfall, sprang up, and danced away. "Now we fight. See, take that and that." He punched and fought until he was on the ground. "Still there? Now for the sword." Once again he danced in and out, this time with his imaginary sword, darting up, making a thrust, leaping back, till he was gasping for breath. "But he is always there to mock me. Only if I disappear . . . That would be his final joke." He left me then and went to get ready for the crowd. In a moment, he would have them in his hands. Too bad they hadn't seen what I'd seen.

Then it was time for the show. "No more fighting with shadows," he said, taking a breath as the orchestra worked up and the Kid came on to announce the show. "Much better to search through the world for a woman to kiss. The right woman. Today, look." He opened up his ragged jacket: a red heart was pinned to the center of his chest. Olga came in to tell him where she would be sitting in the third row of the bleachers. Her eye darted once in my direction as she left, but she didn't say anything to me. Bruno, at least, had distracted me from what I had on my mind—

"Doodles is coming back after the show. The Kid is going to put him into concessions. Maybe he could wear a clown costume while he's selling soft drinks or whatever—get a little confidence. Who knows?"

"Be my apprentice, you mean?" he said with good humor. "Copy my every action?"

"He's doing that already, I have the feeling."

This performance, too, went without a hitch. Now that all the cues were down pat, everybody working at their best, and all the parts coordinated—action, lights, sound, music, it seemed like everyone in the show had to be more careful than ever, careful not to get slick or take things for granted. The only way you could keep the performance fresh.

I'd watched the show from the beginning, that is, those parts where I could stray away from my post and step just outside the thin blue curtain that separated us from the side rows of the bleachers. I'd seen some of the acts over and over again, saw the high points and the little dips and sags. And every once in a while, a performance that shot through the roof, something you could never predict

After the show, when Doodles was back, I hardly recognized him. He had on a clean shirt, blue and white with a pattern of sailing ships, jeans that looked barely worn, and a pair of tennis shoes, fairly clean ones—the whole topped off with a red bill cap. He'd washed, had a shave, combed his hair. Looked decent, even human. Everything about him was lighter. I complimented him.

"You done good, kid."

"Fourteen dollars and fifty cents," he announced proudly, "and I got them to throw in a couple of extra shirts and a change of underwear. Here's what's left."

"You got to eat once in a while," I reminded him.

"A loan," he insisted, "till I get back on my feet."

At the moment, there was no place for him to keep his things or sleep except on the floor of the wardrobe trailer. We'd have to find a mat for him, then figure something out. At least, he was safe there for the time being.

The evening performance went even better than the matinee, if that was possible. We'd had a good crowd for the afternoon show, but this one was bigger. The Kid was exuberant—it had been a great day. And the rest of us stood around for a while congratulating ourselves. Afterwards, I saw the Kid go over to Morgan's trailer. He was there for a long time. Maybe the business with Doodles was bringing a few things to a head, and now that the show had really proved itself, the Kid maybe figured he had some clout.

I sat up for a while, making a pretense of reading. But I kept being interrupted by some sort of waking dream. It was like I was living the show over again, but not that one alone. I caught glimpses of things I'd seen over the years. Flashes of a liberty act with Dimitri astride two horses and a pony running between his legs. Claudette doing a handstand astride a galloping Arabian. Stuff like that. An endless show. It made me restless.

Even though it was dark and getting late and the streets were no place to be, I set out for a walk. A lone streetlight shone on deserted warehouses and empty, rutted alleys. I turned into a street that was pretty well lit and kept on. Along the way, a black church was letting out after some kind of celebration. Clusters of people were emerging, whole families, in a cascade of colors, some of the women brilliant and tropical, the little girls in frilly dresses and dress-up shoes. The night caught the jumbled exuberant sounds, put them into a single shining hubbub, where you could catch the rising scale of a woman's hilarity or the deep boom of a man's heartiness. It all came tumbling about me. A trio of three young men were trying at something that sounded like bebop. I couldn't catch the words—but it kept breaking off into laughter. I wanted to hire them to bring some of it our way. Celebration—the magic the Kid was trying for. I threaded my way along the sidewalk, where people looked at me strangely. Car doors began to slam amid a chorus of calls to one another and goodnights. Motors started up, and the cars started to move off. By the time I looked back, the street was deserted, the lights in the church turned off.

It was late when I got back to the caravan, after midnight. I hadn't locked the door—never did. When I opened it, I wanted to cry out. All the dishes and canned goods and what-not had been torn from the cupboards and broken up on the floor. Something oily was dribbling down the sides of the cabinets. And my clothes and costumes had been thrown down among the broken objects, cornflakes, and coffee grounds scattered on top of them.

For I don't how long, I just stood there staring at the wreckage. Who'd do such a thing? What kind of meanness? Who could hate me that much? Olga was the only one who came to mind. Hard to think of her working up to that kind of rage. Being that jealous. Of me. Pure craziness. But who else would have even the suggestions of a motive? Unless there'd been a mistake, and the whole thing was meant for somebody else. Morgan? From the bozos who'd banged on Morgan's door? But Morgan's caravan was across the lot.

I had to work to keep from sinking into the chaos. For a time, I just sat there in the midst of it all. Numb. I was in shock. Everything torn up. When I came to myself, I'd been clutching onto my old red fringe dress, a piece torn out of the skirt. And then I started crying. The tears just poured out, almost as bad as when Dusty let go of my hand and left me sitting there without him. I felt like some part of me had been ripped in two. Why, those costumes were me, who I'd been all these years. When the comforting voice came, *Don't let it get you, hon—worse things have happened,* I just started bawling harder. It was all over. The costumes. Why, they were me. They were my life in the glory days and even after. Reminders of what I'd been. Torn to pieces. I picked another one up and just let it fall. Done for. A pile of rags and what was I? It was all over and done with—finished. I was like a little kid bawling.

I don't know how long I sat there like that. Finally there were no more tears. My eyes hurt and my cheeks felt swollen. I was beat out. No question of going to bed. The sheets had been ripped and God knows what-all poured over the mattress. Wouldn't be able to sleep on it that night, and maybe I'd just have to throw the thing in the trash. I hung up the costumes as best I could. Couldn't just leave them there. I was dead tired. I pushed a couple of broken blinds aside, shoved a bunch of junk to the floor and lay down on the little couch still in my clothes. Tried to close my eyes. I'd have given anything for a drink. Didn't have anything on hand though—hadn't trusted myself. I'd almost have been willing to go for the cologne or the vanilla—only who could find anything in all that mess?

Finally I dropped off. I think I spent the night trying to sew together my costumes.

VIII.
Confrontation

Morning didn't change a thing. Daylight, and socko! right in the eye. Food making little scrimmages all over the counter and the floor, like somebody had been rummaging in the cupboards and fridge for whatever would satisfy an unknown and desperate hunger but couldn't find nary a suggestion to fend it off. Then had a fit in pure frustration and even have taken some deep gut pleasure in seeing what could be done with mayonnaise, catsup, olive oil, vinegar, mustard, peanut butter, and the jar of good orange marmalade I'd bought. Smashing and trampling. Ripping and dumping. Coffee grounds and crackers stirred into the mess, and all of it mixed with broken glass on the carpet alongside the sink.

I had to leave the blinds pulled down, wait till I could replace the broken ones. At least I had the whole day to get at the mess before showtime. Just how I wanted to spend my time, hone up my domestic skills! I picked up glass and garbage and swept up what I could and took it out to the trash barrel, then sponged up the carpet and washed down the counter and sink and cleaned out the refrigerator. I managed to salvage a couple of pieces of bread in the process. I found a piece of cheese that was still edible. That was breakfast. The coffee pot was broken, so I'd have to get a new one. Double damn!

In the middle of it all, Minna came over to invite me for dinner the next night. I wasn't sure I could manage anything sociable. I must have looked as sour as curdled milk.

"What happened?" she said, noticing first the blinds, then the general upheaval.

"I don't even know. Vandals," I said. "Just found the place torn apart."

"Jesus—who'd do that?"

"I don't know—I'm tossing around a few theories."

"Let me help you clean up."

"No," I told her. Somehow I didn't want anybody coming between that mess and what I needed to do, needed to feel. "We'd just be tripping over one another. And I've got it mostly done. Tell you what, though. You've got a car—take me down to the laundromat. And some outfit where I can replace these blinds."

"Sure—just let me know when you're ready."

I'd taken up the clothes from where they'd been thrown down and sponged off the food and glass. Now I untwisted the sheets torn from the bed and put all the stuff in a pile of what I could salvage to take to the laundromat. And all the while I was building up to fury.

Why not just go back to Florida? I thought, *which I should never have left in the first place.* I floated that idea for a while. Thought about the trailer and my flowers and the kittens. Didn't sound half bad. Just seeing myself looking out over the ocean, sipping my piña coladas. *The Kid doesn't need you any more,* one side of me put in. And who did? For my great back curtain act? *Think of all the inconvenience, having the rest fill in for you*—that was the other half getting in its two cents. *Yeah, but what's a circus performer if he can't do something in a pinch?* That was me talking. *Improvise.*

Improvise. That was the ticket. For them. But for me? Improvise. What would that be now? It would take a damn lot of it to make any difference. *You going to give whoever it was the satisfaction of chasing you off?* No, dammit. *Watch out, Olga—You're in for a knock-down drag-out.* Suppose I was wrong? Only I was sure I wasn't. In any event, I figured I had a little visit to pay—At least I'd try to get to the bottom of the whole nasty business. Only I didn't want to do it when I knew Bruno was by—no point in dragging him into it. It was between her and me. Nor the Kid—Just wanted to keep it simple. See if something could be settled at the source. I hadn't said anything to the Kid about it, though I'd wondered, in fact, how he'd managed not to hear the noise. All that smashing. But if he had the air conditioner on, like everybody else, and had been so beat he'd dropped into sleep immediately, like most of us did, he probably hadn't heard a thing. And just as well. Why have one more distraction?

Minna helped with the clothes, working quietly beside me. She must have sensed my mood. When we sat down to wait for the wash, we talked about everything else but that—just like any two women who'd come to do the laundry. I was grateful to her.

When she brought me back and helped me carry the laundry in, she just said, "Let me know if you need anything else." But I didn't know what I needed.

After I'd tended to the basics, I took out the costumes to examine them more closely. The top of one was ripped almost beyond repair, and the others had big tears in them, not to mention stains. It wasn't just the costumes that were torn. Felt like something I'd put together, lived out, had been ripped past repair. Now that I was looking at them dry-eyed, all passion spent, as they say, I couldn't even feel sorry for myself. *You aren't there anymore* came into my head. *You aren't that anymore.* I was looking at a dancing figure in a photo, the dance all done. All the dimensions flattened into an image without any life in it—just an empty shell. And before all that, in my growing up—I wasn't anything either. And here's the torn-up present. Maybe I'd kept the costumes as relics. Hadn't tried them on for god-knows how long. Knew they probably wouldn't fit.

But something came over me as I was standing there in a kind of stupor, in the midst of all that chaos I'd been struggling through. I had a sudden vision of a great blue space, as though the circus tent had expanded until the whole sky was inside. There were red elephants in a blue day, and dancers leaping up on their backs. Ten horses, black and white, with equestriennes standing on their galloping forms. Clowns and acrobats. Seemed like all the people I knew were there, knew and had known, as though they'd never vanished. Billy and Dusty, the Kid, Grace, who'd been like a daughter, Curran and Donovan, midget and giant. And suddenly, my face was wet with tears. Different tears. Maybe there was only an image left, but I recognized myself, and it evoked all that I'd known and felt in my muscles and bones, liver, head and heart. It was me—*and not all of it's gone.*

I scooped up the costumes and before I knew it, I was climbing the steps of the wardrobe trailer, where I found Jenna busy ironing the costumes for the show that night.

"What've you got?" she said, when I was inside.

"Some old stuff that got some bad treatment," I told her. "I know it's asking a lot, but d'you think you can salvage anything? They're kind of important to me." She took up one, then another, looking at the tears and shaking her head. I didn't go into any explanations.

"It would take a few substitutions," she said. "I'd have to go to the shops and try to find what would match. Or maybe look at some of the antique clothing places. Do you mind a few innovations?"

Suddenly I felt light as air. "Surprise me," I said. "I'll leave it all to you."

She was a jewel, this one—all of twenty-four or -five, but she wielded a wicked needle and thread—was sheer genius on the sewing machine. She kept the costumes all washed and ironed and repaired right up to the minute. Lovely, too, standing there beside me looking over the wreckage. A wave of honey-colored hair and large soft eyes, both curious and intent.

Then she said, "You should try these things on. It would give me a better idea of how to proceed." I felt little embarrassed, not knowing what verdict lay in the seams. But I got them on. So I stood there in my rags waiting for the fairy godmother to reveal me in my splendor. The purple bodice I'd fancied for so long, all embroidered with flowers, with swirls of sequins and little silver knobs, was snug all right, the sleeves all but torn off. Jenna didn't see it as a complete disaster, though the skirt was almost completely wrecked.

"That's a lovely piece of embroidery," she said. "Maybe I can do something with it."

It would be a challenge, but it cheered me that she'd take it on, see what she could come up with. The red outfit had only a couple of rips, but bad ones. It was missing a sleeve, ripped right out of the armhole. I managed to wiggle into the thing, but it wouldn't zip. "I can let that out," she said. "There's some room at the seams." Cheered me no end. Took me back a-ways.

Once I'd been Queen of the Moon, I told Jenna. A long story—oh, how long ago. Of all my outfits, I loved that one the best, the material all silvery and shimmery, the red mantle embroidered with white pomegranates. A crescent moon for a crown. I'd felt like a queen, too. Standing there with Dusty, the Moon to his Sun—oh, it was grand. A spectacle. Took my breath away, just to float in all that beauty. And I recalled a moment when I could just let everything go, everything I'd lived and suffered and enjoyed. In that space, I wasn't anything—I just was. Not long after Billy's death either, when grief had plunged me to the center of the Earth, down into the molten magma. Down to where absence is more than emptiness, but like part of your own death. Maybe that's what led me to that moment—let me stand there pure as water. Maybe that's what let things flow on again.

And what was preventing me now? Some broken glass and torn scraps of old tulle and velvet and what-not? Only where was I supposed to dip for the juice, the old wine?

I stood there just pondering and running on like an idle breeze, while Jenna measured and considered, pinned and made notes.

"You know," she said gently, "most of this material is pretty fragile. See where it's coming apart here. I don't know what happened, but if it hadn't happened . . ."

I caught her drift. "—they'd be falling apart anyhow." She was delicate, that one. Her smile didn't suggest I was being an old fool.

So Olga, if it was Olga, could have saved herself the trouble—if she hadn't needed a taste of vengeance. That was the main fact. Somebody comes in and tears up your things, you can't help feeling violated. Especially if they've made up a whole scenario in their heads. Suppose I did take after her man—at the moment it would be a satisfaction.

When I left Jenna I was feeling somewhat mollified but still in the mood to resurrect some old bad habit—such as taking in a toke of pot or getting sloshed—and work it to the hilt. I thought of going down to the liquor store for something more potent than Concha de Torro, the Chilean red. Just enough to let me flop down and sink into oblivion for a few hours. Sometimes it's what you want most. But then I vetoed the idea. Needed to keep what little concentration I had left.

I ran into Morgan with a fistful of newspapers in his hands. Competition now—the Ringling outfit. Lots of ads with clowns grinning out. A whole troupe of elephants, raising their trunks. Thrills galore.

"Look at that, look at that," he said, as though it were a personal insult. "They'll fill that tent with three or four thousand."

I shrugged. "At least it's only a weekend."

"Only that'll kill the pocketbook and the eagerness to see our show," he said. "Do you know how much that means at the box office?"

"No point getting all riled up," I said. "We're here, we'll be here after they leave—we'll perform and hope for the best. We got past that other outfit and all the hoochie-cooch."

"You were always a trooper, Alta," he said, sentiment rising up. "You've got what it takes."

"Well, you're in this business, you got to work up a few survivor instincts. You ought to know."

"This outfit means the world to me—whatever happens, that's the truth."

I believed him.

"I'm a pretty sorry kind of a shit," he said, and looked like he'd say something else, but the Kid came over—there was some problem with one of the outfits that supplied feed for the elephant. Wouldn't deliver any more until he'd been paid.

"Oh, that guy—" Morgan said. "A pain in the ass. I told Kitty to tell him he'd get his money. Soon as the corporation ponies up. He's got ants in his pants. Don't worry about it—everything's fine."

I was more and more convinced it wasn't. Only as yet, there wasn't any proof. I'd suggested to the Kid we ought to have a look at the books. But I wasn't sure he'd asked to see them, or if Morgan had turned them over. He was always making me jumpy—left me lurching between two minds. Or whether they were in order. Were we so close to the edge we couldn't pay for feed? I could tell the Kid was looking a little hollow too. I didn't like that cast of things. After the check business, Dusty never trusted Morgan again—that was clear. Two of a kind—with an ambition that took them to the skies. Only Dusty never intended to cheat anybody. Morgan ? I could see him pulling a fast one. Big bucks gave him the chance to play the swell.

I was still trying to get a bead on what happened down in Ventura

City. Maybe he tried to pull a fast one down there. A nightclub burning down. Wasn't that in Vegas? Did it happen twice—some kind of insurance ploy? Whatever happened, seemed like he was the sort who could always land on all four feet and leave the rest of us in the lurch.

I had taken down the blinds and put up the new ones. I'd left all the windows open to get rid of the smell. After that, I didn't know what to do with myself. Didn't feel like reading or talking to anybody, so I wandered over to look at the animals. Sometimes they help put you in touch with the earth again, get things in perspective. Especially Babe—she's like a great mound of it, cracked skin reminding you of clay when it's dried and split. The Ringling outfit could boast their elephants as much as they wanted. They'd be hard put to find such a splendid animal. I loved the light of intelligence in her eye, like she had a trick up her sleeve she was just waiting to pull—and her strong will. Always moving in the direction of desire: food—the main thing. But she had loyalties as well. She knew who she could count on, and who she was partial to. And could be jealous if she saw Tony, or even Bruno, letting their attention wander past her to someone else. She was a queen and expected to be treated like one by her admirers. A creature after my own heart.

But what was she to a whole herd of elephants, a whole raft of horses and lions and tigers—if bigger was the main thing you wanted? Three rings going at once, and all the dazzle. Spectacle—they knew how to bring it off all right. You had to hand it to them. And Morgan's nose was a-quiver, like a bear's looking for bees. We had to suffer through his gloom and doom the next few days. Down from the clouds, into the dumps.

Not all that easy for the rest of the crew either. All that weekend we could feel the presence of that great show everybody knows, see it staring back at us from the empty seats. Morgan was tearing his hair, running around in a panic, certain of disaster, rushing off to meetings with potential benefactors—all the while trying to bulldoze the Kid into trying for what would capture an audience when we came back in the fall after the road show. Now it was the teenage market age we had to go for.

"That's where the bucks are these days. They learned that out in Hollywood. Maybe some daredevils spinning around in cars."

"Look," the Kid argued. "We've proved ourselves. We're here to give the kids and their folks a different experience—put them closer to their dreaming selves. Old wonders into a new format—so maybe they'd see some other set of possibilities. They've been sucked into all the distractions."

Sometimes Bruno did a little pantomime in Morgan's presence, rushing off, waving his arms, stopping dead in his tracks, cocking his head as though he had an ear out for the music of the spheres, lightbulbs popping all inside his skull, rushing back, going into a somersault and taking off in another direction. He'd send us all into fits, and even Morgan would be forced into a smile.

"You've been reading too many circus magazines," Wally told Morgan. "The specter of the Big Time has got you by the collar."

The animals were more open with their opinions. If Morgan walked by the elephant pen when he was arguing some new scheme, Babe would blow him a raspberry. The first time it happened it startled the hell out of him. He'd been right in the middle of a sentence and here came a blast of sound somewhere between a foghorn and a trumpet. Morgan had practically leapt out of his skin. She only did it when he was around.

Her sentiments must have caught on with some of the other animals. That gleam in her eye was what did it—got the word passed around. And one of the dogs, a little mutt named Humphrey—without any pedigree, enough poodle in him to give him some smarts, and enough sheepdog for dedication—came over and peed on Morgan's shoe when he was going into one of his tirades.

Morgan pulled back like a snake had bit him, yelled, and threw out a string of cusswords that were a glory to hear, they ran such a range of sexual insult and perverted relationship. All the polish had peeled off his surface, to let out some true raw sentiment. You could see his leg just itching to kick the mutt and send him spinning, and I can't say I blame him. But then Humphrey was a performer, and he had merely expressed an opinion in one of the few ways open to him. Morgan drew himself up into his dignity and took himself back to his RV.

Only the chimps appeared to be on his side. They danced around him whenever he was in their midst, offering him bananas. But Olga was maybe the influence there. She ran a tight ship and expected loyalty. Once I saw one of the chimpanzees make an obscene gesture behind the Kid's back when he told Olga her act was running overtime, but that may have been a purely personal expression. Myself, I kept clear of them, though I can't say they were unfriendly when they trooped by into the chute. Or when they came out. Mostly, they were chattering among themselves, perhaps going over their act and how it came off, the way all the other performers did.

In the midst of all the nonsense, here came a letter from Dollie, still trying to get a take on the future:

Listen, girlfriend, I've had one of my little gleams of inspiration, and it made me hold my breath. Thought I'd try entering the future with coffee grounds. There are many doorways. Besides, I had a hankering for a little Turkish coffee—the stuff that puts hair on your chest and other places you don't want it. Strengthens the inner caliber and resolve. Left the dregs in the bottom of the cup. Swirled them around three times, the magic number, and turned over the cup. What a pattern! Three snakes appeared—one in the grass, one on the sidewalk, one hanging from a window blind. Treachery underfoot, out in the open, and hanging there waiting. All three kinds at once—a bad sign. The rest I read from the crystal. Plots are thickening. Oh, and turmoil. Things all in a mess, broken— in the midst, a sewing machine. You don't sew, do you? The Kid? Couldn't tell. Confusion over money. Bribes, local politics. I suspect a takeover. That's as far as it goes, sweetie. Watch your step. Keep the elephant on your side.

I was glad to hear from her. I think she was onto something all right. A threat in the air. But I wasn't sure I knew any better what to do about it. That's the trouble, I guess, with trying to get a leg up on the future. She didn't have to tell me any news about the state my trailer was in or the turmoil around us. She didn't mention the kittens or Mando.

I let a couple more days go by, meanwhile tried to keep an eye on Olga. Could I tell anything from her behavior?—whether she was held by some tension, waiting for whatever might or might not happen? We couldn't avoid each other entirely. She had to walk past me as she went in to do her act with the chimps, two performances a day on the weekends. I pulled the curtain for her to enter the chute, monkeys loping and gibbering around her, she issuing commands or talking a kind of elaborate baby talk that turned my stomach. I opened the curtain after her act was over, and she passed beside me. I'd just let my eye drift along, following her with my gaze. She didn't bother to notice me—I'd watch the whites of her eyes roll right past me. But every once in a while, one of her chimps would stop and look at me and even offer me a hand. From her I'd get a flash of blue fire. She'd grab the chimp by the other hand, give him a word as sharp as an icicle, and lead him off. I'd give her a little slow smile, leaving her with whatever questions might still hang in the air. Did I suspect her? Was I going to let it pass?

Except for that, things were looking up, if you were in the mood to see them that way. The Ringling outfit came and went. They were there for only a weekend before traveling down to Texas. The weather was sunny and brilliant, calling for the kids to be outdoors, playing in the parks, swimming in the pools. Calling for an afternoon, an evening at the circus. For once our place was packed and the ticket sales were steady. The Kid was buoyant, though he and Morgan still walked around one another like two dogs waiting to see who'd make the first lunge.

"At least we're where we should be," the Kid told me. "If we keep on with a house like this, we'll do it—I'm banking on it. A couple of the backers have been really impressed—they've been to see me. And Morgan's talking them up. Otherwise I'd be thinking he was the biggest mistake of my life."

So I felt a little jolt of optimism. A chance for them to pull things out. I was still up and down about my own situation, sometimes really in the dumps. I'd kept pretty much to myself. Finally Minna came over to see how I was faring. I'd got the place pretty well back in shape by then. I had her come in for a cup of coffee.

"Where've you been keeping yourself?" she asked me, taking things in. "Looks a helluva lot better than when I was here last."

"Yeah, you can't tell anything happened."

She looked at me with a question in her eyes.

"I haven't asked any questions. Figured I'd wait for the right opportunity. But I'd like it all to stay right here between us."

"Sure," she said. "Is it who I think it is?"

"I don't know—I just can't believe anybody would do that."

"Why don't you have supper with Wally and me tonight?" she said. "That's why I came by. I think we've got a new performer in the making."

Doodles had become their protégé—he'd be coming too. First they'd fixed him up with a clown costume and had him working the bleachers, selling soft drinks during the shows. Then Wally and Bruno had taken him on, they were teaching him some simple routines. Bruno had it in mind to make him into a kind of apprentice who twists everything out of shape, not only gets it wrong but sends things into such a cocked hat that chaos is come again. At the end of the routine Bruno would simply pull him up out of the chaos and have Babe carry him out—no other remedy. Doodles was a natural, Minna said. They'd been having rehearsals the past few mornings.

"Good. That'll help get us past the empty slot." Right now they were having to fill in for the dog show. Alex, who had charge of it, had sprained an ankle while he was cavorting around the ring and had to stay off his feet.

"So will you come?"

"Sure, I'll come." I hadn't eaten a decent meal since the trailer had been torn apart, though I had gone out for pizza or had it delivered.

"Maybe you could do me a favor?" I wanted to make a little visit, had worked it up in my mind to do it, now that I had little distance and some of the rage had left me. What I wanted was to have Bruno out of the way, and I figured she could let me know when he and Wally were together. The two of us plotted to make that happen just before dinner.

After the matinee, I looked at myself in the mirror, brushed my hair, hiked up my determination, and strolled over to Olga and Bruno's headquarters. I tapped at the door, and when Olga opened, she said matter-of-factly, "Is there something you want?"

"I think we need to have a little chat," I told her. "We'd better do it inside. I'd invite you to my place," I said, "the scene of the crime, that is, but I think I'd rather do it here."

"I don't know what you're talking about," she said.

"If you don't, I'd be happy to lay out the details. Like the place was a wreck, all torn apart. It didn't happen by itself, and the only person I can think of who's got some kind of mad going against me is you. Now can we talk?"

Her brows gathered—she had two deep creases between them, and she pursed her lips.

"We have half an hour or so," I told her. "He's off with Wally and Doodles. So let's not waste time—unless you want to see me cut loose." By this time, my lather was pretty well worked up—I hadn't figured on getting that wrought up again—and I was trying hard to stay in control. I think I'd have forced my way inside if she hadn't given ground, I was that het up.

She went white, then red. "You come here to cause trouble," she accused me, but she stood aside and let me enter. It was neat and snug inside, like everything had been ironed. I noticed some photographs on the wall, old ones, circus shots, but I couldn't make them out in the dim light, and I wasn't in the mood to study them. Theirs was a big trailer, with a sizeable living room and something more than the little sink, the suggestion of counter and cupboard in mine.

"Comfortable-looking little nest you got," I said, and sat down on the couch. "Nice to have a retreat to come back to when you're all tuckered out at night. Nice to be able to open the door and not find everything smashed inside. Not find all the dishes broken and the food in the cupboard all over the floor mixed with glass. Not find the bed all torn up, so you can't even lie down . . ."

"You are making up trouble—what do you think I did?" she said.

"I'm talking about what I found when I opened the door not

quite a week ago, and I don't have to guess who did it, do I? Nobody else here has the kind of cordial feeling towards me you do. So maybe that's why you had to tear up my things."

She stared at me for a moment. A little smile played on her lip, then she grimaced as though the joke was too absurd even for a joke. "You really think I did that?"

"Do I have to think?"

Suddenly she laughed. "Wait," she said. She got up and went to a drawer in the desk and pulled out the red sleeve of my costume.

"Where did you get that?" A souvenir of the raid?

"Amos had it," she said. One of the chimps. "He got away from me the other night when I opened the cage. For an hour, I couldn't find him. He's very clever. He must have gotten into your caravan," she said. "I am so very sorry."

Gone for an hour and she didn't hear the noise? Her face made a little contortion, as though she was trying to hold back a laugh but held it firmly and finally got things tightened down around the mouth. She looked as though she lived in some spot high above suspicion, but there was still a little twitch at the corner. I'll admit I was flabbergasted, left standing naked on one foot. A chimp could have done it—I never locked the door. But it was her monkey.

"Well then," I said, standing up. "So long as it's not you doing the monkeying. I'll take the sleeve, being that it's my personal property." Nothing for it then—and I'd been put in the wrong. I felt stupid—humiliated, because, after all, she had got the better of me. So I left, figuring she was rejoicing at my back—glad her monkey did what she might have wanted to do. Well, she could have her triumph.

Only by the time I got down the steps and turned at the corner of the trailer, I was hearing what I'd never have expected, the sound of a woman weeping—with her whole heart. Sobbing bitterly and full of rage, as though everything had gone against her, and nothing could set things right. I stood there for a moment, wondering if I should go back and see if there was any help for it. But I figured I was the wrong person—she'd probably fly at me with all her claws—and I didn't want to run into Bruno, who'd be coming along any minute now.

IX.
Stirring the Pot

I went off to Minna and Wally's, trailing a few confusions. Nothing settled. Only the mess in my caravan had got cleaned up. That's the trouble—you can pick up the pieces, find the replacements, rebuild houses after fire and flood, restore the landscape after you bomb the hell out of it—only what gets stirred up inside, all the fret and fever, never just lies down flat and curls up its toes. Now I had to imagine Bruno coming along, finding Olga all worked up into a tizzy. How easy for her then to say I'd insulted her, put something on her that was low and mean. It gnawed at me to think he would believe her. If I hadn't promised I'd go to Minna and Wally's for supper, I'd have snuck off for a quiet sandwich and just sat with that other part of the mess, trying to unravel how I got there. Though maybe it was better not to brood myself silly over it. After all, the mess had been dumped on me, not the other way around.

Minna greeted me at the door with a question in her eyes; dying to find out what came of that little tête-à-tête. But since I wasn't sure myself, or why such a storm of grief was working just under the surface of Olga's coldness and jealousy, I was glad not to have to recap. So I looked into whatever face offered me a distraction—Doodles was it, his expression bright and eager. Nowadays he acted as though he'd just been raised up like Lazarus, a whole new world at his feet, and he was eagerly rushing in.

"Whatcha got?" he asked me when I came in. I forgot I was still holding onto the red sleeve.

"Oh, nothing," I said, "a scrap of an old costume."

"Here, let me see it." I gave it over.

"Funny thing. The chimp—Amos, you know the one I mean?—had hold of it the other night. I'd got out of the truck to go to the donniker, and I saw him coming out of your place with it, shaking

119

it, making a big noise. Then here comes Olga and takes it away from him and gives him a banana."

I must have looked like something hit me on the noggin, while he started imitating the chimp, and then Olga and the chimp, till he had us all in stitches. Only under mine was a huge rage.

Funny, all right. Minna raised her eyebrows. My suspicions had hit the top of the bulb, though maybe Olga was just trying to lure the chimp back to the cage, not just offering him a reward. Would I ever know? It wasn't the moment to belabor the matter.

Doodles was floating like soap bubbles—somewhere near the ceiling, if not the wild blue yonder—for the moment, not a cloud on the horizon. I could recognize the feeling, from soaring up there in the ring. Hard to hold onto afterwards. But he looked like he'd found his natural state. I was happy for him. I could envy him without envy, if you know what I mean. He was light and airy, little balloons the colors of the rainbow or maybe a handful of confetti just hanging there in the blue, never to fall. He'd found a home—in more ways than one. On the level of where to rest your rump, Wally and Bruno had rigged up a tent for him towards the back of the lot. He had a mat and a sleeping bag, plus the use of the washing facilities in Minna and Wally's trailer. They may as well have adopted him. He ate with them several times a week. Sometimes he brought food for Minna to cook for the three of them.

Now he was somebody, part of the circus, set off in the direction of a future. He'd found the genius of folly in his nature that he could bring into the ring and give a shape, piece together bits out of his haphazard life: his penchant for getting things wrong the way everybody gets things wrong, only more so. A great subject for laughter—a treat as good as chocolate cake. He clowned around while Minna was setting things up for supper. I've never known anybody with a more mobile face, like dough. Or anybody more innocent. Even though he'd seen twenty-five years' worth of living and what-all and knew the inside of a jail cell. His comedy was in acting like he'd been born yesterday— If he could just survive . . . He had me laughing over things he never meant to be funny.

In the road show, the Kid told me later, Doodles would take over the slot left by the dog act. Alexis was pulling out to do a gig elsewhere. In a way, all this was owing to Morgan. Only he paid no more attention to Doodles than if he was a dog he'd once petted or kicked. They avoided each other, and I can't think Morgan was all that pleased to have Doodles around. He was all set to capitalize on whatever might bring him a profit, even to selling his grandmother; but he never looked at what was right in front of his nose. Maybe he was afraid the Kid would pick up what he had mishandled and cast aside and rub his nose in it. But we hadn't seen much of Morgan lately—he was too busy with business downtown.

We were a merry crew around the table. Minna brought out the fried chicken and au gratin potatoes and the snap beans that had come from the farmers' market. Real fresh lettuce and tomatoes for the salad. Wally poured out the wine into various sized tumblers. We drank a bunch of toasts—to Doodles's new career, to the circus, to Babe. Wally opened another bottle, poured out more wine. I was getting a little squiffed, owing to lack of sleep, but it felt good. We made short work of the meal and pie Doodles had brought from the bakery. Then we settled into a game of nickel ante poker, and Doodles won about ten dollars. Wally was the heavy loser. It was about ten-thirty when I got back to my place and dropped into bed. It was a hot night even with the fan on, but I slept like a brick till morning.

We had the next day off, so I took a long walk over to the shopping center and went to the hardware store for the new light fixture I'd forgotten the day before. I bought some eggs and treated myself to another jar of marmalade. When I got back, I found Bruno sitting in front in a folding chair he'd brought up from behind the back entrance, reading a newspaper. He must have been waiting a long time. I'd been gone half the afternoon, and I was pooped, what with the heat and carrying my stuff.

He jumped up when he saw me, "I was afraid you weren't coming back," he said, as he helped me carry my groceries and stuff inside.

"I could be sitting on the sand, looking out at the ocean," I said. Life would be simpler. And how come Olga wasn't there yelling at him?

"How about some iced tea—just made it this morning."

"Most welcome," he said, following me inside, sitting down at the table. "A real scorcher today." He wiped a hand across his forehead.

"Think what it'll be inside that tent, if it keeps up."

"That's just what I don't want to think about," he said, taking the glass of tea and holding it in both hands. "Ah, just the thing."

I sat down across from him. "I don't put much sugar in—there's some here in the sugar bowl if you want it."

"Tastes fine." He was silent for a moment. "Something I need to talk about," he said. "Maybe you can guess." He looked at me as though I might fill in the blanks, but I had no desire to close in on the subject.

"Olga told me you accused her of smashing the things here in the caravan—when it was the chimp." He looked around. "Not so nice, eh, to have everything broken?"

"I don't usually go round accusing people," I said, "Only—"

"Yes, well. Olga— Perhaps you've seen—so difficult. Sometimes she gets strange ideas about people." He was making a big circle around the whole business. Trying to excuse her, it looked like. It took something powerful to hold myself back—I was feeling pretty hot under the collar.

"Totally false— You can't imagine. But if you put her, me back into the old regime, you can maybe understand. Then even your best friends . . . even those in the circus," he said with a shudder. "You never knew who might betray you. And it's hard to put the blame on them, the authorities know so well how to threaten your family, and intimidate . . ."

I got the picture. When you can't trust the folks your life depends on—well, could you even have a circus? With Olga and me, something had gotten broken before it was ever in one piece.

"I have tried to take care of her, work with her. Ivana—that was my wife—Ivana would have wanted it."

I was thunderstruck.

"Yes," he said, looking at me— "It's what everyone thinks. I have let it be that way—easier for her. Easier to be in this country. Not so much red tape, questions, objections—she is my wife. Okay. Maybe easier for me, too." He threw open his arms. "You make a great big cardboard castle, put inside the king and queen. That is part of the comedy. No, Olga is not my wife, though that is the part she still wants. The queen is dead—long live the queen."

I was more confused than ever.

"Twins" he said. "Ivana, my wife—Olga, five minutes older. For a while we were all together, still in the circus—after the Prague Spring turned to winter. We could still exist. Not so good, but okay. Then one, two, three—our friends who were fleeing came to us. 'Hide us, help us get away.' It was easy enough. We put them in costume, gave them a place in the circus, helped them arrange false passports so they could be smuggled out of the country. We could still travel then—sometimes to Yugoslavia. If they could get to Zagreb, they could slip over to Trieste on the ferry, then to Paris.

Finally, the secret police caught on—maybe there was an informer. Everybody was spying on everybody else. We had only a few hours' warning. I sent the women to a friend who would hide them, though Ivana pleaded to come with me—" He broke off. "If I had let her, both of them would have had to come. I thought it would be safer to go in two different directions. Only I was the lucky one—that is the comedy." He paused to take a sip of tea, then to lean back. "The terrible choice." He gave a deep sigh. "That is what remains with you."

"I had to hide in the countryside, bribe my way across the border. Then to Paris. Alone—the anguish of leaving all behind. My lovely Ivana, and her sister, taking refuge with my parents in the country. But with the hope . . . Somehow that never goes away." He made a little wry smile.

"Paris was good to me, the circuses there. What would I have done otherwise? I didn't know the language—I had no contacts. But circus is a common language—thank God for that. I did everything—animal acts, juggling, magic—then I became Bruno, the Clown. So the comedy went on."

"So the years passed there in Paris—time suspended. Nothing seemed real," he told me. Only the waiting. Walking into each show and losing himself for a time as Bruno. Walking the streets of the city—

"Next to Prague, Paris is the greatest city in the world for walking"—finding his solace in some café. "I kept eating, putting on weight. Stupid really, but it was something to do. I took up painting. Didn't know that, did you? I was even pretty good."

He traveled across Europe. Rome, Berlin, Copenhagen. But with only one thought: to get the two women out of the country. His father died. He wrote letters, he sent packages of food to his mother. Sometimes Ivana got the letters, the packages—others went astray. They were terribly poor. Finally, Ivana managed to get a job in Bohemia working in one of the chemical plants.

"And that was a terrible thing," Bruno said. "I didn't want her to do it. Breathing in all those toxic chemicals, the air poisoned. But she had nothing. His mother died—the house went to the state. A punishment, no doubt." He shrugged. "There is more than one way to destroy."

Meanwhile he was hanging by a thread. "Always just a thread of suspense, a little hope dangling—maybe they can slip out. Ivana tried all the ways she could imagine. Once she almost had it in her hand—bribes, forged passport, but at the last minute it all fell apart." Occasionally, he got a letter, through someone who was able to travel. "Just to look at that piece of paper," he told me. "To see her handwriting. I couldn't even read it because—"

I thought of him there in the circus, made up of people who've spent their lives focused on an audience for the special thing they could do. For those few moments of being all caught up, of being truly alive. I'd lived for them myself. That swing through the air. The somersaults. Like being high—well, I was high—so high I had no desire to come down to earth. And who cared what was going on outside?

Bruno was sitting in front of me now without his clown's face, and I could appreciate even more the role he'd taken on. He'd been able to clown around, juggle away those few minutes in the ring every day. Maybe look at many things as a joke. But the rest of the time, he'd had to think or put off thinking about what the rest of us could ignore—what had caught his life in a snag. No wonder he was such a great clown.

So he stayed in Paris for thirteen years, trying from his side to finagle some way to get his wife, if not Olga, out of the country. Perhaps Olga held that against him. Losing track of one or the other, connecting again. Sometimes he had a letter from Olga. He'd never been all that close to his sister-in-law, he had to confess. Other people couldn't tell the two apart, but he knew who was who the moment one stepped into a room. Different energies. There was a glow around Ivana—people warmed to her immediately, gave her gifts, did favors for her. Almost a kind of tribute. It was that way even when they were children. Ivana was a warm breeze; Olga was an arrow.

"If she wanted something, she just took it. I had a paperweight once my brother brought me from Copenhagen. Butterflies inside—the most extraordinary blue I'd ever seen. I used to say to myself, *What is this blue?* And sometimes I would think, *it belongs to some lost happiness once known in the world.* I almost believed it." He opened his palm. "Suddenly it was gone. She'd been inside the caravan and I saw her pick it up." He imitated her, picking up an imaginary object, holding it under one eye, then another. Frowning and scrutinizing, till you saw the thing disappearing. "Then—presto!—it was hers."

He stood up with a kind of dark triumph, holding out the trophy. "Oh, but I saw what she was taking. She was taking back what I'd given Ivana, what Ivana had given to me. She wanted it—the blue of our happiness. No, she could not live without it. It had been her secret all along. And she kept waiting," Bruno said. "She was always waiting—there was something in her eye." He paused. "Do you see now?"

I thought I'd caught on. Something had happened to put Olga where Ivana used to be. I was taking it in, trying to work out where all this fit in with what had happened. Yes, I was looking at a different side of her, and though I hadn't yet put aside the shock of seeing my place in a wreck, I could almost feel sorry for her.

"So how did it all come about?" Bruno went on " —I will tell you." For many years they had kept hold of the thread that bound them, their meaning for one another, during the terrible time when Ivana went north to work in one of the chemical plants. "I hated to see her do it—but she had nothing. They paid well, it was such a terrible place to work. The air was poisoned. I was afraid for her health. I hung onto every crumb." Messages from his mother to say whether Ivana was sick or well when she came on her brief holidays. He sent packages of food, never knowing if they arrived. "But between then and now a river flows, and you are changing, too, even as you try to hold on. Time, the old trickster—his part in the comedy. And what you get is not what you see."

"I remember the day—finally she was coming, after all the years and all the papers and requests. I remember it so clearly. The platform at the Gare du Nord. I had walked around the neighborhood for an hour. I went past an old woman from the country selling flowers on the corner of the rue du Faubourg St. Denis. I thought that was exactly what Ivana would want, so I bought half a dozen bouquets of daffodils, with their scent of spring. If she had trouble picking me out from the crowd, she would know that only an idiot like me would be standing there with his arms full of flowers."

"The train pulled in. I waited. I saw her—I'd have recognized her anywhere. The years made no difference. I waved, three bouquets in each hand. We threw our arms around each other. Then I looked into her face, her eyes. And I knew it was not Ivana."

A chill ran down my spine.

He was silent for a time. "Ivana had died, perhaps from malnutrition, perhaps from lung disease."

"Did Olga think she could fool you?"

"No, I don't think so. I think she wanted what Ivana had—she always did. So she gambled. It was her way out of the country. When she saw my expression, that I knew, she broke down and told me all that had happened. She had nothing, nowhere to go. She thought we could build a life together."

"A terrible task," he said—always being reminded of what he had lost. Yet she had suffered, too, and it seemed to him he could offer Ivana's twin sister a place of safety. She wanted him to love her in the same way he loved Ivana. She wanted to take her place. But though he tried, it was not possible for him.

Now I did see it. I knew why Olga had been sobbing her heart out. Not simply because I'd insulted her but because, in her mind, I was just one more reminder of what she didn't have and could never get.

X.

More Trouble

Outwardly, things were going very well. The tent wasn't full to capacity, not yet, but there was an enthusiastic crowd filling most sections of the bleachers. The word was getting around—we were beginning to make up for lost time. Building for the future. It takes a while to get up a reputation, convince people they're having a once-in-a-lifetime experience. But when it starts happening, why that's the exciting part. I was rejoicing for the Kid, for all of us, for all we'd put into the show. Now Morgan could go to the backers with the good news.

Yes, he agreed, though, of course, there were still certain things to be ironed out. They had a few reservations here and there and so on. Big money, that's what he talked about now. Big prospects—a chance at doing things on a grander scale yet. That's what he was gunning for.

"I'll drink to that," I said, though I couldn't say I was on the side of that kind of ambition any more. Yet I know what can happen when a lifetime of practice rises up and becomes an art—when you leap beyond yourself into the dream. And how all the tangles about money, the lurking doubts and suspicions, the jealousies—all the troubles you've been moiling around in just evaporate. No substance to them. I'd known it once. And the Kid knew it. In his haphazard way, I think it was what Morgan was after as well.

I was seeing him in moments of high good humor now that things were going his way. He had more room for *social life*, he told me, giving that a particular emphasis and meaning. "How about my grilling a couple of steaks for us?" he offered. "A little celebration."

"You're on," I told him. I was willing to be pampered. I just wanted to bask in the good feeling surrounded nearly all of us. I wasn't going to allow Olga to poison the atmosphere, if I could help it. She was still complaining to anybody who would listen to her. She'd even gone to Morgan—he'd mentioned it, too, her making out I was some kind of bad apple. Trying to create trouble between her and Bruno. But I figured everybody knew her temperament well enough to ignore her. Whenever she came into my space, I gave her a wave and a smile, and let her eyeballs roll on past me. I was glad she didn't say anything to me. Otherwise, it might have taken very little for me to yank her hair and kick her in the sexus-plexus. If you get my tilt.

I still didn't have anything to wear for a *social occasion*. I was going to have to wait until Jessie found a way to restore what was salvageable now that the cleaners had done their job. I'd picked up a couple of things at the thrift shop to get me by from day to day.

But as it turned out, I was going to have to wait for my steak and the next chapter of our, what should I call it?—relationship? Morgan had been called away, so the Kid told me, for a special meeting with the sponsors, with some new big shot on the scene. I didn't see him for a week.

I began to notice a change in the Kid. He seemed abstracted and distant, as though something weighed heavily on his mind. I didn't like what I was seeing.

"Anything wrong?" I asked him.

"I'm not sure," he said. "Morgan's been on me. Olga went to him—again. Only this time, she told him she was going to take the chimps out of the show unless she got a public apology and that she and Bruno were thinking of pulling out. The way she'd been treated and all— She's fiercely jealous of you—I know that much."

"That would almost be flattering, if it weren't so stupid. She must be out of her mind. Bruno pulling out? I think she's trying to blackmail you. Have you talked to him?"

"I've been waiting until Morgan shows up, so we can get everything laid out in the open. Not just the Olga business . . . Where we stand now on the money side—it's always money with him."

"Where is he anyway? He hasn't been around—not even after the show. Where does he sleep?"

The Kid shrugged. "He said something came up he had to settle with his lawyer."

Where was Bruno in all this? I hadn't really had a chance to talk to him since our last exchange. And what sort of mess was Olga trying to create? Was there something else in the wind? The meeting that had kept Morgan away so long and so unexpectedly—what was all that about? With my head so full of questions, I could barely concentrate on getting my cues right for the curtain, and the anxiety of having to wait for answers nearly made me crazy. Trouble and blame. Jealousy and suspicion pushed to the limit. Things had been turned inside out and were sending up such a stink of bad feeling and inner turmoil, it was hard to stand back and shake loose. Seemed like the Kid, Bruno, and I were all caught in the same lasso.

A minor commotion at the beginning, but now what did it mean for the circus itself—and for the Kid? You couldn't say how much it was affecting the others. They had wind of it—that sort of news always gets around. But somehow everybody pushed aside the turmoil going on behind the scenes and gave their damndest in the ring. Maybe that was what saved us. No let down. Bruno, Wally, and Doodles, the Flying Wonders, the Barclays, the acrobats, the Cossack riders—even the Kid—were all working hard to keep up morale, to make sure the patrons got their money's worth. Professionals every one of them, and when they were in the ring, nothing stood between them and what they were supposed to be doing there.

Morgan was back the Sunday after the matinee, and he came by to remind me of our date.

"Where've you been all this time?" I wanted to know.

"Oh, I had a make a quick trip to Vegas," he said. "Something I couldn't put off." He didn't offer any explanations. "Anyway, I've got those steaks in a special marinade," he said. "A speciality of the house."

"I'll bring my appetite."

"We can have a happy hour before dinner and make up for lost time." He pressed my hand. "I've waited too long for this," he said. I was to come at six.

I wasn't sure what I'd been waiting for beside the steaks. Something to ease the tension. My curiosity had me hanging on tenterhooks.

When I arrived, Morgan was outside starting up the grill. He was looking cheerful in a tropical-looking Hawaiian shirt and tan slacks. His hair was neatly combed over his bald spot. I had on a Florida T-shirt with shells on the front, and my hair pulled back and fastened with a hairclip. I wore some earrings with shells in a little cluster dyed in various colors, and I'd put on lipstick. He came forward, put his hands on my shoulders, and stood looking at me as though for the first time.

"So glad you're here," he said. "I've waited so long for this—too long." He leaned forward and planted a series of kisses along my forehead, then hugged me to him.

It made me feel strange to myself to have a man holding me that way. I'd forgotten the sensation and wasn't ready to remember it now, particularly with Morgan. This was to be an informal occasion with steaks for a centerpiece, without questions rising up from the past, and a round of mixed feelings about Morgan's unpredictable take on things.

"Just a little welcome," he said. "Come inside—it's more comfortable there. The grill needs a little time to rev up."

The steaks were on the kitchen counter on a platter covered with foil, ready to grill. I could smell garlic. "Tenderloins," he said. "My favorite." There was more: a salad with arugula and other greens, tomatoes and cucumbers, to be topped with blue cheese dressing; a mushroom sauce for the steak, and a baguette cut into slices with garlic butter, to be put under the broiler for a moment.

"Your invitations are too much to resist," I said, trying to make it playful.

He laughed, and things were okay.

"Would you like a gin and tonic? Just the weather for one. I got fixings for martinis, too."

"I'm a gin and tonic girl," I said, and sat down on the couch. "I can go either way with lemon or lime."

He brought out some olives, and some brie, spread out some crackers and little toasts, then set the tray on the coffee table in front of me.

There was a kind of nervous edge to his eagerness to please. I was feeling a bit overwhelmed.

"Well, here's to the Big Top," I said, when he handed me my drink. "May we go over the top."

"Yes," he said as he sat down at the other end of the couch from me. "To the future and a new start." He leaned over to clink glasses. "To us."

"Let's hope it brings good things for us all."

"You know," he said, looking at me with a little smile you might call tender, "you've never called me by my first name."

I'd never thought about it. He'd always been Morgan, then and now.

"Juan," I said. "Juan Pablo." Then, "Doesn't seem to fit you somehow." He looked a little surprised when I said that. "Perhaps Don Juan?"

He laughed. "I've been around," he admitted. "but that doesn't change a thing. A few distractions. But I've always known what I wanted. You know, Alta . . ." He paused. "I've done some things I haven't been proud of—somehow I think if you'd have been with me, everything would have been different."

"That's pretty heavy. I don't think I deserve that kind of credit."

His eyes rested on my face a moment before he got up to put on the steaks. "With this marinade," he said, "they ought to be out of this world. I'm waiting for your testimony." He went outside to put them on the grill, while I fidgeted and sipped my drink. He came back in with a winning smile. "I want you to tell me this is the best steak you've ever had."

"Great to have somebody cook for me," I told him. I meant it—I wasn't much into cooking. "Especially such a dinner."

"Anything I can do for you, dear Alta," he said, putting his hand on mine, as he sat back down. "I really meant what I said. I needed something then. There has to be something—a light somewhere, a kind of loyalty, a cord to hold onto."

A chill went through me. I could tell he was deadly serious.

"Otherwise," he said, "you get caught up short. You don't know what you're doing, and you make some bad, really bad, mistakes."

"Well, don't feel pregnant," I said. "Dusty came up with some clinkers along the road." His brows formed a question, but I didn't elaborate. Some things are best left alone.

"That's because he forgot what he had, didn't keep his eyes focused in the right direction. He should have known better—he had you."

That hung in the air for a moment. It could have gone to my head, along with the drink. I marveled. He was really saying those things, sitting there like an old lover. But I'd been around too long. I had to ask what he was seeing when he looked at me. Not what I am—I was sure of it. He was seeing a shapely young woman with a mane of chestnut hair and green eyes—at the top of her form, a bird in flight. But that high-flyer had come down to earth, with streaked gray hair and wrinkles I didn't bother to hide.

"You know, when I first met the Kid and learned you'd been back of him, I felt like I'd been struck by lightning. I didn't know Dusty was gone. It was just like everything had been stripped away. I was back at the beginning. Something was possible."

"Hey," I said, "you're not forgetting those steaks?"

He leapt up and went out again. The drink had opened up my appetite. I downed the last of it and took another olive. So the fresh start. A new fling into the future. Likely it was what drew him to the Kid. Youth and great expectations. I wondered if he'd had a bevy of beauties on his arm along the way. He had the looks for it, the touch of the suave, the old come-hither. Looking for the second chance—or maybe the tenth?

The meal was all I could have asked for. The steaks were just right, delicious, and all the trimmings—the salad, the buttered pecan ice cream and cookies for dessert, the espresso coffee and brandy for the finale. When we moved from the table back to the couch, he sat down and put his arm around me.

"I know things have been kind of up in the air lately," he said, "stuff we need to settle. The whole business with Olga . . ."

"Yes, that's been pretty ugly," I said.

"It's left some questions with the backers," he said.

"They know about this?" I said, surprised. "Why is it any of their business?"

"Well, you have to think about the Kid's ability to keep things in hand."

"What?" I was taken aback. Was he trying to sandbag the Kid?

"Olga's out of her mind."

"Hold on now, don't get upset. Olga's a fragile. Bruno's the stable one, having to keep her placated, keeping things on an even keel. I mean, Bruno is a mainstay . . ."

"Aren't you overlooking a few things?" I tried to remind him. "Like coming back and finding everything wrecked. Doesn't the whole thing raise a few other questions?"

"Wait a minute," he said, using his hand as if to compress everything into the size of a walnut. "That was just the final straw . . ."

"What do you mean?" I set down the brandy and pulled away.

"Please, Alta. Don't get me wrong. You're due an explanation, I'm well aware. I know things haven't worked out as you might want, but please don't think badly of me. Hear me out."

"You see," he said, when I didn't respond, "the Kid's young—hasn't had all that much experience. And he took on—too much."

"Things look pretty good to me. Smashing, I'd say. Everything's been going smooth as butter, except for the Olga stuff, and that's not the whole circus. Seems like if you're behind the Kid, it can all be worked out."

Morgan gave a sigh. "I know that's the way it looks," he said, twiddling with his mustache. "But some of our backers haven't been satisfied with the results. They think the show needs to cater more to public taste—more spectacle— You may remember I said so. You see where we are, practically in a slum. It's too arty for what's here. You've got to get down on their level."

"What's a circus for, damn it, if it isn't for the folks who live here, but maybe to take them into the future in a different way— especially in this part of town— And the rest of the city, too. Sure, the Kid's been trying out some things. But you see how it's going—it's going great."

"We've got to take a larger view, what gets us beyond the things that can wreck the whole undertaking." He shook his head. "And now the thing with Olga throwing a monkey wrench into the works . . ."

"You're back on that? Not trying to be funny, are you?"

"Please," he said, trying to press everything down again. Trying to play up to me. Trying to enlist me as an ally. I was flabbergasted. Did he really think I'd go against the Kid?

"Come off it," I said. "Let's stop beating round the bush and look at what's happening. You're about to pull the rug out from under the Kid, and there are some nasty rumors running around about me. Now say what you mean."

"You've seen how up and down it's been—totally unpredictable. Anyway—"

He waved away my protest. "There's nothing more to argue. I've talked to the city people—they see things my way. We figure we'd better cut out losses and put together a show that'll make money." His mouth closed with that prim, stubborn expression of his I'd seen before—put him beyond any reproach.

Suddenly he was talking about a contract with certain provisions in his favor. What it came down to was that he and the Kid weren't equal partners after all. Morgan would come up with the backing after he and the Kid put in their equal shares to start things up, and then he confused me with a lot of gobblydegook that said he could dump the Kid, if his performance proved unsatisfactory. Despite the good showing lately, the books were still in the red. As far as Morgan was concerned, the show would continue till the end of the run. They'd cut out the road show, and reopen for the last three weeks of the season. Without the Kid.

I could see now what he'd been up to—poisoning the well so he could complain about the water. Cutting the Kid down from the very start. Only I hadn't been able to figure out why. Now I knew. Yes, he had a stake in all this, in the success of the circus, especially if he wanted a shot at the big time. And now he had the means for that success. He just needed the Kid to put the show together, put his money and his heart in it, then whip the rug out from under—take the credit as well as the profit and wham bam he was on to the future.

When I thought about it later, I was sure there was a rat turd's worth of truth in what he had to say about the backers, the city commissioners, or anybody else. He could pitch his lies on both sides about anybody comparing notes. They must have read the newspapers, though. And some had been to see the show. I'd seen them hobnobbing with Morgan. And they came to the Kid to tell him how much they enjoyed the performance. But Morgan had managed to queer all that.

"You know what I feel," Morgan went on, his voice going soft once more. "You know my admiration— I thought you could talk to him, soften things a bit. " A smile. Raising his lips into the side of a smile.

"Talk to him! You want *me* . . .?" I was sputtering with rage. "I won't have any part of this. This isn't circus. This is betrayal."

"Alta, please," he said, blocking my way. "Look," he said, "Think what we can do together. I can get you where you want to go, believe me. Dusty never could. And the Kid can't do it either. There's a sweet life out there. I had it in Vegas. I had circus in the club. The best, and we hit it big. All the celebrities came—they know me. I can do it again. Use your wits. I should have known better than to get into this with him."

"Then why did you?" I wanted to punch him.

"There was youth," he said. "Passion—enthusiasm. He could dazzle an empty box he's so caught up in his dream. Okay, granted—he had one great year. But it wasn't here. So he gets the ball once—then he's nowhere. He's got this drippy idea he can do something *here*. In this slum? Pretty soon he'll run things into the ground. Look at his past—"

"You creepy son-of-a-bitch. What do you know about him? or Dusty? Or me—or what I want? You've been undermining the Kid right from the start. Let me out of here." I picked up a lamp and made ready to swing. And it wasn't his head I was aiming at. "Get out of my way."

"Alta—"

"You don't move, you'll regret it."

He moved.

"Alta," he pleaded, as I threw down the lamp and rushed out. "Give me a second chance."

XI.
Costumes

I figured the Kid needed a good night's sleep before I laid on him the whole Morgan business. I didn't get much sleep myself. I spent half the night playing a re-run of scenes from the past, followed by the most recent batch. What a way to spend your time, things going around like they were caught in a Ferris wheel. Morgan had only proved he was the same old leopard with the same old spots—up to his same old tricks. Second chance, my eye!

The Kid seemed glad to see me. He got up from the table, where he'd been enjoying a late breakfast—we had the day off—gave me a hug, and offered me a coffee and a sweet roll. I joined him at the table. The sun was fingering a little begonia he had in the center of the table, and the morning seemed so fresh and sweet I hated to wreck it. I started in talking about the latest letter I'd received from Dollie, that is, the part about the kittens. "You want a cat?" Suddenly I was asking him. "Good company for you, and the calicoes should be beautiful."

"I might at that," he said.

"Maybe Dollie could send one up."

"But you didn't come here this time of day to talk about kittens or yesterday's matinee," he said after we hit a pause.

I took a deep breath and launched in. He listened to the whole saga without breaking in. "I've been expecting it," he said. "He's a dirty dog, but I'm on to him."

"But is he just going to take over?"

"I don't think so. You remember the guys who came around to tell me how much they enjoyed the show—Jack Garvey and Bill Hendrickson—maybe you saw them. I've had some dealings with them since then. We went out to dinner the other night. I laid things out pretty clearly—how it would take time to build the circus into a real community project, start making use of local talent, getting the kids involved—that kind of thing. And that we might lose money for a while. But they're really committed to what can be done in this part of town. And they know what Morgan's been up too—trying to find out who he might be able to influence—where he could talk up the money angle—how I didn't live in the real world. Anyway, we have a contract for next year and there'll be other meetings."

"What about Morgan? Can he just push you aside and take over?"

"There's something about dissolving the partnership—I don't remember exactly, but I think he'd have to prove I'm doing things in . . . Anyway, Jack's a lawyer. I'm not going to worry about it."

"Morgan's convinced the Olga thing has raised such a stink—"

"Yeah, she came to me. She's worked herself up all right. You had blackened her character, were trying to make trouble between her and Bruno . . . She wants a public apology . . . I know she's fiercely jealous of you. Bruno made that clear."

"I suppose I could feel almost flattered, if it weren't so stupid—and sad."

"I wish you'd have come to me," the Kid said. "So we could've headed her off."

"I suppose I should've, considering where it's got to. I thought if we could have it out, we could lay it in the dust and maybe even come to an understanding. Now she's got Morgan involved, and you know, I think he's taking her side."

"Bruno's upset about the whole thing. Really upset with her. She was here yesterday, saying she was going to leave unless she got her satisfaction—that she and Bruno were thinking of pulling out."

"She must be out of her mind. Have you talked to Bruno?"

"Not yet. I thought I'd give her a chance to calm down—see if Bruno could talk some sense into her. You can't get anywhere with her when she's like this. I've learned that much. You have to let her run out of steam."

I had to hand it to the Kid—he was worth studying. Whatever he'd been through in the past, he'd certainly learned a few things, could rise to the occasion. The circus was now his choice, his fate, and he'd been growing with it.

I felt lighter in spirit after I left him, not that things were in any way settled. But I was restless. To distract myself, I went back to my place to read over Dollie's latest letter. I'd just skimmed it before. Mando had refused all treatment for his depression, Dolly wrote, and finally, after some strong words and legal maneuvering—he was bound by some kind of contract—he had pulled out of the facility where he'd been their star guinea pig.

For a while he'd kept up his guest appearances on talk shows, including some prime- time exposure, and talked to reporters, but he made himself so obnoxious and insulting—"you know how he can do that," she wrote—they dropped him quick as they could and practically ran when they saw him. He struck out in every direction.

The culture had sunk to a new low. Everywhere you looked. Politics was a sunken trough. Betrayal and corruption. Selfishness and greed. Things turned upside down. Where was decency, where was justice? Concern for the widow and orphan, the sick and poor? The pursuit of great deeds? Taste and beauty? (You couldn't even buy a decent pair of socks.) The higher truth? Where was feeling and meaning and authenticity? Where was humanity? He was a snarling animal. "I had no idea what to do with him," Dollie wrote:

He was driving me up the wall. For a while I thought there's going to be three out of our minds. At least Ari was somewhere in outer space. But here was the other half holing up with me, practically starving himself to death and ranting on like a car alarm gone haywire. So out of desperation, I said to him, "Are you going to live or die? Make up your mind one way or the other."

He started in on me then. How could I live in this pig sty, in this clutter—what were all these clippings and lives and why was I wallowing in the mire of humanity? The human race was a flop anyway. All they did was screw and watch television and kill each other. A failed experiment. God's joke on himself—what a laugh that anybody could look around this sinkhole and think there was anything to be called *salvation*, for Christ's sake?

At least there was a certain energy in all those diatribes—though I was afraid he'd split a seam somewhere. Otherwise he was just sitting there in a funk. It's been awful.

Poor Dollie! I can believe it. And poor Mando! Finally she arranged for him to buy a camper and settle on the lot next to hers where, as he put it, he was "content to seethe in midst of my own kind of oblivion." That way she could look in on him, see that he at least got something to eat occasionally. For the rest of his affairs he had no interest. Fortunately, he'd turned all his financial affairs over to his accountant who, after the first time, wouldn't let him go reeling down the streets throwing wads of bills into the air, shouting, "It's all paper. Go fight for it, you dumb pricks." Dollie went on.

I was amazed at the money—it still keeps rolling in. He doesn't have to do a thing.

"At least you could do something with it," I tried to convince him. "You can give it to some worthy cause instead of letting it sit there. Make the world a little better."

"Better just to burn it," he said, "for all the good it would do." When he's in that mood you can't do anything with him. I have the feeling, though, that it lies in your power, Alta, to make a positive change for the future.

Really? It would certainly call upon a set of talents beyond me. I wondered what she had in mind.

"Do you want any of those kittens?" she went on. "I've decided to keep one of the calicoes, if it's all the same to you. There are three. And two males, one black and one white. They're in a tumble all the time—they enjoy leaping all over Timon, who has developed a certain resignation, or indulgence. He's a good cat."

"The elephant still looms large in your future," she added. "You can put your dependence on her. Where there are elephants, there is victory," she ended. I put her letter down and stared out the window. She couldn't keep out of the future. Her domain, I guess. She was certainly stuck on the elephant. First the black Percheron, now Babe—among the other animals in my life . . . I made a mental note and put it out of my mind. I was mostly absorbed in not thinking, sitting there inside with a glass of iced tea and a certain blankness—there was still a stain on the wall that was making me nervous—when here comes Jenna at the door.

She stood there, a slim girl in jeans and a sleeveless striped blue shirt, with a bill cap on, an eagerness in her face, as though she'd come with the news that would make you drop a basket of eggs and run towards your future. "C'mon over to the truck," she said. "I've got something to show you."

The costumes— I'd scarcely given them a thought since I put them into her hands—funny, considering all the tears I'd shed over them. I had scarcely worked up any curiosity about what she might be doing with them. And there she'd been, just working away. She took me over. She had two of them up on hangers on nails along the wall. I couldn't believe my eyes. She'd resurrected that embroidered vest of mine, worked it into a bodice, added sleeves, and stitched on a pale blue silk overskirt with loops around it, and little rosettes at the center of each loop. And the red dress with the fringe she'd made look good as new.

"I couldn't save others," she said. "The material was just shot. And even if I'd redone the seams, they wouldn't have held up. Plus the stains. So—" she said, "I figured I could improvise. You told me about that costume of yours—Queen of the Moon." She looked at me. "That sounds pretty classy. Elegant," she said. "I've never known a Queen of the Moon."

Nor had I, except for one brief moment. She went behind the curtain and brought out the dress, and we stood there a moment, both of us, as though we were looking at a treasure she'd just uncovered.

"You've done this?" I said. "Why—it's stunning—a real creation. How could you possibly?"

"Oh, I've got my ways." She'd called upon a couple of elderly aunts with time on their hands and many a chair cover and pillow case behind them, to make a deep purple cape with a look like nighttime, sewing it with rhinestones to make stars on the front and all around the back. In the midst of appliqueing a series of moons in all their phases. Just below, a night sea, embroidered with dolphins leaping, as though reveling under that moon, and in the center, a ship with sails aloft and two figures in it. The dress was purple and white, purple silk skirts overlaying the white underskirt, with white ruffles around the edges. The white bodice was embroidered all with silver crescent moons. She'd fashioned a crown for me too, silver with two tall white plumes and a crescent moon in front. They'd outdone themselves, all of them.

"All the time I was imagining you in it," she said.

I couldn't imagine that myself.

"Try them on," she urged me. "I want to see if I got the measurements right."

So one by one, I put the dresses on. First the pale silk with the embroidered vest of blue flowers. When I looked in the mirror, I saw a kind of floating innocence that didn't know what to make of itself or anything else, a kind of fog of doubt shooting through with little gleams of raw feeling. Prettified anguish. No substance at all. The second, the red beauty with the fringe I'd shimmied in was sheer bluff and bluster. Only I'd learned then you had to have it. Trying to put out—making a lot of show and noise. Nothing sure underneath, but maybe a certain determination and a few inklings. Call it passion. A hunger. So I'd hung onto both, not wanting to let go of either—at least they were stages I knew about. My life has been a series of costumes.

Then there came a moment that took things up another notch. The moment when I was Queen of the Moon in a borrowed costume in that great festival so long ago. All red and white. I stood there, scepter in hand, Dusty by my side, Billy in my thoughts, and despite the grief and desperation I'd been in, things seemed to come together in some kind of balance. A great moment.

But this new dress was like nothing I'd known before. I stood there for a long moment, the skirts billowing out around me, taking in the regal look of the purple, the puffed sleeves, then turned around to the night sky of the cape lit by moons that were all one moon and accompanying stars, leaping dolphins, and the ship moving from one side of the world maybe to the other. I stood caught up in the impression. If I wore it, I'd have to fill out its suggestions. And what might those be? I had no idea . . .

"It's a marvel, truly a marvel." I turned round, and round again in front of the mirror. "Jenna, I can't tell you— Just tell me what I owe you."

Jenna thought a moment. "There are some items—the material and thread and zippers—you can pay for those."

"That's nothing. What about the rest?"

"Okay—I want a special invitation to whatever event you wear this one to—whenever you're Queen of the Moon again. I want to be wined and dined."

"But you must have spent hours, days. You and the aunts. I can't even imagine, what with all the other stuff you're doing. How was it possible? Where's the magic wand? When did you sleep?"

She shrugged. "It all got done."

As I was taking the costumes back to the caravan, I had to laugh at myself. The pure vanity of it all. Most days I frump around in a pair of jeans and a t-shirt and an old pair of sandals or *huarachas* with the heels worn down I haven't bothered to get fixed. And now all the glitz—What would I do with them—shining without purpose there in the closet?

As I put them away, the various costumes I'd taken on and off over the years were in my head, along with the various shapes I'd grown into along the way, as though the body itself were a series of costumes you keep putting on, taking off. These I was putting away had a strange effect on me, what they called up. Like there was something more than memory, something else stood behind the simple business of covering yourself with clothes.

As a kid, there were dress-ups. That started me off one time during the various wanderings my mother made to one relative and another, trying to find a landing place for her unsettled life. Where my father was, who he was, I never knew. There was family, of which we were the slim pickings. The failures looking for a hand-out. The reluctant taking-us-in. The relieved seeing-us-go. Quarrels, remonstrances, bursts of tears. Packing of suitcases. Harsh goodbyes. Travel by bus, sometimes train. Food hastily bought, hastily eaten. Long faces over money. Cigarette smoke, the breath of booze. This time, a pause with my mother's Aunt Kate, who had an attic with all of her things in it.

She had beautiful things, my mother said. She was a dresser. They told me I could play up there in the attic with the kids' toys, if I didn't bother anything, but the boxes and trunks were pure temptation. Dresses and high button shoes, and velvet cloche hats and hats with feathers. The feathers, oh the feathers. I put on a velvet jacket and fawn gloves and a velvet hat, and wrapped a feather boa around my neck and went down to show off my finery.

Aunt Kate stared at me for a long moment. "Bygone and come again," she said. And the two women went off into peals of laughter. I stood there as though I'd made a debut. I didn't know what it meant to that old aunt to see me in garments that had only been put aside, not cast off. Nothing to wear again; yet perhaps it was the pieces of her life she was keeping hold of.

But my mother seemed bent on casting off the pieces of hers. They were too thorny to keep, and we were on our way to a destination that changed it all. "You're going to love dressing up," she promised me. "You know what, honey—we're going to make you into a star."

She had me all excited. I was going to do what every little girl dreamed of. We were on our way then to the Corning Circus, where her brother Larry had performed on the high wire and the trapeze. As a kid, he'd wandered down to where the Vaudeville performers hung out, and they'd taught him to juggle. All through high school, he worked with circuses when they were in town, and during the summers, and that was his life. High wire and trapeze. He'd been with some big outfits, but he wasn't young any more—had some arthritis. Still performing some, also juggling, and he'd been teaching at the circus school in Florida.

"What a woman needs in this world," my mother told me, "is a way of her own—a way to fly. Wings. And they're hard to come by." Women were supposed to stay home and take care of the kids while their husbands were out earning their bread and butter. Only my mom was on her own, having to make her own way. "But the circus," she said. "That's a place where you can soar. And everybody out there's going to look at you, all in your glory, doing what they'd love to do. You'll fly all right."

She looked at me so brightly as we sat there, the bus wheels pounding under us, I gave a little squeal. But she was faking it, I know it now. Trying to put on a good show. Giving herself a boost. And I didn't know enough to ask any questions. Where she'd be, what she'd be doing. When she'd be around.

Uncle Larry was there to meet us at the station. A slender man, not much taller than my mother, but with big arms and shoulders, a skinny butt. His hair had started to go—big bald spot at the center. Bushy brows, kind eyes. "The little star," he said, swooping me up and swinging me around.

"Limber as a shoestring," my mother said. "Light as a bird."

And I felt as though some glow inside me had given me a lightness, as though I didn't have any bones. "Just what we ordered," Larry said. He showed us all around the circus lot, showed us tigers and lions, even a camel. Showed me where I'd be sleeping in the caravan and where to put my things.

"We'll take good care of her, Angie," he said. "You'll see what she can do." And I thought only of that. Even when my mother had gone, I had it in the back of my mind she hadn't really left, that she'd be there to see me when the time came.

Only she never did come. A couple of letters came instead. She had gotten a job selling hats in a department store. She sent me a winter coat she'd bought at a discount, but maybe she'd stayed there only long enough to be able to buy it, for the next postcard came from Passiac, New Jersey. After that, she was working in a shoe factory in Maine. Then the postcards stopped altogether. She'd disappeared into the last postmark. Maybe she took off for Canada, though I couldn't imagine her living in deep winter. I doubt she lasted long in Maine. And somehow, as one day flowed into another, I guess I'd also come to know she wouldn't be back. Later on, I had an image of her sinking down into a swamp, holding me there above the water. Before she went under, she'd given me one last boost.

But I didn't have time to dwell on her absence. The days were filled with practice, practice, and more practice. I took to it like I'd been born knowing. A natural talent and no fear. Larry was jubilant.

145

He had to restrain me, keep my impatience in bounds, keep me from asking for everything at once. But I wanted to get *there,* wherever *there* was, and I'd have practiced till I dropped if I could manage it any sooner. It was a cradle act Larry and Steve were putting together. Me learning to swing by my knees, hold on by the ankles. Working towards the backward somersault and the catch below. Leaping but not yet flying. And when I stood up there above the crowd for the first time on the bar in my tights and tutu and sequined bodice, I was a single bright wordless glow. How free I was! The crowd ate it up—there I was, an eight-year-old kid who could do a backward somersault into a catch from below. I wanted only to get that harness off me and do everything clean. That night I dreamt that my mother had stolen in to see me perform, because she didn't want me to be nervous about her being there and *that afterwards she came in while I was asleep and whispered in my ear, You're a real trouper, my own—my love. How high you'll soar.* When I woke, I expected her to be there. In fact, I knew she was there—I could feel her there. I sat up and looked around.

"Mama?" It was just a room full of darkness.

"Mama." I must have been bawling it by then, because Larry got up to see what was wrong. I hung onto to him for a while. It must have been a long time. The next thing I knew it was daylight. Time to get up and have some juice and cereal and begin another day of practicing.

So it went on—rehearsal and performance. Hanging around with the other circus kids. And the performers and the crew. They gave us a lot of attention. The only family I'd ever really have. I was developing a sense of myself as a performer, knowing how I wanted to do things, knowing when it wasn't right. I chafed to get out of that harness. I remember how emotional Larry got when I insisted I was ready to go on my own. He was proud of me—scared, but proud of me.

"If I let anything happen to you . . ." he said.

"I'm too good for that." I was joking, but he wouldn't let me get away with it.

"No one's ever too good," he said. "No one's above having an accident or bad luck. Just remember that."

Nor would he let the applause go to my head. "Sure you've got the goods," he said, "but there are lots of gifts. Just think of it. Gift of gab and gift of speed. Gift of a musical ear. Even stealing takes a gift. You've got the gift of lightness, kid. Remember that."

Later on I knew what he meant. Lightness. The glow of youth—energy, when every cell seems alive and you're not afraid, and you're sure the future belongs to you. When your spirit soars with your body. That's before you've been kicked in the slats a few times. When, if you trip, you pick yourself up right quick. And what that body could do, how it could take things to the limit, make the folks below wonder if you weren't some special kind of creature, clapping out their admiration—that was the glow, too. And something else. When I'd gone on beyond anything Larry could teach me, gone to the flying passes and the double somersault with a young partner named Damon—how I loved the pirouette pass—when I'd gone on to twirling by my wrist from a rope a hundred times, it was the glow of full flight. I could do anything. Damon and I were a hit. The costume I put on, the shining blue sequined body suit, gave out the whole dazzling sense of who I was, the impulse that pushed me, that seemed a huge thing, larger than me, propelling this woman through the air. Was that what my mother dreamed of?

After it was clear that she was gone for good and then, only three years later, Larry, too—heart got him when he was only fifty-five—I knew something else. If it was never anybody else, there'd been at least two people in the world who'd loved me enough to want the best for me. Until then I never knew what love was. When it came to me, I knew everything that all the unsettled nature of our lives—when Mama and I were together, all that pitching our tents on the porches of relatives and all the arguments and quarrels and accusations and what she had finally done—had led me to that sense of things. I would never be the same again. I knew what love was, and I wanted some of it. When I'm feeling desperate about things, I have to remind myself, what would I have been without it.

You can forget. Forget the glow and what lifts it into flame. Forget the sequins and the spin through the air. I left it all behind and might just as well have slouched around in an old piece of burlap. Just after Larry went—I was sixteen then—I took it into my head I'd had enough of circus life and I was going to go look for my mother at the end of our run and not come back. The folks around tried to talk me out of it. Damon was sick over it. I was determined. Headstrong. Did I think I'd be any better off? Able to learn something better than what I'd been able to imagine. Far worse, I can tell you. For me, anyway. That time I left the circus and just knocked around was one of the worst in my life. Managed to locate a few of the relatives and went round to ask for a little information. They looked at me like I'd landed from the beyond. Not eager to see me either—offspring of my mother. Had a few choice words. *Crazy in the head—that's all you can call her. Going off and leaving her child that way—in a circus. Without any schooling or proper upbringing. And her going to the dogs. Men, drink. Disgrace to the family. Her and that worthless brother.*

They hadn't kept any pictures of her. I wanted one so I could remember what she looked like. When I tried to see her features, they sort of melted and pooled and wouldn't make up a face I could recognize. All I could remember was her hair and watching her put it up in curlers. Then she didn't look like my mother or anyone I knew. And watching her put on her face. But I couldn't remember *her* face.

One of my aunts gave me house-room for a while. Insisted on it, as though she didn't want to see a bad thing go worse. I connected with her daughter Emily, who played flute in the high school band and liked to cut out pictures of movie stars and paste them in a scrap book and knew all about their love affairs from the Hollywood magazines she read. I even went to school for awhile. Worked as a waitress on weekends. That's when I learned what boredom was. Couldn't get excited about pep clubs and football games and quiz shoes. Couldn't concentrate on a row of facts or documentaries about how to dress for the high school prom.

One night I put my stuff together and went down to the local truck stop and hitched a ride to Philadelphia. I didn't head back to the circus right away. Guess first I had to fill my craw. I went from here to there—you could always find waitress work. Saved up my tips. Moved around in the gray Fifties for a little while.

All the time I'd been with the circus I'd been able to close off the world out there, just pull the curtain shut and concentrate on what was happening inside the tent. Its own little world. Oh, you had to eat and wash your clothes and keep stretching those muscles, working out, rehearsing endlessly. You had to deal with all the stuff that comes up—jealousies, differences. But you had a part in something larger, and maybe it was even more necessary then, working together for something that lived beyond the headlines. I had a costume, and in it I was who I was—forget the sore muscles. I didn't know how cold it could be once you left the tent. So back I fled finally. Maybe it wasn't real, the sequins and dazzle, but it was real enough for me. For what I could imagine. I was part of the dream and Dusty had it, and now the Kid had it too.

That was the second thing I knew. Those who see, who go high or deep, who go dreaming to the heart of things—somehow, through all the obstacles—it works out in time. What a marvel it was to think up a machine that could fly. Chained to earth before that. Now flying to the moon. Who knows what next? Finally when all the costumes go limp in the closet, I hold onto that. Hard put sometimes, things falling to rags and tatters.

I don't know if there is a third thing, what-all you can prove even in a stretch of years. Especially now that it's late in the day and living is a patchwork affair, trying to negotiate with a body whose parts are worn and the performance is a little tired.

But anyway, I hung up the costumes carefully. It would just do me good to know they were there. From now on, when I left the caravan, I'd be careful to lock the door. So that's the story of my costumes, those I'd been in and out of and those I had for the future, whatever that would be. And when I told the story to Bruno, he said, "Well, we came to the circus in our different ways, but they are alike, and the circus is what saved us. And for the future—maybe you'll wear them yet."

XII.

Ups and Downs

I felt nervous and jumpy. Though things were calm enough on the surface during the week, I had the sense that our troubles were seething underneath. Morgan, I could tell, was avoiding me, though he was always polite when we met. A little smile, a little raising of the hand, not really a wave, acknowledging my presence. I noticed that Olga was spending her time over at his caravan. She now glared at me when our paths crossed. Bruno had moved out of their caravan and was sleeping over in the costume truck with Doodles. He and Olga weren't speaking, and though we still bantered with one another when we were in the chute, some of the spark had gone out of it. Otherwise, the show still went on, the Kid still running things as usual.

Yet the air seemed charged. What had gone up hadn't yet come down, and when it's like that, you can't help thinking things will get worse before they get better. Only you don't have a clue about what the *worse* is going to be.

Even the animals seemed to be affected, taking their cues from the humans around them. I think the chimps were tuned into the dynamics firsthand and were acting out all the impulses of the humans around them. Maybe that's where they got their ideas. I'd been watching them in the ring and out of it.

As usual, Amos had been sporting around in the spotlight, winning extra applause from the crowd for his unicycle performance, playing the celebrity. They all had a go at the unicyle, but he was a definite cut above the others. Could ride and clown and mug with the best, the sweetheart of the crowd. Raising his arms and clasping his hands over his head like a winning prizefighter after the countdown, bowing to the crowd, then leaping up and down with explosive chortles of triumph.

But this time, instead of just shunning him, watching him sulking

150

in a corner, then cozying up to the females and letting them dance around him, the males cornered him at the back of the cage and started beating on him. I could understand the impulse. It took the efforts of both Bruno and Olga and a big bag of popcorn to settle them down. One of the females still continued to sit with Amos, stroking him and picking his fleas. The other females shunned her.

I'll hand it to Olga—she somehow managed to collect them together to perform. And Amos continued to do well in his act with Bruno. He was taken off the unicycle for awhile, till things settled down.

The horses had their own loyalties, strong loyalties to their riders—they lived only for performance. They didn't have an inclination for politics—You could tell it was a matter of pride, the way they galloped the ring and tossed their manes and munched their carrots afterwards.

It looked as though Babe stood above it all, there in her pen, and kept to her own thoughts above the chatter. But you had a sense she had an eye out, wasn't missing a trick. Those eyes of hers, set in a nest of wrinkles, you could see only one at a time. A large eye, deep as a quarry lake—but curious, sifting, weighing, working towards conclusions. An imprint in the memory. Plus she had her inclinations, outside of Tony, the strongest being towards Bruno and the Kid.

They were trying to get her to work with Doodles now, and she was obliging, though you could see she was still forming her opinion. A person had to walk around her for a time, subject himself to inspection. It didn't happen immediately. First, you had to get past any fears you might have and take her as she was. Live with feet that could flatten you, her powerful trunk, her curious nose. You had to give her intelligence its due, and her nature, whatever lived in that. You had to court her. Pay homage. Then you were given a sort of opening. And once she came to her conclusions, you had the feeling nothing would change her mind to the contrary. I think she felt friendly towards me. I'd taken Dollie's advice and tried for her goodwill.

Doodles was doing the courting, giving her the proper respect. His dream was to ride into the ring on her back. He was going easy with her, not trying to force the friendship. Tony was instructing him, along with Bruno. It had taken a little doing to restrain him, eager, impatient as he was, with a tendency to throw himself into any antic that crossed his mind.

"Discipline," Bruno kept telling him. "Remember that word—it's the heart of the matter."

Being a clown was an art just like being an acrobat or working on the high wire. Control. Working with the muscles of face and body. Endless practice. The basics—before you could really work on what kind of clown you were going to be and could dip into the heart of comedy. Then you'd know how to paint your face and what kind of outfit you were going to wear—come into your own.

Finally, the moment came for Doodles to make his debut. The test, as he put it. The evening of the performance he was as nervous as a groom on his wedding night. Bruno tried to calm him down, told him to get some rest. During intermission—he wasn't supposed to go on until the second half—he appeared, looking both antsy and scared, coming over to where some of us were sitting outside the tent, between the wardrobe trailer and Babe's pen. We admired his costume—red shirt, pantaloons with red and white stripes, striped socks with the stripes going across, and a pointed hat with a tassel. He sat down and started kidding with the musicians, who were eating hot dogs and french fries. But he couldn't sit still. Wandered over to Jack, the Percheron, waiting to go in, and rubbed his neck, talked to Tony who stood with Babe in her pen, checked back with me to ask about his makeup, whether the sweat was making it run.

"Listen to that crowd out there," he said, awestruck. Bruno had been working them up during the last few minutes before the second half began—you could hear a kind of ocean roar in the background. Then Bruno slid in through the side curtain and came out where we were sitting.

"A few nerves here," I told him as Doodles skipped back to where we were.

"Forget yourself," he told Doodles. "Remember, you're Doodles. Just be Doodles."

Doodles was confused. "How can I forget myself and just be myself?"

"Okay, folks, let's go," the Kid said.

The music started up, bold and sassy, and Tony led Babe into the chute for the chivaree. Nothing like a round of good circus music to get your blood up. Then into the ring came the Kid with Babe, and all the rest followed, acrobats and equestrians, clowns, horses and dogs. A good house again tonight. Things moving at a lively pace. As always, I'd sneak out the side curtain and stand at the end of the bleachers to watch as much of an act as I could. I'd seen most of them dozens of times. You get a different sense than when you're out in front. You get to know when the audience will react, like when Melinda, the youngest of the Flying Wonders does her backward somersault and Marco reaches out and catches her by the wrists. No nets below. The crowd gasps every time. Same with the Cossack riding act. When Ivan works his way under the belly of that horse galloping like fury and comes out on the other side, the crowd goes wild.

I never got tired of watching Bruno, seeing the different people he and Wally pick out of the audience to be part of his orchestra— young women, middle-aged men, grandmother types. Some stiff, some eager to be funny, willing to be the good sport. All kinds. And then the woman who'd give Bruno a kiss. So it went. These days, though, no Olga sat in the audience for a back-up. Once nobody offered him a kiss, but he turned that into such a funny sad-clown routine, it was almost better than before.

And now here comes Doodles onto the scene. Bruno keeps trying to demonstrate how things ought to be done—drives up in a little car, but suddenly it won't go. They both look under the hood. Doodles takes a wrench and a couple of pieces of motor fall out. When he tries to get them back, the fenders fall off, then the tires. Pretty soon, the whole chassis is lying there in pieces, and all you see are the two seats and the dashboard still intact. At the end Bruno brings in Babe, who picks up Doodles and carries him off. The audience loved it.

Doodles emerged breathless and elated.

"Terrific," Bruno said, as he moved out with Babe.

"Well, congratulations," I told him. "You did a bang-up job."

Doodles stood trembling all over. "Good grief," he said. "I can't believe I did it." Then suddenly he was sailing like a balloon. Five minutes of his life on top of the peak.

We worked through the second trapeze act and the Cossack riders. Then the finale, which ended with all the performers doing a little dance before they came back out. Afterwards the whole cast, Doodles among them now, marching out through the front entrance, music still playing, as they formed two lines to greet the crowd on their way out.

When we'd gotten out of our costumes and makeup, we were going off to celebrate at one of the bars close by. I changed out of my black trousers and shirt and waited for Bruno and Wally, Minna and the Kid. Doodles appeared first.

"They really liked me," he said, still on a high. "They kept telling me."

"And how was it being carried off by an elephant?" I wanted to know.

"Whew, I was scared, I have to tell you—but it was exciting, too. It was all right." So we finished up the evening performance as we had so many times.

Doodles started describing an act he was dreaming up—he was full of ideas—when a siren came wailing down the street. We quit talking till it passed, but that was just the first. Three or four of them came one after the other.

"Something big," Doodles said. "Not far away either." —because the sirens came to a halt only a couple of minutes after they passed. From where we were sitting, we couldn't tell if it was fire trucks or police cars. It was the first time anything like that had come that close since we'd been there—fortunately. Didn't want anything keeping people away—it would have been a depressing enough neighborhood without the circus tent to brighten it up and a crowd of show-goers to put some life into it.

"Maybe it's a car wreck," Doodles suggested.

Only it wasn't. I didn't think any more about it. Here came Bruno and the Kid, Wally and Minna, and we all strolled down to the Brass Pot a couple of streets away. Had a good time teasing Doodles about his future stardom. A young couple came up to our table.

"You're from the circus, aren't you?" They'd been to the performance the other night and were eager to talk about it. Doodles looked a little deflated—they hadn't seen his debut. Bruno joshed him after they left.

"Now if you don't get all the attention, you'll be meaner than hornets."

Like I say, I didn't think anything more about the sirens. Wasn't curious enough to go buy a paper the next day. It was Jason Foote who gave us the news. He didn't show up that day to haul away the empty soda cans. He'd been regular as clockwork ever since he started, and he, too, had inherited a series of little jobs that needed somebody in a hurry. Then the day after, he appeared, newspaper clipping in hand. A few blocks away, a drug dealer and one of his customers had gotten in a gunfight. One of them had delivered a stash to the other, only it was nearly all corn starch or talcum powder. The customer who'd been cheated tracked down the dealer. There was a chase, the one running frantically down an alley, the pursuer firing shots. The dealer ran into an abandoned building and started firing back. One of the bullets hit a little six-year-old kid, who'd been out playing in the alley and was running towards her house, scared to death. Only she didn't make it. Her mama came rushing out to find her crumpled on the stoop. The bullet had struck her in the head. Right there in the neighborhood. It was Jason's little girl.

He came to the Kid. I remember once seeing a man standing in the middle of a street in a small New Mexico town where we had a gig. He stood there heaving up the most wrenching sounds I ever heard coming from a human being. Like whatever grief—it had to be from a great loss—would never find its way into words. Pure animal sounds that went to such depths you'd never got to the bottom.

At first we thought he was drunk, and he may have been that too. We never knew what it all came from. When I think of it, I'm always caught between wondering what the trouble is and glad not to know. But this man stood quietly, showing only the terrible effects—. His face was drawn and ghastly, and his eyes looked as though they'd sink into his skull. Voice trembling, he couldn't tell what happened, but only held out the clipping from the newspaper, with a picture of her mother and himself frozen in their disbelief—then above the article a little school picture of their child, Leila Ann. You could see from her grin where her two new front teeth were just coming through. "We had such plans for her," the caption read.

"Oh, my God," the Kid said.

"She just loved the circus," Jason said, as if it was the only thing he could think of now. "I was planning to bring her again—she wanted to come back so bad. She's even been to the rehearsals."

I had just come up, and the Kid handed me the clipping. Then I knew—more than I ever wanted to find out.

"She just loved the acrobats. Told me she wanted to be one."

By then, a whole group of us were standing around him.

"What can we do for you, Jason?" the Kid said. He looked at me. I knew what he was thinking—they'd hardly have money to pay for the funeral.

"Whatever it costs—all of it," the Kid stammered out. "Don't worry about the bills."

"My wife's working now. Got a job in the cafeteria—at her school." He paused for a moment. "There is a favor, though. Do you think," Jason said, "maybe some of the folks could come to the funeral, and the acrobats—"

"Of course," the Kid said. "That's just what we'll do. We'll dedicate the matinee to her, free entrance, and then go to the funeral—the ones who want to. And we'll put on a little show for Leila Ann, just for her. Just something small, a little thing with Minna and a couple of the others. But anyway, you'll need something extra," the Kid said, and gave him the money he had in his wallet. After Jason left us, we took up a collection for flowers.

"Hey, you know, I like the sound of that," Morgan said, when the Kid told him what we were going to do. "Brilliant," he said, "Why it's something I could have thought of myself. Get the newspapers in on it and—"

"Damn it," the Kid told him, "that wasn't what I had in mind. Do you have to try to milk everything? Make it into a publicity gimmick. The little girl's dead. We're just trying to let folks know it's our grief too."

"Okay, it's a sad thing, damned sad. But the world runs on publicity, and we may as well make the most of it. Folks'll lap it up. And we deserve a little help," Morgan said, as though an injury had been directed at us. "All this is gonna put us in a hell of a fix. Scare people off. I don't see why we can't try to make a little mileage out of it. Otherwise there'll be another funeral—ours."

He had a point. That night the tent was more than half empty. Though we weren't that close to where the shooting had been, people get spooked anyway. They're reminded that it could happen anywhere, any time in such a neighborhood. You can't blame them. The Kid couldn't quarrel with Morgan about the results—he didn't need any news the empty bleachers didn't tell him.

"Look," the Kid argued, "this is the time we let people in this neighborhood mean something to us—if we want to mean something to them. We've got a whole bunch of tickets—let's see that every kid in the area comes free. Hell, the parents, too. They don't have it to spend on circuses."

"Okay, a few free tickets, but that's all. This isn't a giveaway," Morgan said.

"We've got a sponsor, don't we? This is our first year. We're trying to do something for the city, remember."

"If we survive," Morgan argued. "We go deep enough into the hole nobody's going to carry us."

We hadn't heard anything more about Morgan getting rid of the Kid and taking over, so they were back where they began, though with a different point of argument. Some of us began to drift away. It looked like the main thing was settled.

"I'm not thinking about next year," the Kid said. "It's what we do now."

Morgan was pretty ticked off—the Kid told me all about it afterwards, but the Kid himself was as angry as I'd seen him. Ready to let the tent come down around his head, if he didn't get his way.

The right way. First he talked to Minna and the others, and they were more than willing. They could do a simple pyramid, with Genevieve, just nine, the youngest performer in the show, on top as usual. Then the Kid went by the church to arrange it with the minister, the Reverend Carter Brown. He told him what he had in mind—he didn't want to butt in, he explained, but Jason worked with the circus, and had asked us to come, and if he was willing, we'd be there for the service, and the acrobats would give a little show in remembrance of Jason's daughter.

"We're not looking for publicity," the Kid told him. "We just want the folks in the neighborhood to know we're part of it."

The matinee in Leila Ann's honor was packed with people. I think the whole congregation must have been there, and probably others close to the family. Others came from the city, some of the sponsors like Jack Garner came, too. I was glad to see a crowd.

Three days later a group of us went to the church ceremony and sat or stood in the back of the church. It was a dark occasion for that summer day, the sun hot enough to blister metal. The church was somewhat cooler inside, with the sort of closed-in smell you get in churches, kind of musty, dust mingling with the smell of old hymnals and the scent of flowers. The men in their jackets stood perspiring, mopping their foreheads with handkerchiefs. Jason and his wife sat in front with their eight-year-old son, along with family members and various friends, holding onto the mother, trying to console her. Her voice, the voice of her tears was a kind of continuing strain that wove brokenly in and out of the minister's words. I don't know how the others took our presence—though we weren't the only white people there. A sizeable number appeared. The little girl's first grade teacher came with some of Leila Ann's school friends and their parents. Her teacher was among those who came up and spoke about Leila Ann, told how eager she'd been to learn and how generous she'd been with her schoolmates. She would be greatly missed. The mayor was there, as well as several other city officials. He spoke briefly about the terrible losses brought about by drugs and violence, the need to exert greater efforts to protect our neighborhoods and fight the evil that had cut off the blossom of a young life.

"It's our youth that suffer most," he said. "And those who love their kids." I kept wondering why the city hadn't done something before.

At the end, they made a place for the Kid to come and speak a few words.

"This is the first time we've been in this church," he said, "so we come as strangers. And we didn't know Leila Ann, who is no longer among us. We don't know how to miss her the way you do. But we are sad her life has been cut short, sad about the way she was robbed of her precious chances. We are sad she can't come to our circus—"

A wail arose from her mother, "Oh, honey, honey—"

"And that we can do so little to offer consolation. But we have come to do the only thing we know—to perform for her spirit and for the sake of remembrance."

The acrobats came forward to the platform in front of the altar—there was just enough room for them in front of the altar. Then Genevieve, with Carl and Mike, did a backward somersault from the shoulders of one to the other. Then the others came in and they made a pyramid with Genevieve at the top. They descended with grace and, bowed to the mourners, and faded back into their midst. The service was over.

The church had been full, and the street outside was crowded with people you'd not have found there ordinarily, both from the neighborhood and outside it. Some curiosity seekers perhaps. Reporters were waiting there as well—there was a strong reaction in the city, and their articles would be appearing in the papers for at least a week, trying to light a fire for some action in the poorer areas of the city. The city center had been losing population and neighborhoods had been going down because the money pulled out of them as more and more people decamped for the suburbs. You looked at buildings boarded up and eyeless windows.

Morgan and the Kid could have saved themselves the heat and trouble of their argument. Reporters kept showing up after we got back to the tent. One of them, a young guy with a shock of flame-red hair, was doing a piece on drug-related violence and was not only

159

working up the human interest side of a senseless death; he wanted to see some sort of renovations happening in the inner city. And a serious young woman with straight black hair came with a crew intent on doing a documentary on decaying neighborhoods and the onset of drugs and crime. They interviewed both Morgan and the Kid.

Morgan was reveling in the attention that had caught us up. His imagination was boiling like a pot.

"It's a shame we didn't think of having Babe in on it," he kept saying. "Part of the funeral procession. You know the attention an elephant gets. You can't miss. Barnum put one on his place in Connecticut—so that everybody passing by on the train would see her. It was great publicity item."

When the attendance continued to slack off, a kind of pall settled over us. You felt for the performers who had to give it their all even though there was only a scattering of people in the side stands, a little clump at the center. But they always put out—no matter if it was for a crowd of fifty or a crowd of thousands. The Kid had to work to keep his head above water. You could tell things were getting to him. Olga was nipping at him, letting out snide remarks in his hearing. Supposedly talking to her chimps. But nobody took her up. Bad for morale, which was bad enough as it was.

"We'll just have to weather through," the Kid said, "—hope that things'll pick up in a week or so."

Morgan didn't help matters any. It was strange the way he was acting now, joking and jabbering away, almost frenetic, like he was trying to distract himself and everybody else. Fill up the silence or keep something at bay. He got on our nerves. He startled easily, jumped when you came up and spoke to him, he'd look over his shoulder as though he was expecting someone. In passing, he'd give me a wink, pat me on the shoulder, say something mindless. I had the sense his attention had shifted. Nothing in the old vein. Like he was trying to gloss everything over—the lousy receipts, the prospects for the rest of our stint. Or maybe he had something else in the wind. I wondered about the two guys who'd materialized out of the blue. Treasure hunting. They hadn't come back around. Was he still waiting for his ship to come in? Right now, it would be most welcome. The odds did not look favorable.

A peculiar thing happened. It was after the show, and Tony and Bruno were standing outside with Babe, talking. In a moment or two, Tony would take her across the street to the lot, but right now she was standing there, moving her trunk along the ground, looking for a tidbit. Morgan came up to tell them they were canceling the next two weekday shows—there weren't enough tickets sold even to pay for the electricity, he said. He was angry.

"I thought we were going to do a couple of kids' performances," Bruno said. "That's what the Kid said."

"No," Morgan said. "Too expensive . . . We're in deep enough water as it is. "

"We've given out tickets," Bruno reminded him.

"So? No law about canceling a show. We didn't invent it."

"What about the weekend?" Bruno said.

"The weekend is business as usual. If it's free tickets you're worried about, we'll give out a few in the weeks to come. Spread it out."

An argument flared up. The Kid joined the others, and their voices began to rise. It wasn't right to renege, the Kid argued. They were trying to win fans, not alienate them. Morgan reeled off a list of expenses. Bruno and Tony gave their opinions. I could hear them from the trailer, but figured they didn't need my two cents. Only I heard Morgan yelling, and then I went out to see what was going on. Bruno and Tony must have been standing just to one side of Babe, Morgan on the other. But by the time I got there, Morgan was swinging in the air. Babe had reached down, curled her trunk around his middle and hoisted him up.

"Goddamn it, get me down," he yelled. "What d'you think this is?"

"Stay calm," Tony urged him. "Don't get her nervous. Babe, put him down," he said severely. "This instant. Put him down." She held there a moment as though she had to make up her mind.

"Quit your tricks, Babe. Put him down."

We all stood there as though frozen. We were afraid for him— Though Babe had never offered any threat, she was formidable, and if her mind had moved against him, no telling what she'd do.

"Babe," Tony commanded again. "Put him down." She did then, taking her own good time, as though to relish the full pleasure of him dangling there in the air.

Then he was on the ground, dusting himself off. Tony was trying to turn Babe in the direction of the gate.

"This is your doing," Morgan said. "You turned her against me from the first."

"Are you out of your mind?" Tony said. "If she thinks you're threatening me . . . Now bugger off." He offered her a handful of carrots left on the table for the horses and led her away.

"I'll bet you had something to do with it, too," Morgan said.

"I just wish I'd thought of it," Bruno said. It was all Babe's idea, he told me afterwards. "She just scooped him up and let him dangle," he said, marveling. "But then we've always known her opinion."

"Since she'd picked up Doodles," I suggested, "maybe she figured she could pick up him as well."

"Yes," Bruno said. "Why not let him join the comedy? It's all comedy."

We couldn't have predicted the next episode. After Olga had her paycheck that day, she starting packing her things. I don't know if the Kid had asked her to leave, or whether it was too hard for her to stay. At first we didn't know what she was doing, she was just awfully busy. What we didn't know until the next day was that she and Morgan had gone off in her caravan, actually Bruno's caravan. She hadn't said anything to him.

It was a hasty departure. He'd pulled his clothes out of the bureau drawers and the closet. But he'd left a lot of stuff behind—food in the cupboards, dishes in the sink. And the macaw. I remembered hearing some commotion as I walked across the lot earlier that evening. A lot of squawking and a string of cusswords that came ripping through the air. Only it wasn't Morgan—it was the bird. Hadn't heard that much language since one of the circus hands backed into Dusty and dropped a hammer on his foot. Maybe Dah was putting up a resistance and refused to go. We heard him next morning screeching his name,

Dah, Dah, Dah. The Kid knocked on Morgan's door, came over and told me he thought something was up. We went back together, and the Kid knocked again, finally turned the handle and we went inside. The macaw was sitting on his perch in all his brilliance, blue and green, red and yellow. He cocked his head and gave us a feisty look.

"You remember us," I said. "We'll take care of you." We got him fresh bird seed and water, then paused to take in the major fact— Morgan was gone. Not a word to anybody that he was taking off, or where. If Dah had any treasure-hunting abilities, Morgan was no longer in a way to get any benefit from them.

"Part of the comedy," Bruno said. At that moment, it looked like the whole show was over.

XIII.
Starting Over

I'd forgotten how hot it could get down in Florida, though heaven knows, it was beastly enough there in the Midwest. Felt strange to be back, like I'd been off in a foreign country. I hadn't really been in the Midwest, though—I'd been in the circus. That *is* a different country. Now I was out of the dream and forced back into the daylight, into the real world, though you certainly get your dose of reality whether you're inside the tent or out. It was one of those hot sultry days, the humidity clinging like a skin, and you felt like you were inside a dog's breath, tongue hanging out, panting for a breeze off that ocean—*c'mon out there, let's give with little stir of activity*—while you fan yourself with the *Herald* and drink your beverage of choice before the ice melts.

A day to be on the beach—and no doubt fifty thousand others are out there, thicker than the sand fleas, suntanned backs and exposed thighs—dipping into the briny deep whenever they got overheated lying on the sand. But Dollie and I were in her backyard under the acacias next to the pond, enjoying a pitcher of piña coladas. An interesting scene of bird and animal life. I wanted to see that Dah had a good home, so I took him over to Dollie practically the moment I arrived. Carried him on the plane in a covered cage. Had to buy an extra seat, but they gave me the little kid's rate. He didn't take to the flight, however, and gave out with some language during the trip. I don't know as my neighbors appreciated, though one of the men kept a smirk.

Dollie was delighted with him.

"Well, look at this," she said. "Isn't he a beaut? A rare one, too, I'll bet. He'll be happier down closer to the tropics."

She walked around him, admired his strong black beak, like polished ebony, and the feathers that gave off their wonderful bluish-green sheen. Dah's eye followed her, as he kept turning to keep her in sight.

"I've never seen one like him," Dollie said. "Not that I'm an expert."

I was a little worried about how he would make out with Timon, but Dollie said, "With that beak, he ought to fend off anything short of a jaguar. I doubt Timon will pose much of a threat."

The next day, when I went over, it was clear she'd fallen in love with that macaw. She was full of news about him—couldn't wait to tell me. I hadn't seen her all that excited since I ran off to join the Kid's circus.

"His real name's Saudade," she said, "old Spanish word. Imagine—all these years he's been Dah—Doddie, like they'd forgotten him, and he'd forgotten himself. Turned him into a blithering idiot. Why, as soon as he told me his name, all sorts of things came flooding to the surface."

"All I ever heard from him was the tail ends of sentences."

"Why he's forgotten more languages than you and I ever knew, and he can swear in all of them."

"Sangre de cabres!"

"Is that all he can do?"

"You wouldn't believe what he knows," Dollie told me, "besides turning the air blue and practically withering the plants."

"May an owl grow in your belly! Get out of my sight or I'll swing by a rope from the cunt of your sister." We turned to see Timon creeping up on him—another long string of vivid expressions and the cat beat it.

"He told me he was of a vanished breed," Dollie said. "I thought as much. It's his ancient past that thrills me," she went on. "Don't know where he got it—inherited it maybe. He goes back to lines of kings down there in Central America. Said his ancestor belonged to 18 Rabbit—strange name, killed in a battle at Quirigua. Don't know where that is either. A great king—he told me, and that he'd stood in the doorway between this world and the world of spirits and even the watery world below and had spoken with the ancestors."

"Well, you'd never have known it watching him there in Morgan's corner."

It was the original intelligence, Dollie explained. Of the days when the shamans listened with an ear to the world. That night she'd heard him singing: "The sea has a heart of fire—I am a child of the sea." He sang of the moon, the wandering moon, and the stars and the sun whose rays were wings.

Even as she described it, the world seemed to expand—he'd kept the knowledge of it, she said. Knowledge of its ebb and flow. Of the things that happened under the sun. He could send out the frozen words of ancient wars, sharp as spikes that split the air like lightning.

"I had the TV on and he really cut loose," Dollie said. "As though each of his tail feathers was a whole book of knowledge where he kept everything in store." She shook her head. "Only now it's all in fragments. Garbled and corrupt."

"Morgan said he'd belonged to sailors."

She snorted. "Typical! All hot for treasure—clear as day."

"Pieces of gelt, pieces of gelt," Saudade screeched from his perch. "A bottle of rum and ye better not water it down." He was looking at us like he wouldn't mind a little liquid refreshment. While Dollie was wondering how many generations of sailors had owned him, I was wondering how often he'd been drunk.

"All those languages and foreign parts," Dollie went on. "All the stuff he picked up. A regular polyglot. Maybe that's how he got his name—means a longing for unknown places and people you've never known."

"I've had something like that in my blood too." *Takes you off in the direction of adventure*, I thought, *or maybe just a life full of longing*. For which, I decided, there is no cure. "Wonder why he started talking to you."

"Because I could see—just looked at him and I could see he'd been around. I think he's been traveling for the last four hundred years."

"But that's impossible—parrot-types don't live that long."

"Not usually," Dollie said.

"Then how do you explain it?"

"I don't," she said. "The more I know, the less I can explain."

I didn't know what to say to that.

She leaned over and patted my knee. "It's all a mystery, darling."

I figured I'd let things go at that. We sat back with our drinks, pausing now and then to wipe our foreheads. Calypso had a box outside the trailer, where she was nestling with her kittens. They were pretty independent now, big enough now to climb out and go wandering in the grass. They still nursed a little, but it was pushing her patience—time for them to be weaned. She still tried to assert her mother's will. Sometimes she'd leap up out of the box and pick up the wandering kit by the scruff of the neck and put her back where she belonged. That is, till they got too much for her. Then she'd stretch, flick her tail, and head off on her own—let the kits shift for themselves, she'd done her duty. Each of us had a kitten on our lap, and the rest were frolicking in the grass, rolling over and biting each other's ears. You'd hear a little squeal. Every once in a while, we'd set our kitten down and hoist up a new one. I love the eyes of fresh-born creatures. Couldn't tell which I liked best, but we were each going to keep one of the calicoes and give the rest away. I was filling Dollie in on all that had happened, when I could get past her interruptions. She had to explain to me in all the symbols along the pathway to the future.

The macaw sat there dreamily while we talked. Then he spoke, softly this time: "Ah my love, let us be true. My heart is yours alone, my poor brain is only aphid's milk."

We sat listening for more, but nothing came. "You can tell there are worlds of experience in those brown eyes of his." Dollie shook her head. "Too bad it's all in fragments."

Seems you spend your life clawing around, then trying to put together what you've come up with. Trying to make a necklace out of a few rare beads. Love, too. Throw that into the pot. My ideas were floating off before I could settle them down. I could have gone off into a little haze, a combination of heat and booze. The air was beginning to waver before my eyes. Love again. It sets your flesh tingling, all the dogs barking, the wind blowing, stars falling. Just when you think all the colors have faded.

"Just think of all that's brought us to the present moment," Dollie said, throwing in another distraction. Even the outlines of the moment weren't clear to me, at least not at that moment. Another moment right on its heels.

"And here's my reward," she said, indicating Saudade. "I knew something like this would happen. I knew the elephant would prove the answer. I'm sure she was the one who gave Morgan the final push. Now other things can come to light." She was full of triumph over her powers of prophecy. Infuriating.

So maybe she was right—if you could understand her language and what she'd set herself to interpret. Still I felt I was dropping in after the fact, trying to piece things together. And how much Babe had been an instrument I wasn't sure. She certainly weighed enough to tip the scales—a hefty eight thousand pounds. Morgan might have figured the odds were too much against him to try to maintain himself with a group of performers who carried around the picture of him dangling up in the air, red in the face, his dignity at the mercy of an elephantine whim.

But there were about ten different directions to come at the whole business. I put myself back to those nights in Morgan's trailer, when he was wooing some fancy from the past that seemed real to him and even sounded genuine. Whatever I'd stood for in his mind. Could be he, too, really had some ideal of what he ought to be and kept trying to grab hold of it. Only the past seemed to grab him up and pull him back.

He'd certainly tried to talk himself out of the past. The bad check and what had happened with Dusty. The woman he'd never captured. The nightclub that had burned down. After things had unraveled, we found out it had been owned by a syndicate with connections in Las Vegas as well. There was some suspicion the fire was set to collect the insurance. For a while the insurance company stalled in paying, but no concrete evidence showed up, and whether Morgan had any part in it was only speculation. Very likely, it wasn't his money that had opened the place in Vegas. And the house he boasted about—no doubt sheer invention. He'd spent some money on suits, left behind a dozen pairs of shoes. But he wasn't living like a former dictator. He had money from somewhere. Treasure hunting or something crooked—who knows.

The neighborhood, it must have sent him into the twitches. Things evened out when he won over the corporation to sponsor us. Hell, they could write it off as a tax loss. A way to buy time. But he'd been pitching around in all directions, looking for the rocket into the future.

Then it occurred to me that maybe Morgan had been working another angle, creating a kind of smoke screen, just waiting for the right moment to clear out. Because it looked like some planning had gone into it. He took off quick as a fox, but it hadn't been on the spur of the moment. When he left we were $250,000 in the hole. And how to account for that.

What a mess! The figures for the tickets and receipts didn't jibe in any of his accounts. We knew what the contribution of the city was, and the board with various backers, private and corporate, could reconstruct the amounts of money they had put up. But for the rest, there was only confusion. Only one figure was clear: the show was $250,000 in the red. Whether owing to poor returns at the box office or Morgan's having siphoned off that much of the loot, it was impossible to say. I had my opinion. Morgan could juggle anything—he'd had experience. Why not the books? And his effort to dump the Kid. The only thing I could figure was that since we were riding high then, he felt he had a clear track to try for the big time with the kind of show he was convinced would make a pot. Only when things took a dive with the shooting, he figured he'd get out with his loot.

Where he'd gone was the next question. Whether it was with Olga and were they still together? Or had she just been a cover—to give him a ride out of the gate and make it more difficult to track him down? Dollie could see palm trees and a stretch of ocean, but whether that meant the coast of Cornwall or Mexico, or Spain or the Hawaiian Islands, or Madagascar or any of the other hundreds of places with palm trees along a stretch of beach was entirely open. Could be he was around the corner in Daytona Beach. They put out a search for him through the police and the FBI—he was wanted for questioning. But they didn't have any proof he'd taken any money, and very likely they wouldn't find it if they got him. Either he'd have spent it or stashed it already. I hear they have a few banks down in Grand Cayman that'll wash it for you.

On to what mattered. What mattered was that we were in the hole and needed a quick fix. And since Dollie had written in her letter that I had the key to Mando's future, to getting him out of his depression, I'd come back to see if I could make it come true for real. He was rich—maybe he'd let go of a little cash. That was the most immediate consideration. But I had another idea too. It had made me even more fidgety than the first.

When Mando came over, I was shocked by his appearance. Not only painfully thin, almost pigeon-breasted, but haggard, the skin tight over his handsome cheekbones. His mustache was scraggly, his mouth had the same drooping curve. Looked like none of the letters of the alphabet would lead him to anything to his taste. Looked like he didn't give a damn. Like he was miserable down to the bone marrow. I wondered how he managed to provide Ari a shoulder to lean on. If anything Ari looked more peaceful than ever—you know, the way children do when really soundly asleep. Ari was out of it, all right. And if Mando got any thinner he'd walk the two of them right out of the picture.

He brightened when he saw me, gave me a big hug.

"Well, the wanderer's come back," he said. "And what's the news from the world of marvels?"

"The circus is great," I said. "—if we can only keep it going."

Dollie asked him if he'd like a bite to eat or something to drink, but he shook his head. "You in your minus-quantity phase? Come on, I've got some wonderful chicken pie, your favorite. I made it last night."

He thought it over.

"C'mon," Dollie insisted. "Don't give me a hard time."

"Sounds tempting," he said. "Maybe a little piece."

"Of course," Dollie said, and brought him a plateful.

"So you've hit a snag," he said. "Receipts down?"

When I told him what had happened, he said, "Peanuts, Alta. I have a low opinion of the crook. He needs some apprenticeship in government so he can mis-locate or steal millions. Pooh, $250,000.

170

I've known rank amateurs that have racked up half a million without batting an eye."

He ate tentatively, as though he were eating fish filled with bones. Ruminated.

"A little embezzlement, huh? Well, it's a naughty world. You see my little retreat over there?" He pointed to his trailer. "No TV, no more newspapers, no radio. Just a stereo with Mozart playing. Let the world go roaring on to the next great scandal and public uproar. What'll it be next? Sex or money—take your pick." He ate three or four more bites and put the plate aside. Dollie frowned.

A whole blank white fog of indifference—that's what I was up against. It didn't look good, and I knew I'd leave there that afternoon without asking him for a cent. I just couldn't do it—at least not then. I'd brought over a whole batch of clippings, from the early reviews to recent developments—the one headed, *Show Comes Up Short*.

"Well," I said. "I had reason not to trust him. Guess it all figures in with the neighborhood. They can certainly see we're one of them. No matter what sort of glitz you put on, you can't forget it. If you're lucky, you'll just have a mirror ripped off your car—You don't think one of your own family might rip you off. At least money's just paper." I told him about Jason's little girl and how he'd come to us and what he'd asked for. I should have known better.

Mando just sat there in a funk. For a long moment, he didn't say a word.

"She was a sacrifice," he said finally. "Look around at all the sacrifices—what we've done—made sacrifices of our kids." There was anger in his voice now. No wonder he'd quit listening to the news.

"And what do we do?—we go on doing it. Like I was. Blind," he said. He had tears in his eyes. "Worse than any freak. You know what I think," he said. "I think that's why Ari left me."

Dollie and I just looked at one another.

At that moment Saudade began to chant softly, "O the grass grows tall in valley. The wild geese fly above. In the colors of the rainbow I see my love."

He was a rainbow, that bird, the sheen breaking from his feathers, the blues playing into one another, shearing off into green, sliding into yellow, the bands of red. He was a whole symphony of color.

"What was her name?" Mando said. "What did she look like?"

Curious he'd want to know. "Little heart-shaped face, dimple in her chin. Large eyes, big grin, front teeth missing. I've got a picture of her among the other clippings. I brought all the newspaper stuff."

He took the folder and went through the articles one by one, glanced over them, indifferent.

"Gave you a good write-up," he said—that was all. I remembered how excited he'd been when I was going off, envious even. Dollie sat in a nervous fidget alongside me. You could tell she wanted to give him a poke or say something to rouse him, but she kept quiet. When he came to the picture of Jason's kid, he sat there studying it for several minutes, almost as though he were memorizing her features. Then quietly he set it inside the folder, stood up, handed it to me, and without another word went off to his trailer.

"That's like he is," Dollie said. "Now he'll probably just go and sit there in a stupor till it's time to take himself and his other half to bed. At least there are no quarrels between them about who's going to do what when."

Which I was prepared to do as well. The heat and the piña coladas had combined to make me sleepy.

"Well, I could do with a nap. Think I'll go back and turn on the fan."

Well, scratch that one, I thought. I really wanted to be able to tell the Kid some good news. For all the troubles hatching around us, I'd gotten used to being back in the middle of things. I missed being there with the show. I decided to call the Kid anyway. To my surprise, he was in good spirits. Since I'd left, they'd had big crowds for the performances. Maybe the breath of scandal had excited some new interest.

"You think that corporation will help us out some more?"

"There was no corporation," the Kid said. "That was just another of Morgan's red herrings. But there may be one now—to give us some matching funds," the Kid said, "but we need something more than seed money."

"I don't think there's anything coming from this end."

"Forget it then. Just hurry back."

He filled me in on recent news. Olga, it turned out, had gone back to Europe, to a circus in Paris. No sign of Morgan—though they'd found checks made out to a marine recovery operation working out of Tallahassee. When they'd tried to trace it, it kept disappearing into another location and set of phone numbers, different bank accounts with the name of the company changing along with it. From Tubby John's Marine Recovery Operation to Treasure Ahoy! An operation with as many ins and outs as Morgan himself. As for him, the search kept turning up various and contradictory results. He was linked to a travel agency in the Seven Cities, taking people to the famous "lost" city, with connections to some smugglers of artifacts from various ruins in Mexico and Latin America. A woman who claimed to be his wife had provided several leads, so far none of them successful.

The Kid was undaunted, was ready to pick up from where he'd been thrown down. He'd finish the season, then try to regroup. I told him I'd be back the end of the week in time for the Saturday matinee. No point in staying here any longer.

The next day I went down to the beach for a little relaxation, set up my umbrella and spread out my towel, and spent some pleasant time watching kids build sand castles and grownups play volley ball and badminton and dogs chase sticks into the water, and gauged the progress of various suntans. I went in for a dip, took in a little sun, and opened up the newspaper I'd brought with me. A picture on the front page drew my attention: a couple of fellows the Coast Guard had brought in. They'd located a Spanish galleon and brought up all manner of bullion. Only they'd been doing it on the sly. Then I knew who they were—the pair who'd come looking for Morgan. They mentioned a third partner, whereabouts unknown. Name of John Porter Marigold. Seems Morgan was good at disappearing acts.

Towards the end of the afternoon I stopped at a little seafood place I like and treated myself to a meal of red snapper and trimmings. Then I went home and turned on the TV to see if I could catch a movie.

I was hardly inside the door when the phone rang. Dollie, in a state of high excitement.

"Listen," she said, "something's happened. I've been trying to call you. Come over tomorrow—around ten. Late breakfast." She wouldn't give me any details, so I had the rest of the evening and a good share of the morning to feel irritable wondering what was up.

I managed to while away the morning doing some work in the garden, pulling stuff out right and left, creepers and vines. Go away for a few weeks and you come back to a jungle. Then I washed my hands, changed into some clean slacks and a fresh shirt, and strolled on over. Mando was there, and again I was surprised. He looked transformed.

"That child's face haunted me all the night before," he said. "I kept seeing her—it didn't matter whether I was asleep or awake. And other children. Faces. As though I was looking out over a crowd." He reached into his pocket and handed me an envelope. "This'll at least put you back in square one," he said. "God knows I don't need it."

"Something's happened," Dollie said. "My left heel starting itching like crazy. And it's not the weather."

"You know," Mando said, "I got the strangest feeling there in the middle of the night. I got up—I was hungry for the first time in I don't how long. I sure could have used a piece of that chicken pie," he said to Dollie. "I had the feeling Ari was going to come back."

"I knew it," Dollie said. "I just knew it."

I was flabbergasted. I just stood there looking from one face to the other.

"Why don't you come with me?" I said to Mando. The idea suddenly struck me.

"Whatever for?"

"I don't know. Just come. You don't have anything better to do."

"That's right," Dollie said. "I'd come along myself, but somebody's got to feed the cats."

"You can give this to the Kid," I said, handing back the check. "That's one thing you can do."

"I'll take it under consideration."

After a flurried afternoon and an evening of packing and getting ready, Dollie took us to the airport the next morning.

"I've seen something else," she said. "I think there are a few more surprises." We were itching to go. I was taking one of the calicoes with me.

XIV.
Return

Minna, Wally, and Bruno were on hand to pick us up at the airport, waving and clowning. I was eager to see them all—they were family. I was a little nervous at first, bringing Mando into the picture. There's always that awkward dance till you get used to somebody, and he'd become pretty savage in his isolation. I hadn't had a chance to tell anybody he was coming. We'd collected stares enough on the trip to put him off, either because there were those who recognized him or because of the two heads.

"Sometimes I wonder if people think I'm really human—the same as they are." Mando said. "Sometimes I wonder if I am myself." I was glad he didn't get riled. He settled back with the book he'd brought along, *A Hundred Years of Solitude.*

"That's a pretty long time," I said.

"Sometimes I think there's no such thing as solitude any more," Mando said. "Where do you go to find it?"

He glanced down at Ari. "Maybe the best way to get from this world to the next is to sleep through the passage."

Then it became clear that a number of the passengers recognized Mando from television, or else they'd read his book and were passing up their cocktail napkins and various scraps of paper for autographs. One girl, who had a cast on her arm, wanted him to sign that. He signed his name for a couple of kids just behind us, then announced he was so taken with his own signature, he couldn't afford to give any more away. The stewardess, an older woman trying to serve the usual complimentary beverage, was having a hard time keeping folks in their seats and from blocking the aisles now that the rumor had gone back that a celebrity was on board. But finally a general announcement from the captain helped her get things calmed down and Mando was able to take refuge in his book. He'd always been a reader.

I was glad there weren't any reporters hanging around when we landed. The trip, as well as a certain anxious excitement, had left both us pretty well bushed. It was certainly no big occasion, and maybe they didn't want to tangle with him. Mando had just about scotched any interest in himself by his fits of bad temper.

I introduced Mando and he shook hands first with Bruno, then Wally and Minna. "You're shaking Ari's hand as well," he told them, "even if he isn't around. He's the brains of the outfit. I came along for the ride, figuring two heads are always better than one. Even if one of them's out of commission."

He'd invited them to laugh, and they did.

"Do you do everything by halves?" Bruno wanted to know. The ice was broken, if it needed breaking. It was Mando's way.

"I always figured we might as well make sport of ourselves," he told me once, "instead of leaving it to everybody else. One less chink in the armor." But I don't think he had a lot to worry about. They were used to oddity—they were oddities themselves, and we all had seen a goodly share of it in one form or another.

After we got Mando checked into the motel where some of the other circus people were staying, I took him to my place. I didn't have a thing on hand, and he was itching for a gin and tonic, so I started off to get some refreshments. I knocked at the Kid's door, but he wasn't in—Minna told me he had business in town.

"You're all having dinner with us tonight. I'm going to barbecue some hamburgers." We had the day off and could relax a little before showtime tomorrow.

By the time I got back, the Kid had returned. He gave me a big hug, told me he was relieved I was back.

"You wouldn't believe the mess we've been in," he told me. "My head has been going in so many different directions, I hardly know which way is up." I could believe it.

"Things were bad for awhile," he said. "When we found how deep the hole Morgan left us in, I was afraid we'd cave in. Morale, for one thing. Everybody wondering if they were going to get paid. Me trying to see how much I could beg or borrow to tide us over.

Fortunately, we're still getting good crowds, good reviews." He looked worn out.

I didn't tell him right away that some of his worries were over—I didn't want to take away from Mando's meeting with the Kid himself. So first I told him about the two fellows arrested down in Miami for the salvaging operation and that Morgan was partners with them.

"Now they think Morgan might have gone somewhere in Eastern Europe," the Kid told me. "Maybe Bulgaria. They've got Interpol on the case."

What would he be doing in Bulgaria? I wondered. Maybe there were a few things he could juggle in the government.

"Mando's come back with me," I told the Kid. "I think he's going to do us some good."

The Kid brightened. How often it is that the whole notion of luck comes with money. Seems like you can't climb very far without it. Whatever you're doing, seems like you're standing on somebody's shoulders.

"Come have a drink with him," I said. "I just bought the fixings."

"That's the best offer I've had all day."

I took him over, made a little small talk as I put together a couple of gin and tonics—even remembered the lime—and left them. I thought I'd head down to the little cafe on the corner and have something cool. Another of those hot, humid midwestern days. I thought of the beach. The ground here wasn't firm yet under my feet. I'd been away less than a week, but once you step out of the stream of what you're used to, it takes a little doing to get back in. Fortunately, I ran into Bruno coming across the lot—on his way to ask me if I wanted to go for a lemonade.

"Sounds good to me." I was happy to see him. I'd been so occupied with Mando, I hadn't had a chance to miss him.

"I am so glad you're back," he said, as we started off down the block past the warehouses.

"You don't know how much trouble you caused me," he said, "lying there at night thinking, *Will she come back, won't she come back. Will she, won't she?*"

"Oh," he said, exaggerating even more. "The nights of *Will she, won't she?* You can't image."

I tried to get back into the kind of banter we both enjoyed.

"What?—me leave and not see how things turn out? You know me better than that. I've got too much infernal curiosity to hang there with not knowing how the game ends. Besides, things wouldn't go right without me. Who's on the curtain, by the way? I'm indispensible. Think of Doodles—he might get lost in the streets, fall over his shoelaces, and lie in the gutter for weeks."

"And me?" Bruno said.

"It's a rescue operation all around." We walked along, neither of us saying much.

"The Kid says things have picked up some."

"Yesss," Bruno said, thinking about it. "A little notoriety. People do come out for that. In one way, I'm glad. Glad not to have to play to an empty house. Yet, I don't know. There's something more I'd like to see happen with the show. The acts are there—wonderful all of them . . ."

"You think there's something missing?"

"For entertainment, no. But there is this thing that keeps nagging—when you start to draw people in, ask them to imagine, you start thinking, *Where does this go now? Is this all?* Out of all the possibilities, maybe there are certain ones that make the art rise a little higher . . . Only sometimes you need a little help from outside—sometimes it's only a little pin prick. Or some that just happens, like a star falling or comet flashing past. And you know what you have to do."

I thought I knew what he was talking about. There was all that rush of feeling at the beginning of the show, and there were high-lights, but maybe the whole picture hadn't been imagined yet. I don't know—it was hard to follow. And I'd only seen the show once all the way through.

"You think of it, what the Kid got going," he said. "It's about the dream you keep trying to follow—and everybody's in on it. Through all the obstacles you're tripping over, the pratfalls. When your car falls apart, you keep on patching, inventing all kinds of little tricks. Through all the comedy of having it run away just as you are about to seize it, as you fall on your face, land on your butt, you allow people to reach the laughter inside them—that's what you're there for. You've even got the bumps and bruises to prove it. You bear the marks, but . . ."

He opened the door for me, and we stepped in out of the heat into the heat. No air conditioning inside, just a ceiling fan stirring up the heavy air. The place was full of people, mostly from the shipping houses down the alley. Nearly all men. I didn't feel like sitting at the counter.

"Let's go to that place on the other side of the bus station," he said.

"So back to where you were—at the heart of this circus," I said, when we were out on the street again. "You're still not satisfied, longing for something." Some kind of Saudade whispering to the blood? Maybe there wasn't a word for it yet.

"I don't know—I can't quite get the whole thing in mind," he said, as though he were deep in a puzzle. "When the show is over, I want those who've come to leave thinking that there might be something more to their lives, something they haven't yet imagined but might awaken to."

"Oh, that's asking a lot."

"Yes, I know. But when it comes, you might see it beckoning right before your eyes."

He paused and looked at me. Then he smiled, hitched his shoulder.

"Maybe there's something even for a clown," he said. "Something he can imagine—a place for a little satisfaction. A happy pause before the next pratfall. Maybe it just happens—like that." He snapped his fingers.

"You think so?" We hadn't moved. We were blocking the passers-by.

"Well, you know," he said, taking my hand as we walked along, "when I go roaming around the crowd, wearing my heart on the front of my shirt, looking for a woman to give this baggy monster a kiss, suppose I should find one sitting there, like you perhaps, just sitting there with maybe an old pocketbook on her lap, a straw hat sitting on her head with some wild curls sneaking out from under, and when I come she throws her arms around me and gives me a splendid kiss and won't let go, and maybe gives me another. Think of the laughter. But for Bruno—" he looked at me, "it would be a celebration."

He was smiling as though he'd put forward a joke but was unsure how the punch line would go over.

"You mean, like this?" I threw my arms around him and kissed him. I didn't let go.

"I think," he said, "that might do the trick. How about tomorrow? Would you be too tired?"

"I'm sure we can manage it," I said. "I can do it straight, but if Jenna can come up with something nifty by way of an outfit . . ."

Always the one for costume—that's me. Put the old racehorse back on the track, and she's off and running. Obviously, they had somebody else on the curtain.

"I guess I was moving up in the world."

"Absolutely," he said.

Well, the Kid had said to improvise, I thought, as we were walking along, holding hands. Only when you opened the door, suddenly the wind rushed in and landed you in the midst of a whole new welter of feelings I hadn't expected to have again. Only I felt a sudden new lightness of heart. With all due respects to Dollie, I'd leave the future alone, just ride with the moment. When we finally got to the place near the bus station and sat down in one of the booths, trying to avoid the cracks in the imitation leather, the lemonade was watery and warm as piss. But it didn't seem to matter—the moment was sweet enough.

After we got back, I went to see Jenna.

"I need another costume," I told her—I wasn't sure what. "For tonight, if you can dig something up."

"Look over what I've got hanging up," she said. "There's more on the shelves. I've been rummaging around in some used clothing places," she said, "looking for odds and ends I could use. I've got a whole box full of stuff."

We spent a little while going through what she had. Bruno and I had talked some about what sort of figure I should make. As we worked things out, I didn't have to be just one type—it could change as we went on. After Jenna and I had looked over what she had, we decided on a sort of busty Florida type, with slacks that were made of different colored squares and a flowered shirt and glasses with rhinestone frames. The wig she came up with looked like something Harpo Marx would wear. We were both laughing once I was in that get-up. The whole idea tickled me. I made her go and get Bruno.

"I want to make sure you recognize me," I told him.

He looked me over, made his eyebrows dance. "I'd flirt with you anywhere."

When I got back to the caravan, both the Kid and Mando were nicely set up on their gin and tonics. I saw that they'd helped themselves to another, and that they'd scarfed up most of the peanuts and crackers and cheese I'd gotten for them to snack on. The Kid was buoyant.

"He's dug us out of the hole. Just in the nick of time."

"Something to do with a little spare change," Mando said, tossing it off. To me: "You know how I've always loved the circus. I said I envied you when you came up—I meant it. Can't wait till I see the show."

"This calls for a real celebration," the Kid said. "Tomorrow night after the show we'll have a feast. Have everybody come—we'll celebrate."

He and the Kid went off to the motel to let Mando get a little rest before dinner. It was almost five, and Minna told us to come at seven. I ate the last of the crackers and cheese to tide me over till dinner and lay down on the couch. I was sound asleep in five minutes. Did me a world of good.

I was glad to have a little time to work up to the performance. I had to unpack and lay in some groceries, get settled in again. There was a different cast to things with Olga and Morgan gone. The ingredients had shifted around, left a couple of holes that needed filling in. It was like we were waiting for something else. You could sense an excitement gathering. Mando had given us the sort of boost it makes you dizzy to think about. Just goes right to your head. Everybody was full of talk. The adrenalin was up. And we were going to hit it high and go out afterwards.

It was like champagne bubbles were tickling my nose. I laughed to myself every time I thought about what I was going to do. Bruno and I had agreed we weren't going to tell anybody about it. And Jenna was in on the secret. Just before the show, I got into my outfit and wig and went to sit in the seat Bruno had found for me after he and Kitty checked through the tickets sold. I kept my rhinestone glasses in my purse. Didn't want to call too much attention to myself right away. I was feeling nervous as hell, as if I were about to take off on the trapeze once again. Tried to steady myself by watching the folks coming in. Looking at faces. I've always liked doing that. Watched a family with three little tow-headed kids come in, the littlest in a Day-Glo collar, maybe to keep him from getting lost. They came in with boxes of popcorn and sacks of licorice and cokes and made a nice little file into bleachers, where they finally all got assembled, the parents on either side, a set of grandparents in the middle. Another older couple, white-haired, sat down in front of me. Glad to see them. Still ready to be on hand for a circus. Like me. Young couples, kids, a wave of faces, smooth with youth; older folks lined and spotted with age; dark-skinned and light—all the shades and variations between. A couple was speaking Chinese on one side of me, and a Mexican family came in, with some cute teenage girls, their hair long, a lustrous black, dressed in jeans , speaking rapidly in Spanish.

Jason Foote came by just in front of me, a tray strapped on in front of him, walking among the crowd, selling sodas. He was one of us now, like Doodles. But where would he go? He stood like a reed, tall and skinny, clothes too big for him; looked like a man walking in his sleep. He'd been knocked awake, and what was there for him now? He stood at the end of my row, offering his tray of drinks and snacks, but he didn't recognize me. Didn't expect me to be there. I just let him go by.

I'd told the Kid I wouldn't be there for the back curtain tonight, and he said, no sweat. They'd got it figured out, taking turns, using a couple of the crew when they weren't needed elsewhere. Once again there was a good crowd—all on hand for my debut.

I enjoyed being in the audience for the real thing, watching the show from the opening announcements and the charivari up until Bruno made a series of sour notes on his trumpet, accordion, and flute, threw down his musical instruments and went looking for love in the audience. This time he worked things a little differently. He went up to a middle-aged woman, showed her his heart, clasped his hands, declared himself in pantomime, held open his arms. She rose up laughing. He pointed to his cheek, and she gave him a little peck. He stood there as though enthralled, touched the spot, thought about it, then just shrugged, opened up his palms. Went on to the next, a young woman, maybe in her twenties, who got so caught up in giggling, she couldn't do a thing. He waved his hand to dismiss her. I slipped on my rhinestone glasses. Then he came to me, seized my hands, kissed them, tried to go down on one knee, staggered, righted himself, stood there scratching his head, then seized my hand again, made me go down to the center of the ring, slipped off my glasses, held open his arms, and we went into a clinch. I was a little breathless when I got back to the bleachers.

There was a kind of exuberance in the performance that night. Something extra. You could sense it in the air. The crowd had caught the feeling, and it seemed like performers and audience were caught in one spirit, forgetting everything but the show. Heady stuff. Nothing you can manage beforehand—that buoyancy. We'd been given a fresh start, a new life, and all that remained was to go on with that in mind. I went out with the crowd after the show, didn't wait to stand with the other performers. I was just a member of the audience after all.

"Who's the mystery woman?" a couple of people asked Bruno. Alas, she had fled, and he would have to go in search of her again.

He found me readily enough. After we'd taken off our makeup, we stood around until we could arrange cars and taxis to get everybody to the restaurant, a very nice French restaurant that had Bruno saying, "I must go back soon now." He looked at me, winked.

Bruno and I got a lot of kidding.

"I talked her into it," he boasted. "I had to have a little incentive for the job. I mean the pay's lousy—you can't even get a decent meal back there."

"I knew you belonged here," the Kid said. "Looks like you've got it all figured out."

Figured out? It just happened. But here I was, having the time of my life. Was even thinking about more costumes.

"What did you think of the show?" I asked Mando, as we were riding over to the restaurant in Wally's car.

"Terrific," Mando said. "I liked all the acts. Exciting and funny—all of it. Beautiful. Only it's got me thinking . . ."

"Not a good sign. You found something wrong?"

"No, it's not that—I don't know what I'm thinking. Something keeps stirring in my head—I can't make it out," he said. "I feel the flow of it in my mind—at night I've begun to dream. After so long. Strange," he said. "Can you imagine?"

I was sitting across from him at the table as we ordered. He wasn't saying much. He seemed to be deep in appreciation of his red wine, but he could have been in another space entirely.

"Everything all right over there?" the Kid said. Maybe he'd noticed something too.

"I know Ari has come back," Mando said slowly. "His thoughts have been running with mine. We've been sharing the same dreams." He paused, as though listening for something. "And I think he's waking up."

XV.

The Awakening

With an extraordinary focusing of attention, we watched Ari open his eyes, raise his head, and look around. Don't know what was going on at the other tables, whether they'd noticed anything peculiar. We'd gotten stares enough when we came in through the main part of the restaurant, but we were off to ourselves in the back—secluded. He woke up with a start, looked around like another Rip van Winkel trying to figure out where the hell he was. But then his eyes steadied down like liquid settling in a cup and moved over our faces one by one as we sat there stunned.

Dead silence.

We'd laid down our forks, broken off the conversation in mid-sentence, and sat there there like statues. We could hear whispers from the other tables. Tension like you wouldn't believe. Then he said, "I hope there's food coming—I'm starved."

A roar of laughter—we were all of a common mind. Our stomachs were practically digesting themselves. The place was crowded with folks out for the evening; people were standing three deep around the bar. They must have been short-handed. The one glass of wine I'd been sipping on had gone straight to my head. Fortunately, here came the waitress with our appetizers just then, and Mando told Ari, "You can have mine—go to it."

Since they had only one set of digestive organs and one set of arms and legs, but two heads and two mouths, they used to take turns for meals back when they'd been with us. Mando liked to do breakfast, Ari lunch, though sometimes they swapped around. They took turns for supper.

"Glad you could join us," Bruno said, as though Ari had just breezed in from across the street. "An unexpected pleasure." We'd got back our voices and added our welcome. The Kid did introductions—clowns, acrobats, himself. Doodles came up to be introduced, and some of the others too. Manners before the salad. Then we dug in.

"You remember me from the old days?" I asked him.

"Of course," Ari said, "—you've been running through my dreams here and there."

How about that? I thought—*the way we're always popping up in each other's nightlife.* Folks you see every day, people you haven't seen for years, and the forever dead coming alive. Even those you've never seen in your life—who you don't know if they're real or not or how your mind created them. Or if it did. Like they're waiting there in the wings for a call for just one more show. And what you make of it? Dollie would say they are the material of the future, bearing signs, but I've never been sure myself.

"Thought maybe you weren't coming back," Mando said. "Hey, save me the cucumbers, will you, and a couple of olives."

Ari smiled, a sort of tender smile, and said, "You can have half if you want it." Mando forked a cucumber. "Well," Ari said, "I didn't think I was coming back either."

I know it was rude, but I couldn't take my eyes off his face. The others, too, were snared by fascination. When I'd seen him asleep, caught up in whatever dream was going through his head, his face was relaxed, but closed. No connection to anybody. Now he was present, all there, looking at you with interest, a soft attention. And you waited for words to follow. Something different from Mando's. Shaped by a full, almost girlish mouth but that still kept a kind of firmness in the lips. Mando was drier, scrappier, with a sharp tongue, a wicked wit. But he'd certainly drawn a blank when he was sure Ari had abandoned him. Funny how they belonged with one another. Ari looked much younger than Mando, but you had the sense he'd come through a different kind of experience. Maybe he'd been somewhere beyond us—I was dying to find out.

The Kid passed over what was left of the bread. Wanted to put in an order for another entree, but Mando restrained him. "We can eat only one meal between us," he reminded him. "Have to watch the weight, you know."

"I hope you're in the mood for a filet," he said to Ari.

"I'm in the mood for just about anything."

In another moment they'd all but forgotten us. As we devoured our snails, herrings, and fancy eggs, they were reuniting with each other, truly after such a long separation. Mando could hardly contain himself.

"Now tell me where've you been, for God's sake," he demanded. "And why you left in the first place. I was worried as hell."

I'd paused, fork in the air, not wanting to miss a word. He certainly had an audience.

"It was the atmosphere," Ari explained, "So thick with pollution I was choking."

Gee, I thought. *What a sensitive type.* I'd been down there in Florida for several years now, had managed to escape. Must be I had tougher lungs.

"I could hardly breathe. Not just the exhausts from the trucks and SUVs and all the other traffic and smoke and dirt and garbage, coal fumes, and poisons in the water—that's only a part of it. It's the other half—the stuff you can't see," he continued. "Only you know it's there—you can feel it. It comes and blocks your pores like slick—and the thoughts in your head. Worse than Bunker C oil."

We looked at each other.

"It's all the impulses and thoughts that blacken the atmosphere," he said, his voice rising, "—the hostility, hate thoughts, corruption—all of it. I decided I'd just sleep through it for a while. Only you wouldn't leave me in peace—," he said to Mando, "you had to go off and let all those *-ologists* poke around, put gadgets on my head, open up my dreams . . ."

"I know," Mando murmured. "It was fascination. Thinking, dreaming—it's all such heady stuff. And when all those boys and girls wanted to study us . . . Well, I thought maybe we had something to offer."

"And you loved all the celebrity stuff," Ari said, gigging him. "It just went to your head."

"I don't deny it," Mando said. "You realize my book sold over two million copies? And nobody else could've written it." He looked around, sizing up the response. Were we on his side, even a little?

"Put a few new suits on our common back, didn't it?" Ari said. He had a bit of the Mando in him.

The Kid winked at me, and I understood that wink. Whatever had happened between the brothers, we were certainly reaping the benefit. The grease that made the wheels go round. No, we couldn't knock it. We'd be dead on our feet without both of them, without Mando's book and the cash rolling in.

"Well, knowing you, I'm sure it's a helluva book," Ari said. "I'm not against it. Only some things you don't get from books."

"Is that why you left then?" Minna asked, widening the conversation.

"It was getting on my nerves all right," Ari said. "I hated all those interviews and appearances. All that smirking Mando was doing— sometimes I wanted to bust him one. I tried to shrug it off—figured he was going to get tired of it and come back to his senses. It was the election that was the last straw. Bad enough around the country—but down there in Florida . . . So much meanness in the atmosphere—all the lies and subterfuge, and twisting and turning and finagling. After the final decision, everything just went gray. What was going to happen to the culture. Just couldn't stand it anymore. It's never been easy, the two of us in this one piece of equipment. But I'd had it up to here. Just wanted to leave, get out of my body and never look back. And one day, suddenly I found I could do it."

Food—there it was. And we were torn—we wanted to hear the rest, but we were more than ready to dig in. Fortunately, Ari and Mando were starving along with the rest of us.

When the waiter brought more wine and filled our glasses, the Kid said, "We need a toast. First to Mando, who has saved our necks. And to Ari, who's back among us. To both of you—we couldn't do without you." We clinked glasses all around. "I think we'll need at least another bottle here," he told the waiter. "The other tables, too. We're celebrating. And we'd better do it up right."

Ari ate hungrily, but every now and then, Mando had a bite—for the sake of the flavor. "Great food," Ari said. "It's been awhile," and offered his glass for more wine. "One meal, but the wine can go to two heads."

"He's a cheaper drunk than I am," Mando said.

"So how was it?" Wally said, eager to begin again. "What did you do—out there?"

"Traveled a lot," Ari said, "To Europe first. Hadn't been there in years. Used to be something of a Francophile. And I loved the food. Great place even if they can't get over the fact they're no longer the center of culture. But I still love Paris, in spite of some dark spots in the atmosphere. I spent a lot of time wandering around the city. Then on to Italy. Only the atmosphere kept getting worse the farther east I went. Finally, I thought, *I'm free to go where I want—there's no gravity holding me down. Why not up?* Visited the moon, lots of stars, some of the more distant galaxies."

"Was it all real?" Probably what we were all asking. He spoke as if it had all happened just as he said. We sat there trying to take it in.

"What was all that like?" Wally said. "What was out there?"

"It was—I don't know . . ." Ari said, "Spellbinding. Just to be out there that far—in space, no beginning or ending, and all those stars—seemed like millions. Just floating there, one small mind like a grain of sand—you couldn't take it all in . . ."

"Go on," Mando said.

"It was beyond my imagination—just beyond. And yet, it's funny, after a while, it got boring. I mean, there are some differences in the stars, the craters in different places, hills, pitted surfaces, but you get tired of looking at all that matter."

"No other life out there?" the Kid said. "I've always thought there had to be."

"I had that feeling too," Ari said. "I think there is, only maybe you have to look for it in a different way. I don't know. Only I just couldn't keep on. I kept thinking, there's no color out here. I think I'd lost the ability to see it. There were all those fiery stars. I was dying for color. I thought, I've got to get out of this and find some or I'll die. I knew it was true. Only you've got to have water to get color, and light, a sun shining through it."

I knew exactly what he meant, being I'm a fiend for color myself—couldn't live without it. All the reds and yellows moving towards me,

190

mating up and getting to be orange. And blue and green. The reds stepping back into violet, drawing up a little. I was thinking flowers and woods and the animals in their costumes . . .

"I don't know what happened then," Ari said. "There was a kind of feeling in the atmosphere, though I couldn't make anything out. But I had the sensation of being helped, arriving somewhere else, inside another moment, like being inside a light ray. Suddenly I was standing under a great arch," he said. "A rainbow."

"How can I believe this?" Mando said.

I didn't know what to think.

Ari shrugged his particular shoulder. "You don't have to believe any of it," he said. "You asked me where I was and what I saw—I'm just telling you."

"You've got a great imagination," Mando said.

Ari ignored him. "Only it wasn't just any rainbow—it was like a mother of rainbows. There were all kinds of rainbows—if you'd wanted to put together a heaven made all of rainbows, it was like that. Making up the whole atmosphere, each one a particle of that, belonging to that." He grew more and more excited. "And the light was behind it all. Lights flashing, little gold points. They just kept flashing. And there were rainbows all of flowers. And butterfly rainbows. I just can't tell you." His forehead was shining with sweat.

"So what the hell are you doing back here?" Mando said, and everybody laughed. You could see he was nervous.

"Something kept pulling at me. I couldn't ignore it—believe me I tried. It was you," he said to Mando.

"Me?"

"You were down there—crying out in the desert."

Mando looked embarrassed. Then he said, "I missed you."

"Something else." Ari frowned in puzzlement. "Just before you left Florida and came wherever this is. Something you were feeling—there were these big splotches I kept seeing, a lot of ugliness, and then in the middle of it, there was this—I don't know—I think it was a face. A small face—only I couldn't make it out. Now you tell me what's going on—what you've got yourself into."

We were ready for another bottle of wine. We'd eaten the steaks and chops and chicken and au-gratin potatoes— polished off the works. Now we were all talking at once, giving out with the struggle we'd had, the shooting of Jason's kid, Morgan taking off with his money and ours, my return to Florida—all the ingredients that had gone into this particular moment—the bunch of us of sitting around with Ari in our midst.

But Mando wasn't satisfied. "Okay, so I brought you back. But what made you decide to wake up?"

"Funny thing," Ari said. "When I came down, I got as far as the tent. As long as I was up there, I figured I might as well watch the circus. From up around where the trapeze hangs. Great location. And I was looking down at all the faces—like little lights down below. All that crowd sitting there, putting everything else aside, all the stuff that trips you up during the day and turns the atmosphere black. Here they were, letting their minds open, their eyes and hearts lift up a little. It was happening to me, too. Not that you can say what it is exactly—It all kept running through my head."

"It's the magic," the Kid said, and raised his glass, "Here's to the magic."

But Ari hadn't finished. "And the Downtown Circus," Wally said.

"That's not right," Bruno said, speech getting a little slurred. "That's not right. You can't stick with the downtown. You gotta go up—up."

We were all getting quite a little drunk. "To the circus in the air," Bruno said. "Up in the air." He raised his glass.

"Why not?" the Kid said, raising his glass. "After all, things are still up in the air."

Ari was still trying to say something, only the wine had got hold of us. We were in high spirits, plentiful spirits. Something had broken loose, and the rest of the evening we were joking and laughing. Bruno kept offering wine to anyone who passed by the table, and pretty soon we'd left our table and were drinking with the others at theirs, making quite a hullabaloo. Even some others from the main part of the restaurant wandered over to join the party.

"Come to the circus," Bruno kept saying, waving his glass. "Come

come come come. We're downtown now, but the sky's the limit."

Jeez, it came to me—he sounds just like Dusty.

"That's right," the Kid said. "More drinks everybody. Here's a fellow who's gone beyond gravity. Give him a toast. Here's to Ari."

"Aerialist supreme," Bruno said, waving his glass.

"Our dreamer," Mando said. He turned towards Ari. "What if that's all it is—just a dream?"

"It doesn't matter," Ari said. "Doesn't matter at all. What you can see is what you get. And you can *choose* what to make of it." He smiled. "I've seen wonders."

XVI.
Finale

Ari had seen wonders, and he was determined to bring them back so the rest of us could see them, too. We had a great show—terrific, but we weren't finished. I'm trying to pick up the voices, the actions, the shape of events, as I have all along. The whole thing is like trying to see a painting in somebody's mind. But not just one person's—it took all of us putting in the hues, dark and light, as we moved along, not even knowing what we were trying to create. And the larger picture didn't reveal itself all at once, but in flashes. Fits and starts. Something being created out of what we knew, what we were doing, even when our intentions were hardly clear to one another. Yet once we had it together, it seemed like it was there all the time, right before our eyes, waiting.

First the voices—what were they? Sometimes a chance remark from Doodles, a speculation from Mando, a reverie from Ari, or the Kid spinning magic—all that came to be one voice.

You could say it had started with the Kid, the Dream of Circus, his underlying passion to create magic. And where had that notion come from? Dusty was at the back of it somewhere, but then you could keep going back. They say there were acrobats back in ancient Egypt doing summersaults and pyramids at people's funerals. And circus itself goes way back. So the Kid had come up with his own take on it. And there was Bruno, who wanted his comedy to lift from the ground rise "above gravity," he would say. And you can't forget Morgan, who presented a challenge to everybody. Nor Olga and her frustrated longings.

But Ari was the one who, in his reveries was trying to reach for something that took us beyond what we were sure of. You set something new in motion, out of a combined effort, and it's like you've shot a ball out of a cannon, and you have no idea where it's headed.

"But you see," Ari kept saying, "You've got to think about every color of the lights, every sound in the music, not just for what it is, but what you're trying to aim for, how the folks out there are going to respond."

"And where are we trying to get to?" Mando demanded. His voice made a little scraping sound—a kind of reminder. "You have to make it real," he insisted. "And you can't tell where it's going to take you."

It was some kind of sense or emotion Ari was trying to get at. What he'd felt when he was hovering up there above the faces, having come from whereever he came. It was why he'd come back, he said—to make what he'd seen real, so the folks below could join in. That's what he was trying to get the Kid and rest of us to see—to go farther than we'd gone. The right colors, the right sounds. Taking what you had, then going for what you didn't have. Only how could you lasso it, that mysterious feeling and get it to the rest of us? That was the struggle.

Lots of talk about the various acts, the reactions of the audience—what you were seeing, the way it drew people in. What they might be imagining. The play of the lights and the music, what they added to the spirit of it all. How it was to take all we live with—the animal, the human body—and put it in a shape that swirls the dust off the everyday round we know and have got so used to it sticks in the craw, and frees you, lifts you up, till a voice inside you makes you yell out, *My God, I'm really alive*! Life! New energies down there, new thoughts, a new excitement. Creating a new spell of wonder. And after the adventure, after your heart has quickened a few beats and you've looked at what the human body can do when it's taken to the edge, and you've put it inside the story all of us are somehow living, each in their own way, then somehow . . . could you add just a quantum more to the total for the folks to take away? something they could live with, see again in their mind's eye so that it could continue to quicken the blood and continue to start up something new, again? Jeez, that was a tall order. I'd gotten enough kicks from performing and watching to last a lifetime, I suppose. Only it doesn't last—you have to be continually reminded.

The Dream of Circus. A dream more than real. Nobody was sure yet. Ari set something stirring in the Kid's head—he kept saying it was just the boost he needed. He felt driven to experiment. Various acts. Costumes The reds and yellows, the blues and greens. He didn't want to say anything more yet—it might be premature.

Bruno is still at the center, the heart of the show. He has his episodes—his attempts to get somewhere, tripping over the obstacles in his path. And his story sets up the acts, animals and people, sends us to the acrobats and the aerialists, takes in our comic efforts, finally wraps things up with the thundering horsemen, the sense of adventure and daring. Everything you might expect, everything you could enjoy.

Only finally it dawned on the Kid that Bruno's search, Bruno's experience took him only part way. He remained only a spectator. Maybe he points out something for them, but where does it leave him? Could you take a step beyond that? The Kid walked around with the question for a while. Then something clicked.

"Now there's something new," the Kid said. "You keep pointing to a cardboard heart, asking for a kiss," he said to Bruno. "But what's up now? You've given away your heart, at least for one show. And the lady disappears with the crowd."

"You think there's more to it than that?" Bruno said. "You never can tell."

"More for you or more for the circus?"

"Couldn't it be both?" Mando said.

So that was in the air. First thing, the Kid started having Ben, on the lights, play more with the colors. What were the colors of longing and confusion—those at the beginning. And the music that went with that. Maybe the long call of a flute, with the yearning of the violin, the sassiness of the sax—the drums a part of the bumbling mistakes. He had to work things out slowly, not disturb what was in place, because what we'd been doing was really good—it always had been.

"What I'd like," the Kid said, "is to end the season with something really special, something that would promise towards the next."

"Don't you think we should give the Kid a little help?" Bruno said to me a couple of weeks after the famous dinner. We'd been spending a lot of time together. He'd told me the history behind all the photos that hung on the walls of the caravan. "They're the only things I rescued from my past," he said. "The only things I wanted."

We talked a lot about the show and he had a few ideas. "After all," he said, "comedy means finally that you go home feeling better than when you came."

"Even after all the pratfalls along the way?"

"Especially then."

"What did you have in mind."

"Usually there's a celebration."

"I thought that was the whole show."

"Yes," he agreed. "But think of the grand finale."

"When everybody comes out and dances and juggles?"

"That's part of it. Only I was thinking of something even grander."

He had me there. He leaned over and took my hand. "Now that I've found you there in the audience, I can't afford to lose you." He gave a shrug. "I'd have to start the search all over again. I'm not getting any younger," he said.

"You're younger than I am."

"What does that matter?"

"So what do you have in mind?"

"Suppose we got married."

"For real or there in the tent?"

"I mean for real and for the circus—but maybe they're both the same."

But could they be the same? Was it that way with Dusty and me or Billy and me? Love and the circus. I guess it was.

"Sometimes when I listen to Ari, I think everything on the horizon is what is being dreamed now—but . . ." he added, "but . . . all the turmoil it comes with, deep within. I just can't account for that. All that sent me here. I wonder, is the air clearer up where he went, or did he just dream it all? Is there a higher dreaming—and you're just trying to find your place in it? I have no answer, but I have this one small dream of my own." He stood up, took me in his arms as though he was about to lead me into a waltz. "—to make something matter, out of matter, even if," he gave a shrug and danced around himself, "even if it doesn't matter in the least."

Mando saw things differently. "It's all wheels within wheels," he said, "and those of the gods grind slowly. I think I'm into my c-phase for circles—for going around in them. I don't know what we're trying to do down here in this little ring. If only it makes you forget time for a moment— I guess it can't hurt. Those rainbows of Ari's have gone to my head. Trying to pin them down in the circle of time, well it's a crazy business."

"Come on," Ari said. "You're the practical one—that's what our mother always said. 'I'm glad you've got someone to keep things in hand,' she was always telling me. 'Otherwise you'd never come down to earth.'"

That's how we ended up changing the name. Next season it'll be The Circus of Rainbows.

And so the day comes, the last day of the season. And everybody's there. We had Dollie fly up, and she's on hand with Ari and Mando. After all, she'd been the one to read my future, even if none of us could quite see what it was. She had her eye on the horse and elephant aspects. And lots of folks from the neighborhood are there for the show. A number of the congregation from the church down the street, including Jason and his family. Even various officials from the city. And I saw to it that Jenna had a good spot in front to go to after she gave me her assistance. The place is packed. None of the ads said exactly what would happen, but they promised a spectacular conclusion to the dream. Nothing like a little suspense to build up to the climax.

The sequence of the acts unfolds. Then after the thunder of the horsemen and things are at a pitch of excitement and the crowd roars and claps and the riders come in for their bows; after the clamor has died down a little and the band has struck into something joyful but not so full of drums, the little girl Genevieve, dressed prettily in a long white frilly dress and lace cap and ribbons, comes in carrying a basket trimmed with ribbons, and scattering flower petals. Then the minister, the Reverend Carter Jackson, dressed in a light blue robe enters, approaches the altar decked with flowers and takes his place behind it.

And here I am riding in on Jack, the Percheron, just as Dollie might have seen it, all decked out in the splendid costume Jenna made for me, the purple cape embroidered with moons and stars and leaping dolphins. Regal all right. And to top it off, the feathered crown with its crescent moon. I'm holding a scepter with a silver head embossed with dancing figures. Finally the occasion has turned up. I take a turn around the ring on that beauty of a horse, the crowd applauding. It's a pretty impressive costume all right. But now here comes Bruno on top of Babe, her head crowned with red roses and irises, pale blue, yellow, and lavender. She's quite a sight. The crowd is cheering now.

When Babe kneels and he gets down, they can see he's wearing a tux several sizes too big, and his red tie looks like a great big tongue. Of course he has to trip, go into gyrations to right himself, then pick up his hat, which has rolled to the ground. He puts it back on his head in a jaunty angle. He acknowledges their presence with a little bow and joins me at the altar, while one of the crew takes charge of the horse, and Tony takes the elephant.

I look out and see the wave of amusement ripples across the faces. But it's a marriage after all—Bruno's and mine—and though she's taken some liberties with the ceremony, the words are there to join us together. Babe is a part of it too, though she has other interests at the end of her trunk and keeps reaching up to pick off the flowers decorating her head and eating them.

The minister is saying a few words about the joy of the occasion, bringing together all those presences and what has led up to the occasion. He gives his homage to Babe before she gets to us: "Where there are elephants there is victory," he says, the light gleaming benignly from his forehead. At that moment Babe cuts loose with a mighty large dump. Happens now and then in the ring. The crew has to run in and clean it up. Just another part of the painting. But here are the words that bring us here, the kiss to unite us. I toss the bouquet to Babe who swallows it in one delicious gulp. Maybe she'll have her chance too.

The band strikes up again. All the performers appear dancing, around the ring, juggling pins, and when it's all done, we walk out to greet the crowd.

A great feast afterwards—tables loaded with food, piles of ham and roast beef and chicken and potatoes, fruit salad and all the champagne and wine you could drink. Then we cut the cake, Bruno and I, and feed each other a bite.

Well into the night we feasted and celebrated.

My head was in a whirl. Could I have thought at the beginning that I'd be standing here? I couldn't believe it. Tears sprang to my eyes. I couldn't help thinking of Dusty, and Billy too—the others I'd known who'd come and gone. I was the one left behind, and for how long? The body may not be everything, but you wouldn't be here otherwise. And I can't imagine floating around without it. Yet Billy still exists for me, and Dusty. And all that's happened—for good and ill. I wouldn't have been me without it, whatever I am out of costume or in it.

Something Dusty said before he took the final leap came back to me and struck me once again. "I'm an old man," he said. "A bunch of scraps—that's all that's left. Lungs scarred—can't breathe. Heart nothing but a rusty old pump. Hell, I don't know why, but I feel light. None of that awful straining and pushing. Light—the way I used to feel when we were up there on the trapeze. How great it was, Dream Girl, with you, the way we were together, into all that risk and joy." I think Dusty had it right. Maybe it's love that moves you in that direction, and the lightness is all you can ask.

Gladys Swan has published seven novels, *Carnival for the Gods*, (Vintage Contemporaries Series), *Ghost Dance: A Play of Voices*, (LSU Press, nominated for the PEN/Faulkner Award), *A Dark Gamble*, *Ancestors*, *Small Wonder*, *Dancing with Snakes*, and *The Dream Seekers*, as well as seven collections of short fiction. Her poetry and essays, and short stories have appeared in many literary magazines and anthologies. Much of her work is set in New Mexico, where she grew up. Though she has spent most of her career as a writer, she has devoted much of her time during the last two decades to painting and exploring the creative process. She was the first writer since the inception of the Vermont Studio Center to receive a fellowship for a residency in painting. She also received a fellowship from the Lilly Endowment for a year's study of Inuit art and mythology and a Fulbright Award as a writer-in-residence in Yugoslavia. Her paintings have appeared as the cover art for various literary magazines and books, including the most recently published, *The Tiger's Eye: New & Selected Stories*. She has twice been a Guest Writer at the Vermont Studio Center and has held residencies at Yaddo, the Chateau de Lavigny in Switzerland. the Fimdacion Valparaiso in Spain and others. She has taught literature and creative writing at various colleges and universities, notably, in the MFA Program at the Vermont College of the Arts and at the University of Missouri-Columbia. She received an Honorary Doctorate of Humane Letters from Western New Mexico University and gave the commencement address. *The Carnival Quintet*, an outgrowth of her first novel, is being published by Serving House Books. The first volume, *Carnival for the Gods*, appeared in September, 2014. She has done the cover paintings for the series.

www.ingramcontent.com/pod-product-compliance
Lightning Source LLC
Chambersburg PA
CBHW031338170626
46807CB00002B/759